'I could wish you had not come here, Helen Faraday.'

'No one calls me Helen.'

The utterance had a husky quality. Without volition, he turned his head. 'What do they call you?'

'Nell, sir.'

The instant it was out of her mouth, she knew it was a mistake. His gaze became intimate, probing hers. She wanted, needed, to look away. She could not. What had possessed her to speak of her name she could not imagine. Except that his expressed wish so closely mirrored her own. It should have distanced her that he said it. Instead it had created the opposite effect. As if a kinship had sprung up between them.

His voice came softly. 'If I were not an honourable man, Nell, I might well be carried away by the romance of the occasion.' A wisp of a smile curled his lip. 'Moonlight and a pretty girl—balm to ease a troubled heart. It is unbearably tempting.'

Dear Reader

I have often thought with sympathy of that army of sad spinsters in bygone days whose lot in life was to be a governess. Without means, marriage was out of the question, and so they entered alien households to work as a tutor.

In the Georgian world of my creation, three such young ladies, devoted friends, are just emerging from a charitable seminary in Paddington where they have been prepared for just such a life.

First comes Tender **Prudence**, a soft-hearted creature, who is hopelessly outclassed by the enterprising twin nieces of Julius Rookham. Resentful of his amusement at her struggles, Prue finds her unruly heart nevertheless warms to her employer.

Then there is Practical **Nell**, buoyed up by a common-sense approach to the strange goings-on in the Gothic castle of a brooding widower and the erratic behaviour of his little daughter. Yet she is drawn to the mystery of Lord Jarrow's tortured past, and all Nell's considerable strength of mind cannot prevent her from falling into a dangerous attraction.

Lastly, there is Fanciful **Kitty**, the only one of the trio to escape the future mapped out for her. But her reality is a far cry from the golden ambition of her dreams.

I dedicate these stories to those unsung heroines condemned to a life of drudgery, who deserve all the romance they can get.

Elizabeth

Look for Kitty's story, coming soon.

NELL

Elizabeth Bailey

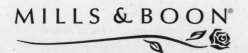
MILLS & BOON®

First published in Great Britain 2002
Large Print edition 2003
Harlequin Mills & Boon Limited,
Eton House, 18-24 Paradise Road, Richmond, Surrey TW9 1SR

© Elizabeth Bailey 2002

ISBN 0 263 17992 3

Set in Times Roman 14¼ on 15½ pt.
42-0303-81028

Printed and bound in Great Britain
by Antony Rowe Ltd, Chippenham, Wiltshire

Elizabeth Bailey grew up in Malawi, then worked as an actress in British theatre. Her interest in writing grew, at length overtaking acting. Instead, she taught drama, developing a third career as a playwright and director. She finds this a fulfilling combination, for each activity fuels the others, firing an incurably romantic imagination. Elizabeth lives in Sussex.

Recent titles by the same author:

THE VEILED BRIDE
A TRACE OF MEMORY
AN INNOCENT MISS*
THE CAPTAIN'S RETURN*
PRUDENCE†

The Steepwood Scandal mini-series
†*Governesses* trilogy

Chapter One

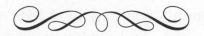

An overcast sky threw gloom across the world, and the wind bit. Huddling into the warmth of her cloak, Miss Helen Faraday blessed the foresight that had led her to line it with an extra layer of flannel. It was chill for mid-April and the long sojourn in the stagecoach had left her numb, ill prepared for further travel in a one-horse gig.

She glanced at the aged retainer who had been sent to Ilford to pick her up, a wizened, bow-legged creature attired in worn black livery, with a battered hat placed upon lanky grey locks tied in the nape of his neck. He was not precisely surly, but his conversation was meagre and to the point. An attitude that was at one, perhaps, with Miss Faraday's new situation. Indeed, her first situation. One, she reminded herself, that she had been eager to obtain. Could it be the unfortunate dullness of the day that was causing her to wonder if she had made the right decision?

The Essex country was pleasant enough, and the sleepy villages through which they were passing must be pretty when the sun shone. It could only be her imagination that set shadows dancing in covered nooks, and an unruly rustling in the leaves. She was become as fanciful as Kitty! She could not repress a smile as she remembered her friend's boding words at parting.

'If there should be wraiths, Nell, and strange whisperings of a night, you had best lock your door and hide under the bed. And whatever you do, don't venture into any vaults or dungeons for fear of skeletons!'

A sage piece of advice that had effectively driven away the pricking at Nell's eyes, setting her instead to laughter. 'If I should discover any such thing, my dearest Kitty, I shall steal one of its bones for you as a souvenir.'

Kitty had shuddered. 'Don't dare! Only do take care, Nell. You may laugh, but even Lord Jarrow said it was a very old castle, so it is bound to be haunted.'

The ghoulish delight beneath the apprehensive tone was not lost on Nell. 'Have no fear, dearest. I shall write for your advice the moment I encounter a spectre.'

Upon which Kitty had fallen into laughter—which had broken in the middle into a distinct sob. Nell had caught her into a convulsive embrace, knowing that with her departure poor Kitty was going to be desperately lonely. It had been bad enough when Prue, the first of the three friends to secure a post, had gone off to Rookham Hall. But now—

Here her thoughts suffered a check as the gig at last turned off the main highway on to a lesser track. She looked towards her escort, who had given his name as Detling, announcing himself to be his lordship's groom.

'Where are we?'

He did not glance at her. 'Whalebone House.'

'Have we far to go?'

'Nobbut a mile to forest. 'Bout mile and half more to Hog Hill.'

Nell was conscious of a slight feeling of apprehension, and instantly quashed it. That was what came of reliving memories! But the sensation persisted as a belt of trees came into sight to one side of the carriage-way. It was thick. And dark.

'Is that the forest?'

A sidelong look was flashed at her. 'Mark Wood, that is. Hainault be our way. Know it when you see it, you will.' He pointed with his whip to the country opposite the wood. 'Padnall Place.'

Automatically Nell cast her eyes in that direction. Some distance from the road, the outline of a large house could be discerned above a smattering of green. A mansion of some note, perhaps? It struck Nell oddly that the servitor, who had volunteered no other information, should have pointed it out. She eyed him.

'What is the significance of Padnall Place?'

Detling cast her another enigmatic look, and replied with only a grunt. Nell felt a rise of irritation. Was this a sample of the manners obtaining at her destination? It bordered on insolence, calling to mind the oft-repeated words of her preceptress at the Seminary.

'Be under no illusions, girls. You will meet with rude treatment. Your defence must be to ignore it. Retain your dignity at all costs. To give way to a natural vexation can only serve to make you ridiculous.'

All the long years of her incarceration at Paddington Seminary, Nell had striven to cultivate that all-important dignity. Mrs Duxford's teachings had inculcated within her a sense of self-worth that had nothing to do with pride. They had all made fun of that dread word *independence*, which the Duck—as they reprehensibly dubbed her—had so strongly underlined. But Nell suspected it had been the saving grace of many of the genteel but indigent females who passed through that lady's hands. They were all of them condemned to a life of drudgery. No bones had been made about that, for the Duck had ever been ruthlessly truthful of their expectations. But along with the candour, for each anticipated slight or harshness that life might deal out, there had been advice sound enough to enable one to endure it with no lessening of self.

It was not always successful, Nell decided. Dear sweet Prue had ever a low self-esteem. As for poor Kitty's hopelessly impossible ambitions!

Nell thrust the thoughts away. She must not dwell on the past. Putting her attention firmly on the road ahead, she became abruptly aware that Detling had been right. Spreading as far as she could see in either direction lay the forest. One could not mistake it. Like a vast sea of green, thrusting waves into the air.

Endless it seemed, waiting in menace. A swamping mass destined to swallow her up. Nell could not repress a shiver of fright.

'Hainault,' announced the groom.

Was there a note of satisfaction in the cracked voice? Had he seen her alarm and taken a perverse pride in it? Not that he was directly responsible for its sinister aspect, but she would stake her oath he regarded the forest as his own since he dwelled within its relentless folds. A characteristic, the Duck had said, often to be found in those whose condition in life gave them little other source of pride. One must recognise the type and refuse to be its adverse effect.

'It is certainly overwhelming,' she conceded, choosing to pander to him. 'How far does it stretch, do you know?'

'More'n two mile up. Near four east to west.'

Nell met another of his testing looks with determined calm. 'And the castle lies deep inside, I take it?'

''Bain't nothing close 'cepting Lodge. Nor you can't see it neither from castle.' A grin creased his leathery countenance, and he became positively loquacious. 'Hog Hill be that high, 'n trees be that thick, bain't nothing to be seen but forest nigh on mile an' mile.'

'Indeed?'

At a loss how to respond suitably to such depressing information, Nell turned her attention to the village they were entering, which sat on the edge of the looming bank of trees, becoming larger with each passing instant.

'What is this place called?'

'Collier Row.' Having opened up at last, her guide was inclined to converse. 'Over t'west be village o' Padnall Corner. If'n we went thataway—' pointing off to the right '—we'm to come to Park Farm to fetch supplies mostly, milk n' such.'

Come, this was more encouraging. 'Then you are not completely isolated. Where do you go for your hardware then, Ilford?'

'Rumford. Three mile mebbe to Rumford.'

Nell began to feel a little more cheerful at the warming thought of a large town nearby. But as the gig left Collier Row behind, and they began to penetrate the forest, she could not repress a resurgence of apprehension. She knew it to be absurd but, as the dense foliage closed over them, she felt more and more hemmed in. It was, besides, excessively dark under the trees. Yet it could not be much more than four o'clock. She had arrived at Ilford as expected at a little past three and Detling had been late by a half-hour. They could not have been travelling all that long for it was only something over five miles to her destination, so she had been told.

She cast a glance upward, looking towards the ribbon of muted light that followed the road. If only it had been sunny, with brightness splashing through the leaves, the atmosphere would have been far less intimidating. She must not allow her fortitude to be shaken by a mere manifestation of the weather.

And then an eerie prickling came over her, for it sounded as if another set of hoofs had begun to overlay the steady clopping of the sturdy cob that pulled the gig.

For an instant, Nell dallied with the random thought that a ghostly stallion had invaded the creature in front. Common sense immediately told her that this was ridiculous. If she could hear hoofbeats, then another horse must be on the road, either before or behind. She glanced back.

No rider was to be seen. Yet the sound of hooves was steadily growing, and travelling faster than the gig. Nell looked at Detling, and saw by the tilt of his chin that he had heard it too. She quelled a stupid sensation of fear, and glanced this way and that, looking for any sign of a horseman. It was not a carriage, for there was no sound to mirror the whoosh of the gig's wheels upon the forest track.

And then a rider burst out of the trees and into the road ahead.

The cob balked, and the gig bounced uncomfortably. Clutching the side, Nell tried to control the gasping shock that gripped her. The man was in black from head to foot, matching the mount, which he had brought to a stamping halt, his head turned towards the gig. Below the wide-brimmed hat set low over his forehead only his eyes could be dimly seen, for the rest of his face was concealed by a loose black mask.

Under the furious thudding of her heart, Nell became aware that the gig had been brought to a standstill. The cob was snorting disagreeably, but the ancient servant at her side had his attention wholly on the footpad.

Recognition of the man's calling thrust Nell into a cold sweat. Her mind reeled, and a long-forgotten image rolled into sight: *A gloved hand through the window of the coach, a discharged pistol smoking...the heavy smell of sulphur...and the blood that seeped from the hole in her father's head.*

The present vision shifted. The black-clad rider was turning his horse, making for the gig. He rode close, coming up on Nell's side. Her pulse shot into high gear and the memory faded, the old terror leaping up anew.

Did he mean to rob her? Then he must be disappointed, for she had nothing worth the taking. Realising that he held no pistol, Nell felt a lessening of fear. Boldly she met his eyes as he halted his mount so that he looked directly into her face. They were wild eyes, frowning and open, although there was not light enough to see what colour they were.

A guttural laugh sounded, but he addressed her in tones unmistakably genteel, a trifle muffled under the cloth that hung over his mouth.

'I need not ask whither you are bound.' The eyes travelled slowly down her person and up again. 'Nor for what purpose.'

Too astonished for speech, Nell concentrated on keeping her countenance, ignoring the commotion at her breast and the peculiar rigidity of her muscles.

His gaze dwelled for a moment on her face, and the expression in his eyes altered. A low whistle came. 'Fortunate Jarrow! I would I were in his shoes.'

The man then executed a low bow, which Nell took to be ironic, and, turning his horse again, cantered off ahead of them and was soon lost to sight. Nell drew a steadying breath, and turned wrathful eyes upon Detling.

'And who, may I ask, was that? Pray do not attempt to tell me that he is unknown to you. It is obvious that he is fully conversant with your master and all that pertains to my arrival.'

A disparaging snort escaped the groom, who gave his horse the office to start off again. 'Bain't no call t' take no account o' the likes of Lord Nobody. Been maraudin' these parts nigh on three year.'

'Lord Nobody? What in the world do you mean?'

Receiving one of the fellow's sidelong looks, Nell drew on all the authority at her command. 'I am in no mood to be trifled with, Detling! It is no answer to tell me he is a highwayman, for that I know already.'

Detling gave vent to a cackle. 'I'd like fine t' see as how Master deal wi' you, missie. Bain't no one thrown tongue at Master since Missus took and died.'

Interesting though this theme was, Nell refused to be drawn by it and merely waited, her eyes firmly upon the man. He eyed her, wrinkled his face in a grimace, and gave in.

'Bain't no one know Lord Nobody for hisself. Could be any one o' they gennelmen round about seemingly. Knows owt as there is t' know do Lord Nobody.' A sly grin was flashed at her. 'Could be as Lord Nobody is Master hisself for owt I know.'

'Lord Jarrow a highwayman? Don't be absurd!'

Nell had spoken out of instant reaction. On the other hand, was it so absurd? He had evidently known that she was a governess, and bound for Castle Jarrow. Which meant he must have recognised Detling, for he could not have seen her before. Oh, it must be nonsense! What had he said? That he wished he had been in Lord Jarrow's shoes. Which she was to take for a compliment, no doubt?

Too used to be an object of interest to the gentlemen round about Paddington—on account, she understood, of the unusual shade of her blonde locks and her distinctive green eyes, for she was certainly not accounted a beauty!—Nell found the discovery neither discomposing nor alarming. She was the more interested that the highwayman's remark argued that he was not Lord Jarrow, which Nell devoutly hoped would be found to be the case. The last thing she wanted was to become an object of amorous interest to her employer. Mrs Duxford had given dire warnings against widowers!

Yet the incident had done nothing to relieve the sense of unease that had attacked her in this place. So unlike herself. Had she not been known for her sang-froid all these years? Even now there were echoes of remembered pain in that wicked image that had sprung up from its banishment in the depths of her subconscious mind. Nell thrust them down. She had long conquered that hurt, and she would not permit of its returning to torment her now.

Turning her attention back to her surroundings, she found that they were slowing as the gig began to climb. The track rose steadily and she spoke aloud the thought in her mind.

'This must be Hog Hill.'

Detling gave forth a grunt. 'That it be.'

The foliage all around was denser than ever, every tree heavy in spring leaf and thick with underbrush. A scent of damp and moss was in the air, and the muggy feel of a threatening storm. Nell repressed an inward shudder. Was it the chill of evening that sent ice racing down her veins?

She could see a turn ahead on to a narrow track, and felt no surprise when the gig slowed to a walk to take it. The way was deep with ruts with a steep rise ahead. Nell felt for the cob as it trudged gamely upward, encouraged by a blandishment or two from the dour groom. But as they breasted the rise, Nell's thought for the horse disappeared as she caught her first sight of Castle Jarrow.

The track was a deep cleft within the encroaching forest, leading directly to a monstrous shadow, standing four-square against the world. Lowering above the gig, it looked like a child's fairytale nightmare, a gross battlemented monstrosity, towering into the sky. The pit of Nell's stomach had vanished, and she found herself wishing with all her heart that she had not come.

In this light, the carriage was a slow-moving speck upon the road below. From the battlements, the view was both spectacular and all encompassing. In ancient times when the forest had not been permitted to encroach upon the hill itself, the most cunning of invaders could not have made an unseen approach.

Watching the advancing gig with a sensation of weary cynicism, the present Lord Jarrow at length identified two figures within. She had not yet turned tail, then. If his tolerance of Toly Beresford had been as it was in the early days, he might have laid a wager with his brother-in-law upon how long it would take. Not that he could find it in himself to blame either of the previous women from escaping as fast as they could. Would that he might do the same! Only this one was little more than a girl.

Had his need not been so desperate, he would never have offered her the post. Only Miss Faraday came highly recommended. He had written to the Paddington Charitable Seminary for Indigent Young Ladies upon the advice of Lady Guineaford, for whose neighbourly kindness he must ever be thankful. She had continued to visit until she had left for town for the season, notwithstanding the unfortunate circumstances and the inevitable scandalmongering. Lady Guineaford's own bevy of daughters had been educated to advantage by one of the women trained under the formidable matron who had replied to him from the Seminary. But although she had allegedly offered him her best pupil, Jarrow had balked at the girl's age. It was only after both of the older females he had engaged through an agency had refused to remain at Castle Jarrow upon any terms that he had once more written to Mrs Duxford. By good fortune, Miss Faraday had been still available, and Jarrow had decided— much against his better judgement!—to try her. And here she was. Utterly inexperienced, and but two and twenty years of age.

Jarrow sank back, and his jaundiced glance swung to the back parapet where the pale gleam of the overcast sky yet cast shadows from the battlements on to the rooftops below. The girl was bound to hate the place. What female would not? And if by some miracle she did stay, how could he reconcile it with his conscience to condemn another young creature to an indefinite incarceration within these walls? The familiar ache of distress started up again.

If only Julietta's condition had not forced him to it! Had he been wrong to bring her here? But what else could he have done? They could not have continued in London, full in the humiliating glare of the public eye. Whether the *ton* looked in contempt or compassion, Jarrow knew he could not have endured it. For good or ill, he had brought Julietta home. And ill had prevailed.

Sighing, he turned from the parapet and made his way around the roof walkway to the study his father had fashioned long years ago out of the top of one of the back turrets. Jarrow had caused it to be refurbished, along with the other, which had been his own schoolroom for a time before he had been sent away and must now serve Henrietta—if he could find a governess who would remain long enough to begin upon the child's education! God send it would serve the purpose. The sorry example of Julietta left doubt— and pain—at his heart.

For several moments Nell was unable either to speak or move, only one thought revolving in her mind. She must have taken leave of her senses!

Yet, as they drew closer to the castle, dropping down into a slight valley before coming up again upon its other side, she began to see that the mammoth sight had been an illusion. A trick of the light, perhaps, throwing shadows that doubled the place in size. Her breath calmed as the building came into better focus.

Sitting on the brow of a hill, surrounded on all sides by the vastness of the forest, Castle Jarrow was nothing short of a medieval fortress. Nell recognised the style. Simple but intimidating, built of massive stone, a round tower at each of the four corners, with a central entrance to this side that must once have held a formidable gate or drawbridge. The roof was solid with battlements, which, together with its commanding position, must have ensured security for the Jarrows of ancient times. It was not these days the sort of accommodation one expected the gentry to inhabit. And Nell had laughed at Kitty's prognostications of spectres and dungeons!

The gig rattled up to the entrance and carried on through the unbarred opening without a check, its wheels clanging on cobbled stone as if to signal Nell's arrival. Thankfully, the courtyard within had been laid with gravel, and the gig rattled more quietly and came to a halt at a pair of arched doors on the opposite side.

Nell did not immediately alight, her interest caught by the huge stone edifice that surrounded her. The darkening skies above did nothing to lessen the feeling of being dwarfed, and Nell could scarcely blame her predecessors, who, it was said, had turned tail and run at first sight of the place. There was not a light to be seen at any window, and no one came out to greet her. It was as if the castle was untenanted. But that could not be. Indeed, an aroma of cooking emanated from one side of the building, and, as Nell roused herself to descend from the gig, the massive wooden doors were pulled open by an unseen hand.

If Nell had been as fanciful as Kitty, she might have supposed a ghost had been responsible. But as her feet touched the ground and she turned again, she discovered someone standing in the aperture. The butler, if she was to judge by his clothing of formal black, and the neatness of his neckcloth.

Her unease began to dissipate. She must not let her imagination run away with her, for there was normality here. Above all, she must try to give a good impression. After all, her future here depended upon her acquitting herself well, not to mention upholding the reputation of the Paddington Seminary. Putting back the hood of her cloak, she moved forward with a smile.

'I am Miss Faraday. How do you do?'

Detling, who was retrieving her portmanteaux from the gig, volunteered his usual scrap of information. 'Keston that be.'

The butler ignored him. He stepped to one side. 'Pray enter, Miss Faraday. Detling will see to your luggage.'

Nell stepped into a cavernous hall that evidently ran the length of one side of the castle. Ahead of her was a wooden stairway, clearly of much later date than the building itself. It rose in a single flight to a landing halfway up, and turned back on itself to reach the floor above. Beneath her feet was solid wood, upon which a regular pattern of light spattered shadows from several high windows. The shaft in which Nell was standing shortened, and disappeared altogether as the butler shut the main doors. They closed with a thud and left her in relative darkness, reawakening her earlier misgivings.

She was requested to wait, and dismay crept over her as she listened to the echo of the butler's footsteps treading away down the hall. A door opened and shut. Nell was alone.

Silence engulfed her. Try as she might to quieten her rising apprehension, the uneven rhythm of her heartbeat prevailed.

This was absurd! She was allowing herself to be overwhelmed by nothing more than imagination. Nell walked purposefully to the stairway and back again. At least she was creating noise! If only her own footsteps did not sound the more eerie for the echoes she made in the empty space. For all she could see in the dim light, the hall appeared to be devoid of furnishings. And that was indeed odd. Should there not have been at least a chair or two? One might look for a pew, a suit of armour or some other manifestation of bygone days.

The scroop of a door opening caused her to jump. There was an abrupt access of light at one end of the hall. Behind it, a silhouette caused Nell to gasp. The highwayman!

Then it vanished and the door shut, leaving her again in darkness that enveloped the more for the contrast. Had it indeed been that masked and black-garbed figure she had seen? It had certainly born a remarkable resemblance to the man on the horse—if she was to trust her eyes in that brief moment of light. Dared she trust any of her senses in this disordered frame of mind?

Before she could decide whether the apparition had indeed been reality, she was thankful to see the butler returning, bearing a lighted candelabrum. The hall immediately appeared darker again and Nell was glad of his escort up the stairs. They entered one of two rooms at the top, where she found herself in a neat parlour. Keston set down the candelabrum on a table to one side, and once again left her, saying that he would inform the master of her arrival.

Alone for the second time, Nell crossed to the window, looking out into the courtyard below. At this height, the fading day still afforded sufficient light to see that the gig had been moved to one side, the horse already taken from between the shafts. There was nobody about. The castle might as well have been deserted. For several minutes her gaze roved the unresponsive walls, searching for any sign of life. The inside windows were all casements, except for those in the slight curve formed by the corner towers between the walls. But for that, and the silhouette of the battlements upon the rooftop, one might not know it was a castle at all.

Time lagged by. No one came, and Nell felt the stirrings of exasperation. She hardly knew now what she had expected, for the reality overshadowed all her previous imaginings. It would seem that she had come to a place of loneliness and silence. Unless it was the thick walls that made it so. What price the life of the little girl she had come to teach, growing up in this relic of the Middle Ages?

Although she was obliged to admit, turning from the window to look about the parlour, that here at least the pervasive sense of ancient days did not hold sway. The light from the candelabrum cast shadows across chairs set neatly against the walls. They looked to be aged and sturdy specimens, but of a style more recent, with cushioned seats the colour of dull gold. An oriental carpet warmed the floor, and near where she stood at the window was the table where the butler had placed the candles. It was of walnut, set between two chairs more delicate in shape than the rest. A marbled fireplace at one end led up to panelled walls inset with damask hangings whose gold matched the upholstery. A portrait of a woman hung above the mantel, drawing Nell's eye. Putting off her gloves, she dropped them on the table and, picking up the candelabrum, crossed the room.

Depicted within the gilded frame was a woman of exceptional beauty, of full red lips and dark eyes, lush curls of black falling *en négligé* from an alabaster brow. About her white neck lay an intricate collar worked in gold with a gleam of green jewels.

It was puzzling, for the style of the portrait looked to be modern, while the necklace appeared of much older origin. Was it an heirloom?

'Miss Faraday?'

Nell jumped violently, almost dropping the candelabrum. She turned quickly, righting the candles before they could drip upon the carpet below her feet. In the doorway stood a gentleman in black.

A vision of the highwayman flashed across her mind and was as swiftly banished. As the man moved into the room, his features lit by the single candle he held, it was to be seen that his attire was rather for home wear than riding. He wore a suit of unrelieved black, and as Nell noted the black of his neck-cloth she recalled that he was in mourning.

She moved to the table and laid down the candelabrum. Turning, she dropped a curtsy. 'How do you do, Lord Jarrow?'

Unmoving, Jarrow stared at the slender figure of the girl. Above the dark cloak that concealed her shape rose a halo of fair hair, mellowed perhaps by the candlelight into the colour of warm honey. Within it the light from the table fell upon features distinctly pleasing, if a trifle strong, and a smile that radiated warmth. Even as he felt himself responding to it, Jarrow noted with dismay the youthful bloom on the girl's cheek. It was worse than he had expected! Her age was bad enough. Why must the creature be so personable into the bargain?

Forgetting that he had not answered her, Jarrow moved into the room. As he crossed to the table, she shifted to one side and he received an impression of unusual height. He laid his candlestick down and turned to find himself being regarded by a pair of frowning eyes of an odd colour, which he could not immediately determine. Distracted, he extended a hand.

'Forgive my abstraction, ma'am.'

Her fingers were chill, and she withdrew them quickly. The frown did not leave her face, and there was little warmth in her voice, which had a mellow timbre.

'You looked, sir, rather critical than abstracted.'

Her frankness did her no discredit. 'I think surprised would better describe it. You are not what I expected.'

Nell felt herself bristling. Her self-possession had faltered as he had stared at her in that rude way. It was not the sort of look that flattered. She had read disappointment in it and felt an immediate rise of annoyance. She gave him back look for look.

'I made no secret of my age, sir, if that is what troubles you.'

A faint smile relaxed his features. 'It does trouble me, but that was not what I meant.' He must have spied the spark in her eye for he held up a hand. 'My concern at your youth is more on your own account than mine, I assure you, Miss Faraday. This is scarcely the sort of place one would wish upon a young girl.'

He wafted the hand as he spoke to encompass the castle, shifting a little away from her. Nell detected a note of disparagement in his voice and wondered at it. Did he dislike living here? He was not, she judged, all that old himself. At first sight, there had been an impression of severity, which had made him appear older—the black clothes, perhaps, or the dark hair worn unfashionably long and tied in a queue at the back. Close up, Nell could see that he was relatively young. A wide brow above eyes set deep, a straight nose and a well-sculpted mouth. It was a lean-featured countenance, furrowed by suffering rather than years.

Nell caught at her own thought. What had made her suppose such a thing? Lord Jarrow was turning to her again, and she consciously searched his face, aware at the same time of what he said.

'If at any time you feel yourself unable to stay, Miss Faraday, you must tell me at once. Do not be deterred by concerns of losing either money or reputation, for I shall make all right. I should be sorry indeed to think of so young a female remaining here against her will. Indeed, I am surprised that you are still here!'

A spurt of laughter was surprised out of Nell. 'So am I, Lord Jarrow, if the truth be told. The journey to this place was decidedly eerie, and your castle more so. But you had given warning of it, and I should think myself a poor creature to be put off by what must be, after all, but the stirrings of imagination.'

'Then you have a good deal more courage than your predecessors, ma'am.'

Jarrow had spoken automatically, but his own words echoed in his mind. She clearly did have courage. What was more, she had an open manner and a forthright way with her that argued strength of personality, and maturity beyond her years. He perceived that she was eyeing him with curiosity.

'There is something you wished to ask me?'

'I was wondering whether the ladies you mention truly ran away at first sight of the place, as you wrote to Mrs Duxford.'

Jarrow sighed. 'I cannot blame them. The first refused even to alight from the carriage, and Detling had to drive her straight back to Ilford.'

'And the second?'

There was a light of amusement in her face, and Jarrow was obliged to smile. 'I believe she got as far as the hall.'

She nodded in a decisive way. 'Yes, I must say that the hall is not endearing. It would be the better for some furnishings.'

'If we had any.'

The dryness of his tone drew Nell's immediate interest. She was tempted to question it. Was he purse-pinched, then? She held her tongue. It was hardly her business to be enquiring into his circumstances. Yet she was intrigued by the hint of a troubled life in shadowed hollows under his eyes—eyes of light brown, she thought. The hollows were repeated in clefts below his cheekbones and beside his mouth. She wondered how long he had been a widower.

Lord Jarrow had picked up his candlestick. 'I will show you to your chamber.'

He would show her? Why not ring for a servant? But it was not for her to argue. She went to the table with the idea of taking up the candelabrum, and then hesitated.

'Should I take this, Lord Jarrow? Or do you wish it to be left in this room?'

He glanced where she gestured. 'Take it by all means. No one is going to be using the parlour now.

I dare say you will feel more comfortable, for there is precious little light in the passages.'

Nell retrieved her gloves and lifted the candela-brum. 'It is certainly dark in this uncertain weather.'

Her employer halted in the doorway, turning on her with a look abruptly fierce. 'It has nothing to do with the weather. You may count yourself fortunate to see the light of day at all in this hellhole!'

The startled look in her eyes caught at Jarrow's conscience. He thrust down on the rise of his own deep frustration. 'I beg your pardon.'

His voice was stiff, but Nell's interest had quickened at the further evidence of disquiet. Impelled by an absurd wish to ease him, she made light of it.

'My dear sir, it would be wonderful indeed if your temper was not impaired through living in a place like this.' She was rewarded by a lightening of his features, and pursued the theme. 'Indeed, since you are so clearly aware of the disadvantages of your own home, I am obliged to acquit you of testing me.'

The intensity of Jarrow's feelings had eased, but they gave way now to puzzlement. 'Testing you, Miss Faraday? How, pray?'

Her gesture encompassed the parlour. 'Why, by keeping me waiting so long in this room. It had occurred to me that perhaps you were wishing to discover if I would grow too frightened to remain.'

He laughed out at that. 'Not at all. I apologise for keeping you waiting. The case is that though the way to my study is short, there is a difficult winding stair to be negotiated and Keston is a good deal too elderly to be either careless or hurried.'

Nell smiled. 'It was not my intention to complain, Lord Jarrow.'

'I know it wasn't,' he agreed. 'But it will be, Miss Faraday. Believe me, it will be.'

The way to Nell's allotted chamber was simple enough. She had only to follow the passage that led, so Lord Jarrow informed her, all around the castle.

'There are two floors, and you will do better to confine yourself to this one, and the schoolroom, which you will see tomorrow. I would not wish you to come to grief falling unwary down one of the mouldering stairways within the turrets. Some sections are safe enough, and we have attempted to lock the doors and block off those that are suspect.'

As she followed in his wake, Nell made a mental vow to avoid the turrets. They passed two bedchambers down one side, the second allotted to her charge, the honourable daughter of the house. Then, after negotiating the curved portion that must lead about one of the towers, Nell found herself standing in a niche that overlooked the road.

'Ah, I see. We are at the front of the castle.'

Lord Jarrow opened a door behind them. 'You are in here, Miss Faraday.'

Her chamber was the middle one of three, set directly over the castle entrance. It was larger than she had expected, testament to the great size of the edifice, and positively luxurious—for the quarters of a gov-

erness. Opposite the window that let onto the courtyard, its shutters open to let in what little light there
was, stood a bed of good proportions, hung with curtains of heavy brocade, considerably faded, in a pattern of red on a yellow ground. Her two portmanteaux
had already been placed beside it, and she noted a
carpet on the floor that echoed the oriental style of the
one in the parlour. A heavy linen press was set in a
corner, together with a simple dressing table, above
which a wood-framed mirror had been attached to the
panelled wall. On the floor below were tucked a basin
and ewer, but Nell stopped short of searching in the
bedside cabinet or under the bed for the necessary pot.

It was a great deal more comfortable than her shared
accommodation at the Seminary, and far grander than
she had thought for. She set the candelabrum down
upon the cabinet by the bed and turned, astonished, to
see Lord Jarrow cast a disparaging look about.

'I suppose it will have to do,' he muttered. 'If you
find anything wanting, I beg you will let me know.'

Nell could only gaze at him. Why in the world
should he concern himself with the needs of a mere
governess? A horrid thought threw her into speech.

'I should not dream of troubling you, my lord. I
dare say your housekeeper will supply me with anything I should need.'

He gave her the oddest look, and Nell's suspicion
deepened. A nervous flutter disturbed her stomach.
Surely she must be mistaken? There was nothing for
it. She must ask him outright.

'You do have a housekeeper, sir?'

Lord Jarrow's unnerving gaze did not shift from her face. Her breath shortened. Driven, Nell demanded, 'My lord, is this an all-male household?'

He started—almost as if he had not heard her earlier question. But his immediate answer belied this. 'Of course it is not. Yes, I have a housekeeper.'

Nell's breath escaped in a relieved whoosh. That had been more alarming than her apprehensions of the castle! To be alone in any sort of situation with only his lordship and a parcel of male servants must have been impossible to endure. The Duck would have advised her to remove herself, and that right speedily. If there was one thing more certain than another, had asserted that worldly wise lady, it was that one's personal safety lay in the presence of other female staff. And senior female staff at that.

Nell knew her lot to be unenviable. Gently bred, but yet confined outside one's proper station, a governess could expect to make few friendships. Only the housekeeper had a status remotely equal to one's own. There was no guarantee that one could befriend the woman—which Nell suspected had been proved with Prue, whose letters had let fall a hint of trouble from that quarter—but one could always seek her company for protection, if subjected to importunities from the gentlemen of the house.

Jarrow noted the relief, and had no difficulty in interpreting it. She had no reason to fear him, attractive though she undoubtedly was. He dared say he could

also vouch for Toly, little though he trusted him on
other counts. But there was poor comfort in that. Her
questions had made him realise that he had not
thought beyond a certainty that she would not stay.
How little she knew of the situation here. The ominous
nature of Castle Jarrow was the least of it!

He moved out of the room and into the recess over
the front entrance. It behoved him to tell her the exact
state of affairs. Yet he hesitated. Was it reluctance to
give her any other cause for distaste? Perhaps it was
better that she discovered it little by little. At least he
must explain the oddities she had evidently perceived.

He found Miss Faraday at his side, and realised that
she was not as tall as he had thought, for he topped
her by several inches. Her gaze was trained upon what
little of the view was visible. Was she looking at that
part of the road illuminated only by spill from lamps
within the castle, and regretting her decision? The
thought pushed him into speech.

'You little know what you have taken on by coming
here.'

Nell jerked round. The black mass of the forest had
made her feel once again distinctly menaced. The fretful note in Lord Jarrow's voice grated on her nerves.

'What is it you mean, sir?'

In the light of his candle, she saw his features had
grown tight. 'You are so young.'

Impatient, Nell nipped this in the bud. 'We have
been over all that, Lord Jarrow. If you have something
to say, speak plainly, if you please.'

A sigh escaped him. 'Perhaps I should have been plainer at the outset.'

'That is past mending, sir. But the present will do very well.'

He was obliged to admit that she was right. He smiled faintly. 'Since you will have it, Miss Faraday, you must understand that we are informal here. Circumstances—into which I shall not drag you—are such that there are but five servants.'

Nell could not help the shock. 'Only five! In a place of this nature?'

She then wished she had held her peace, for her employer's features closed in. She noted the tightening muscle at his jaw and resentment in the dark eyes. Had she not guessed he was purse-pinched? She had not meant to embarrass him.

'I beg your pardon, sir. I was surprised just for the moment.' She saw a slight relaxation in his face and hurried on. 'I have met the butler and Detling, and you mentioned your housekeeper. Who are the other two?'

Jarrow answered her smoothly enough. 'Duggan, my daughter's nurse. And then there is Grig, who is best described as a general help.'

Nell felt absurdly guilty for his discomfort. 'I dare say your household is small enough for them to manage?'

'There is only my daughter and my brother-in-law beside myself. But, no, they can't manage. Which is why I would not trouble Mrs Whyte, who is busy cooking dinner, with the trivial task of showing the new governess to her chamber.'

Aware of sounding irritable, Jarrow made an effort to control his voice. Was it the girl's fault that he had come to this? She was eyeing him with a look that he was at a loss to interpret, and he made a discovery. Her eyes were green. Not that blue-grey colour that was often taken for green. They were a clear and dark-ish green, like the forest just before dusk.

She did not speak, and he felt all the more conscious of his unnecessary harshness. It behoved him to soften what he had said.

'The truth is, Miss Faraday, that neither Toly nor myself make many demands upon the servants. Keston valets us both—which is to say he looks after our clothes. Neither of us is so pampered that we cannot dress ourselves, I am happy to say. We keep to these upper rooms for the most part, and our visitors are few and infrequent. We do no entertaining. Indeed, we have been quiet here for some time, even before—'

He broke off. The governess was silent, and only a slight frown between fair brows showed that she had noticed his jarring halt. There was no reason not to say it. With difficulty, he resumed.

'We could hardly have been anything but quiet here—since the death of my wife.'

The compassion in her face repulsed him even before she expressed it.

'Naturally you could not, sir. I am so sorry.'

It was out before he could stop it. 'Why the devil should you be? You know nothing of her!' He caught himself up, clamping down on his hasty temper. 'Don't heed me, pray.'

Nell felt the more sorry for him. She could not doubt but that Lord Jarrow was still raw from his loss. She wished she knew how long it had been. Not that it mattered. It had taken years before she could think of Papa with any degree of calm, with the result that she had banished all thought of him for fear of breaking down.

There was nothing she could say to mitigate her employer's pain, so she had as well hold her peace. His grief had best be left to himself.

But Jarrow, having recovered his temper, was disgusted with himself. 'You must think me a boorish creature, Miss Faraday, but I promise you I am not always so well fitted to this hideous castle of mine.'

This was absurd, and Nell could not repress a reproving look. Lord Jarrow was moved to grin at her.

'You are not come to be governess to me, Miss Faraday. You need not think to begin your reign by reprimanding your employer!'

Nell had to laugh. 'Indeed, no, sir. But I wish you will tell me about my charge.'

She then wished she had not spoken, for again he pokered up. Heavens, but the man was difficult! She put a tentative question.

'Did I understand correctly that the child will need careful handling? I assure you I am not inexperienced,

sir. I do not wish to boast, but I have for years past
been relied upon to pour calm on troubled waters, and
to deal with the more difficult of my younger com-
panions at the Seminary. Indeed, one of my particular
friends has been much in my charge, for she cherishes
ambitions that have no place in her future.'

Jarrow listened with impatience. If she supposed
such actions fitted her to deal with Hetty, she much
mistook the matter! God, why had he engaged her? It
was never going to work. He should have known it.
Fate was merciless, and there could be no quarter. The
bitterness erupted.

'Miss Faraday, I would not wish to belittle any particular assistance you may have rendered among no
doubt troublesome chits, but you can hardly have had
experience of dealing with what now lies before you.
Unless you happen to have spent some time in an asy-
lum for lunatics?'

Chapter Two

Nell stared, unable to credit the evidence of her own ears. If Lord Jarrow had said what she thought! There was a blaze in his eyes and a white shade around the tight-lipped mouth. For an instant, it struck her that it was her employer and not his daughter who was—as he had intimated—insane. The absurdity of this thought brought her out of the shock. Wrath replaced it.

'Am I to understand, sir, that you believe Miss Jarrow to be deranged?'

He flinched, turning his eyes away. But Nell was too angry to heed his hurt.

'If that is indeed the case, I can only say that the matter should have been made clear and laid before Mrs Duxford at the outset. To have concealed such a thing must be detrimental both to your daughter and to any female who had taken on this post!'

Jarrow shifted uncomfortably. 'I know it.'

'Then why—?'

He turned on her. 'Because it is not what I know to be the case. It is only what I dread!'

'Heavens, but *why*?'

Jarrow shrugged. Why beat about the bush? She must discover it sooner or later. Yet he could not bring himself to make a recital of those disquieting signs that tortured him. He prevaricated.

'There is reason enough. We have—' he drew a painful breath '—instances of insanity in the family.'

She was looking at him in a stricken sort of way. God, but he had thrown the cat among the pigeons now! He must do what he might to mend it. Only the words that came out of his mouth did little to further that intention.

'You need have no apprehension. You will not be expected to deal with the violence of Hetty's tantrums.'

Nell glared at him. 'Tantrums? Is that all? And upon this you base the wicked supposition that the poor child has lost her wits?'

'It is by no means all! But let that pass.'

Watching as he shunted restlessly across the passage and back again, Nell's temper began to cool. Had it been shock that had caused her to lose her sangfroid? It had been the crowning horror to a singularly difficult day! But she had been wrong to attack him.

'I should not have spoken to you so. Only what reason have you for supposing Miss Jarrow to have inherited the trait?'

'She may not have done so. My hope is that she will grow out of it, but it cannot be gainsaid that there is room for doubt.'

'But why do you fear it, sir? What manifestations have you seen?'

He halted before her, the dark eyes hard. 'I would prefer to let you see for yourself. You will find out soon enough.'

But this would not do for Nell. 'Sir, I must insist upon knowing at least what I may expect. You spoke of tantrums, but—'

'Miss Faraday, I will say no more! I would not wish to prejudice you either one way or the other. Indeed, I will welcome the opinion of an outsider when you have had an opportunity to judge of Hetty's condition.'

There was some sense in that. Yet it laid her open not only to unknown horrors, but also to dealing awry with the child due to ignorance. 'Surely there must be something I should know—at least that which may help me to deal with the situation when it arises?'

Lord Jarrow shook his head. 'Duggan knows just what to do, and she will call upon my aid if she cannot manage.'

Nell was not at all satisfied, but it would be futile to argue. It was evident that her employer's mind was made up. She temporised.

'May I not meet the child then? Hetty, I think you said?'

'Henrietta. She is likely preparing for bed. For to-night, you need only make yourself at home. I dare say you will wish to wash away the stains of travel. Do not trouble to change, however. We rarely do so.

Dinner was put back to await your arrival, but we dine in half an hour. I will come myself to fetch you.'

Nell began to offer a word of thanks, but Lord Jarrow was already walking away. She watched him turn into the tower curve, and nearly opened her mouth to call him back. How dared he leave her flat after what had passed? The least he could have done was to try to calm such spectres as he had raised! Then she recalled that he was her employer and there was no question of his daring anything. He might do as he chose.

Turning into the bedchamber given over for her use, she sighed as she shut the door. Why in the world had she not taken up the promising position that had been offered to her on the very day the Duck had received Lord Jarrow's letter? Had she been blinded by her own pride, or seduced by an ambition that must be counted as silly as any that Kitty had voiced?

'A widower, Nell! And a baron too. The two of you alone together in a Gothic castle! What could be more romantic? I do wish the Duck would let me go instead. I know you will never take advantage of such an opportunity, whereas I should be at pains to make Lord Jarrow fall in love with me!'

But it had not been the impossible dream of romance that had lured Nell. Nothing could have been further from her mind. It was the idea of a challenge that had caught at her. Not for Helen Faraday the cosy domesticity of a country house, with two or three sedate little girls to be brought up to take their chances in the marriage mart. Oh, no. She must needs throw away a secure tenure in a respectable family, which could have kept her employed for the next fifteen years. Instead she had opted for the glimmer of danger, the excitement of chance and hazard. What a fool, preening herself upon her capabilities of management! Allowing her head to be turned with the oft-repeated notion that Nell—and only Nell!—could be counted upon to deal with the *difficult* girls. And it had brought her to this!

'I have a good mind not to unpack you at all,' she informed the two portmanteaux. They, naturally enough, returned no answer. Nell sighed again. 'All the same, I shall have to do so, for I need my night things. It is far too late to run away today.'

Yet as she lifted the first one on to the bed and began to undo the straps, that devil of pride within her raised its head. After all, even if Henrietta did prove to be unbalanced, she was only a little girl. Was it beyond Nell's powers to learn how to deal with her? She did not think so. Besides, she did so hate to be thought incapable!

She thrust the portmanteau open with determined hands. His lordship supposed her to be too young, did he? A little demonstration for his benefit might not go amiss.

The butler served the meal, receiving dishes from an unseen minion outside the dining-room door. Contrary to Nell's expectation, the atmosphere was both lively and convivial, for which she undoubtedly had to thank the presence of Lord Jarrow's brother-in-law.

Mr Beresford—Bartholomew by name, 'but everyone calls me Toly'—had greeted her with a jocular reference to her continued presence in the house.

'By Jove, Eden! Haven't you managed to scare her off yet?'

'Toly, do try for a little conduct,' had begged Lord Jarrow in a weary tone.

'But, m'dear fellow, I am positively bowled over!' He had executed a neat bow. 'How de do, Miss Faraday? Deuced glad to see you here. Prettiest sight this barrack of a place has seen in a twelvemonth!'

He had continued in this strain as he bustled to a chair opposite his own, pulling it out for Nell and begging her to be seated. She was more bemused than gratified by this show of attention, wondering a trifle uneasily at the wisdom of dining alone with two gentlemen. Her position in the household should preclude any charge of impropriety, and she must suppose that any other arrangement would cause difficulties for the shorthanded staff. Better two gentlemen than one. And since it seemed to be Mr Beresford's mission to be as amusing as possible, she was at least spared the difficulty of finding inoffensive topics upon which to converse with her touchy employer.

His lordship had not, true to his promise, made any adjustment in his dress beyond, as Nell suspected, donning a fresh neckcloth and retying his hair. She could not think, on the other hand, that Mr Beresford was accustomed to sport a satin waistcoat and a suit of black broadcloth throughout the day in the country. Nell was glad she had ignored Lord Jarrow's instruction—only because she had felt grubby from the journey—and exchanged the warmer gown of brown kerseymere for one of green dimity, its design modest as befit her station, but with a hint of current fashion in the raised waistline. Nell had prepared her wardrobe with care, riding a neat line between simplicity and elegance. Circumstance had forced her to earn her bread, but it would not force her to be drab!

It was noticeable that Mr Beresford did not hold mourning as strictly as his brother-in-law, for his neckcloth was snowy white and the waistcoat grey. Nell judged him the more handsome of the two for the planes of his countenance were more uniform and better rounded, and he had not the other's marks of a troubled existence. He had hair as dark as Lord Jarrow's, although it was shorter, sitting just on his collar, with an unruly slick that fell forward across his brow. He smiled a good deal and had an open gaze, with an odd trick of widening his eyes in an unblinking stare whenever he laughed. Nell found it disconcerting.

The food was simple fare, but well cooked. A roast, from which Lord Jarrow carved, formed the central dish. Two pies—one of them broken—flanked it, together with a platter of sliced cold meat, boiled spinach and stews of both mushroom and cucumber. That this was the normal diet of the household became obvious from Mr Beresford's remarks.

'Ah, still working our way through the pork, are we? Keston, has that wretch at Park Farm no notion of slaughtering cows?'

The butler had picked up Nell's plate, and was holding it while his lordship placed several slices of meat upon it. 'I believe this is the last of the pork, sir. Mrs Whyte has the intention of sending for beef tomorrow.'

'Thank heaven for that!' Mr Beresford turned mock indignant eyes upon Nell. 'You will scarcely credit it, Miss Faraday, but we have had nothing but pork for at least a se'ennight. Mrs Whyte attempts to dress it up, but I am not deceived.' He took up his knife and pointed. 'That pie is ham, for I remember it well. And if those slices are not brawn, you may call me a dunderhead. What is in the new pie, Keston, or dare I ask? Not pork, I beg of you!'

'Artichoke bottoms, sir.'

Mr Beresford made a disgusted sound and laid down his knife. 'There now, Miss Faraday, you have a delightful choice. Pork, pork, pork or artichoke!'

Nell accepted her plate from the butler with a smile. 'You will not find a sympathiser in me, sir. I am used to the plainest of food, and have besides been taught to appreciate whatever falls to my lot.'

She did not think the statement merited the loud guffaw that emanated from Mr Beresford, and noted the frowning glance thrown at him from the head of the table.

'It wasn't a joke, Toly. Miss Faraday hales from an orphanage of sorts.'

Dismay spread over the other man's countenance and Nell felt obliged to interrupt a flood of apology. 'I beg you will not mention it, sir.' She turned to Lord Jarrow, bottling up an unwarranted rise of spleen. 'You paint a false portrait of me, my lord. While it is true that the Seminary was set up to aid orphans, we were never treated as charity cases. Indeed, Mrs Duxford was at pains to give us respect as females who had a rare opportunity to be useful in the world.'

Mr Beresford's jaw dropped. 'Gad! If I didn't know better, ma'am, I'd take you for a governess! A rare set-down, Eden.'

'And well deserved.' Jarrow directed a rueful smile at the girl. 'I did not mean to belittle you, Miss Faraday. My sole desire was to silence my rattlepate of a brother here.'

He eyed Toly's grinning enjoyment. Damn the fellow! Was this determination to be the life and soul of the party due to Miss Faraday's undoubted attraction? He had best find an opportunity to warn him off. The last thing he needed was to lose her services through unwanted attentions from his brother-in-law. Not that she had yet had a chance to prove herself up to the difficult task.

While she made a selection from the dishes Keston presented—taking, he noted, sensible portions without showing greed—he watched her surreptitiously. Her attention, as she began to eat, was held by Toly's constant flow of spirits so that she was mercifully unconscious of his interest. Since, despite the deprivations to which his household was subject, he refused to dine in near darkness, both wall-sconces and two large silver candelabra were lit and set upon sideboard and table. There was thus sufficient light to see Miss Faraday's features clearly, although her profile was for the most part turned towards him.

It was a singularly interesting profile, with a line of strength in both jaw and nose. But the golden hair, which she had somehow piled into a knot behind, softened her face. It had been unruly before, likely from the exigency of a day of travel, but its neatness now did nothing to dull its effect. She could never survive the life to which she was condemned, for men were never going to leave her alone. A recollection of some of the things she had said to him caused an inward smile. Not that Miss Faraday would fall readily. She would give as good as she got. Perhaps he need not trouble to speak to Toly after all.

As if she felt his regard, she turned her head and Jarrow quickly withdrew his gaze. He signed to Keston.

'Will you take wine, Miss Faraday?'

Nell was given no opportunity to answer, for Mr Beresford immediately broke in.

'You had best do so, Miss Faraday. About the only worthwhile boast this mouldering ruin has is the quality of its cellars. Thanks largely to mine host here's dear father, who thoughtfully laid down several pipes of the best claret long moons ago.'

The butler was already pouring, and Nell signed to him to stop when the glass was only half-full. 'That will be sufficient, I thank you.'

'Well, you may give me a refill, Keston. At least it will serve to take away the taste of pork.'

His laughter jarred. Already tired of the incessant humorous assaults upon her employer's dwelling and the dull nature of the repast, Nell wondered at Lord Jarrow's patience. In his shoes, she would have been tempted to ask why his brother-in-law remained if the castle was so odious to him.

As if he read her thought, the culprit threw a sheepish grin across the table. 'I had best hold my tongue before Eden takes it into his head to eject me from these hallowed walls.'

It was too much! Nell erupted. 'Indeed, I wonder that he does not, sir! Since it is apparent that Lord Jarrow is not overfond of the place himself, it might be kinder in you to refrain from poking fun at circumstances that are clearly beyond his control.'

There was a brief instant of silence. Then Mr Beresford broke into a shout of laughter. 'You've a new champion, Eden. Spoken like a true governess, ma'am!'

But Nell was listening to the echo of her own words in her mind with growing dismay. Without volition, her eyes strayed towards the head of the table. Lord

Jarrow was watching her with an unreadable expression. Was that an ironic gleam in his eye? Recalling the way she had spoken to him earlier, Nell could not in all honesty blame him. Involuntarily, she smiled.

'You must be wishing me at Jericho, my lord. I see that I have been too used to speak my mind to be capable of minding my tongue. I shall do my best to mend, I promise you.'

Unexpectedly, he grinned. 'Don't. I like it. Besides, I thought I had explained that we have dispensed with formality.'

'And a good job too!' came irrepressibly from his brother-in-law. 'It would be a great deal too bad if we were obliged to add ceremony to the tortures we endure in this abominable hole.'

Exasperated, Nell turned on him again. 'Then why in the world do you stay, sir? I refuse to believe that his lordship holds you here against your will.'

Lord Jarrow broke in before the other man could answer. 'Far from it. But you do not perfectly understand, my dear Miss Faraday. My respected brother-in-law has not a feather to fly with, and, much as he loathes it, this abode is better than none.'

Nell could scarce prevent herself from wincing as Mr Beresford responded with another bout of hearty laughter, that eerie wide-eyed stare prominent. It struck her suddenly that his amusement was feigned. Why he should be at pains to pretend left her at a loss. Although he took his host's words in good part.

'Perfectly true, old fellow. No notion how I'd manage if I didn't batten on you.'

He took up his wine glass again and drank deep. Nell wondered whether she ought to apologise for taking him to task. She looked to Lord Jarrow again and found that he was engaged in a low-voiced conversation with his butler. A hissing sound from across the table drew her attention. Toly Beresford was leaning towards her. He signalled a wish that she should come closer. Intrigued, Nell leant forward.

But before he could speak, a sudden shrieking broke into the silence. Nell jumped and dropped her fork. The noise was muted, but there could be no doubt that it emanated from within the castle, and close at hand. It sounded like a fury at full sail, repetitive and urgent. A curse was drawn from Lord Jarrow.

'Hell and the devil!'

He laid down his utensils and rose quickly, brushing past the butler towards the door. Nell turned her startled glance upon Mr Beresford in mute question.

He threw his eyes heavenwards. 'Your charge, I believe.'

Hastily getting to her feet, Nell made to follow her employer. He already had the door open, and the immediate crescendo of the shrieks threw Nell's heart into her mouth. Lord Jarrow paused when he saw her, looking back. His voice was sharp.

'Stay where you are! I will not be long.'

Nell hesitated, but Keston settled the matter by closing the door behind him. She listened in a good deal of dismay to the continued emanation of the distressing cries.

'If you take my advice, you will sit down again, Miss Faraday. Nothing you can do.'

She turned, utterly discomposed, to find Mr Beresford had come around the table and was once more holding her chair. Unable to think what else to do, Nell returned to it, taking her seat in a bemused fashion. She supposed that he and the butler were too used to such happenings to be troubled by them. She looked at her plate, where the remains of her meal lay congealing. Her appetite deserted her.

She glanced towards Keston, who was busying himself in clearing dishes from the table to the sideboard, presumably in preparation for the remove to the second course. Nell found a glass of wine in her hand and discovered that Mr Beresford had put it there, having refilled it from the decanter.

He smiled as he moved back to his own seat. 'No need to look so distressed. She'll stop in a moment.'

Nell frowned across at him. 'Does this happen often?'

'Oh, yes.' He took up his knife and fork again. For all his complaints, he was making a hearty meal. 'Regular little madam is Henrietta, if she don't get her own way. You'll get used to it.'

Did he not know then of Lord Jarrow's fears? Surely he must. If there truly were signs of insanity, no member of such a close household could possibly be unaware of them. She eyed him uncertainly and surprised a look of sympathy in his face. He shook his head.

'Poor old fellow. Don't like to say it to his face, but you can see now why I remain. It's what I was about to say to you when Hetty started her yowling. Positively inhuman to leave Jarrow alone at such a time.' He grinned brightly. 'You'd written me down as unfeeling, Miss Faraday, now hadn't you? I do it to tease him, y'know. Keep him from brooding.'

Nell pounced. 'Why should he brood, sir?'

He looked taken aback, but she kept her eyes on his face. 'Don't you know? Gad, you must do, ma'am. Can't have escaped your notice that we're both in mourning.'

She was disconcerted. 'That, no.' On impulse, she shifted her plate to one side and leaned forward. 'How long ago did she die, sir?'

'M'sister? Oh, must be seven or eight months now. Lose track, y'know. Every day the same.' He frowned as if in thought. 'Let's see. September '95 it was. Seven months, isn't it? Yes, seven. And young Hetty turned six in February, which is what started Eden off on the idea of getting her a governess.'

Which drew Nell's attention back to the cries yet to be heard, even through the thick walls of the castle. Her nerves had settled, however, and she was able to listen without flinching inside. Only she knew that she could not endure to hear it and be forced to sit inactive. Not for long. Even now she itched to run to the child's rescue, convinced that she would find a means to help.

No, she must not allow pride to rule her. Those in the household could not but know better than she how to allay whatever distress had been stimulated. Her gaze focused again on Mr Beresford, now calmly sipping his wine, having evidently eaten his fill. Could she with propriety pump him for that information which Lord Jarrow refused to give her? She glanced at the butler, who was snuffing candles, which had begun to gutter in the holder on the sideboard. He was elderly, and hopefully would not hear her. She leaned a little across the table again.

'Mr Beresford.' Was that a start he gave? His mind had evidently been elsewhere. 'How often does this sort of thing happen?'

'You mean Hetty?' He shook his head vaguely. 'Now and then, y'know. Once or twice in a month, I suppose. Perhaps more. So used to it that I can't properly recall.'

'What is there besides tantrums?'

Mr Beresford stared at her, a frown gathering at his brow. 'What else?' Then he struck a hand to his forehead. 'I see what you're getting at! Eden mentioned that, did he? No, no, my brother's mistaken, ma'am. What else is to be expected of a little girl who has lost her mother? Perfectly understandable, and so I keep telling him. Can't suppose it possible that the poor mite has inherited the fatal Beresford tendency.

Why, I myself am perfectly free of the taint. And as for Julietta...'

His voice died, and he shifted into a reverie. Reluctant to disturb those memories that she might inadvertently have evoked with her questions, Nell watched him in a good deal of distress. The fatal Beresford tendency! Free of the *taint*? Heaven help her, there was some substance for Lord Jarrow's fears.

Even as she thought it, she became aware that the shrieking had ceased. How had it been managed? She recalled something her employer had said to her earlier, about the nurse only calling him if she could not manage on her own. Only she had not called him. He had chosen to go immediately upon the sound breaking out. Forgetting her resolve, she addressed Mr Beresford in urgent tones.

'You think Henrietta is merely expressing her grief? Has no one sought to talk to her of her mama? Is it she whom you meant by Julietta?'

He regarded her as if he had not understood. 'Julietta? Talk of her to the child? No, no—what could you say? Too horrific by half! Frighten the girl into flinders, and for what? Best to say nothing. If you take my advice, ma'am, you'll leave well alone on that score.'

Before Nell could think how to reply to a speech that hinted at unknown horrors while giving nothing away, Lord Jarrow was re-entering the room. In silence, she watched him resume his seat. Was it the duller candlelight, or did he look worn?

'Settled again, has she?' enquired Mr Beresford sympathetically.

'She is half asleep.'

'Capital. Best thing for her. Duggan tends her, I expect?'

Was that a narrow look Lord Jarrow gave him as he nodded? Or was she indulging her imagination again? She stiffened warily as his gaze came around to herself. His voice was curt.

'I am sorry this should have happened on your first evening.'

Irrationally, this remark annoyed Nell. It was not as if she were a guest.

'It is as well, sir. I only wish you might be more forthcoming about what has occurred.'

'Time enough for you to find out.'

Nell resented the snap in his voice, but reminded herself that she had no right to do so. It was best that she made no reply if she could not school herself to talk to him with propriety. She was saved the trouble by the laughing intervention of Mr Beresford, once more adopting the teasing tone of his earlier remarks.

'Plain as a pikestaff why he won't talk, Miss Faraday. He's in hopes that ignorance may induce you to remain above a few days.' That irritating laugh came again. 'Can't blame the old fellow if he don't want to put you off.'

It was obvious that Lord Jarrow was in no humour for this type of thing. He threw his brother-in-law a look that caused Nell's conscience to wriggle. It was not her place to be discussing her employer's affairs. She'd had no business to ask questions of Mr Beresford. As well as gossip outright!

To make things worse, the wretched man chose to take his lordship up.

'I see what it is, Eden. Jealousy! While you've been off beating that brat into silence, I've been privileged to enjoy the sole company of the first interesting female to grace this disgracefully Gothic edifice of yours in months.'

Nell heard only vaguely the rest of this nonsensical speech, for her attention had caught fatally on that one horrible word. Lord Jarrow *beat* his daughter? He could not have done so. Particularly if he suspected that her intellect was disordered. As well send the poor child to Bedlam!

She became aware of his voice, clipped and cynical.

'If you have designs upon the new governess, Toly, you had better leave. It must be terrifying enough for Miss Faraday without having her virtue endangered.'

The other's eyes glinted. 'What, and leave you the field? I think not, old fellow.'

Nell met Lord Jarrow's icy gaze as it returned to rest on her face. 'I beg you will ignore my brother-in-law. His notion of banter leaves a good deal to be desired.' Turning back to the other man, his tone became acid. 'As for you, Toly, I wish you will hold your tongue before you give Miss Faraday an entirely false impression of my character as well as your own.'

* * *

Contrary to Nell's expectation, she woke in the morning feeling considerably refreshed. It had been long before she had slept, the events of the few hours she had spent in Castle Jarrow travelling round and round in her brain. On the other hand, she had gone to bed exceptionally early, driven thence by the constraint that had reigned throughout the remainder of dinner.

Even Mr Beresford's determined gaiety had worn thin at last. After the second course had made its appearance, beyond a few jovial remarks upon its content, he had lapsed for the most part into silence. He had stigmatised as meagre a spread of tarts, coddled apples and a selection of fresh fruits augmented by a syllabub, commenting that Mrs Whyte must have swiftly whipped up the syllabub in Nell's honour.

Unwilling to cause further dissension, Nell had dutifully laughed, feeling all the hollowness of putting on a false front. Lord Jarrow had made no attempt to engage in any further conversation. Instead, he had sat in a brown study, eating nothing more, and staring in a vague way at the fruit bowl.

Nell had forced down most of the syllabub and toyed with a slice of tart. Prudence had soon dictated a swift retreat. When she had risen to leave, his lordship's gaze had jerked up abruptly.

'Where are you going?'

'To bed, sir, with your permission. I am very tired.'

Mr Beresford had reached for the decanter, raising a last grin. 'Should think you would be. Don't forget to lock your door!'

Nell had frowned. 'For what reason, pray?'

Lord Jarrow, who had risen politely, had intervened, impatience in his voice. 'No reason at all. No one will disturb you. But by all means lock it if you choose.'

To her annoyance, Nell had been rendered apprehensive by the exchange. She had said a brief goodnight and made for the door. Her employer had stepped out to detain her. Taking up the larger of the two candelabra, he had held it out.

'Take this. Tomorrow Mrs Whyte will give you a supply of candles and some holders.' He had hesitated, the brown gaze searching her face. 'Shall I escort you?'

Nell had shaken her head. 'I will be obliged to find my own way about, sir. I may as well begin now.'

In truth, the eerie darkness of the passages had done little for her peace of mind. She'd been glad of the five candles that spilled light in all directions about her. But there had been no difficulty in finding her way. She had indeed felt excessively tired by the time she had dropped into bed, but her ruminations had kept sleep at bay.

Strangely enough, they had been less concerned with the fate of her prospective charge than with the distresses of the child's father—despite the misgivings engendered by Mr Beresford's mention of his using force to quiet his daughter. If his lordship's suspicions of his daughter's state of mind had any foundation, his lot was indeed tragic, and coming after the loss of his wife, which, if the intriguing words of Mr Beresford were anything to go by, had been a disaster of no common order.

But let her not begin mulling through all that again! Flinging back the bedcurtains, she thrust herself out of the stifling interior and went to pull back the shutters. Relief flooded her along with the sun. It looked to be a glorious day. Her spirits rose and she pulled out the basin and ewer. She could have done with some warm water, but no matter.

Upon the thought came a knock at the door. Nell caught up her robe and shrugged it on. Outside the door she found a harassed-looking woman of middle years, bearing a large jug and dressed in bombazine covered by an apron, a mob cap framing plump features. Its frills rippled as she nodded, smiling.

'I've brought you some hot water, my dear.'

'How very kind!' Nell said warmly. 'You must be Mrs Whyte. Do come in.'

Taking the jug from the older woman, she went to place it on the dressing table. Turning, she saw that the housekeeper had bustled in, and now stood sniffing.

'Still a trifle musty. Hasn't been used for ever so long this room. I've kept it aired, but there's little a body can do when everything in the house is as old as Queen Anne. Have you blankets enough, Miss

Faraday? We've plenty of those at least, whatever else is scarce.'

Nell immediately expressed her satisfaction with her allotted quarters. 'Indeed, I have nothing wanting, I believe, bar an impatience to meet with Miss Jarrow and begin upon my duties.'

A look of distress passed over Mrs Whyte's plump features. 'The poor little mite! Though she's well enough this morning, Duggan tells me.'

Then the housekeeper clearly knew what had happened last night. Nell smiled. 'Then the sooner I begin the better.'

'We'll hope it will be for the better.' The woman fetched a sigh, and then shrugged away her clouded brow, smiling again. 'But that's for later. I'll leave you to your toilet, ma'am. When you're ready, knock on that wall and I'll hear you, for my chamber is next door and I've yet to make the bed. The gentlemen like to get off early, so I do their breakfast first.'

Consternation caught at Nell. She crossed quickly to the bedside cabinet, taking up the essential pocket watch that had been Mrs Duxford's parting gift to her.

'It is past ten! Heavens, I must have been more tired than I thought!' She turned quickly to the housekeeper. 'I do apologize for having inconvenienced you, Mrs Whyte.'

Moving to the door, the older woman tutted. 'You haven't at all. A body couldn't blame you for sleeping a little longer on your first day. So much to take in— and not all of it pleasant, I'll be bound!'

None of it pleasant, Nell might have said. Assuring the housekeeper that she would not dawdle, she closed the door behind her and began swiftly to strip off her night attire.

The ordinary domesticity of the kitchens did much to raise Nell's mood. Refusing to increase Mrs Whyte's burden, she had opted to accompany her and eat below stairs rather than await breakfast in solitary state in the dining parlour.

'You must have quite enough to do, and why in the world should we stand upon ceremony? Lord Jarrow assured me that you are informal here, and I should much prefer to take breakfast in your company, Mrs Whyte.'

The housekeeper had been touchingly grateful. 'Well, it would suit better, Miss Faraday, and that's a fact. There's no gainsaying it's a toil, whether you come through the hall or use them horrid winding stairs in the turret. Can't abide 'em myself, which is why I use the proper stairs, longer though it is. And Mr Keston, the dear, has gone in my stead with Grig to the farm, for you can't trust that noddy on his own. Bound to bring back the wrong joints, and let himself be swindled into the bargain! There's no depending on Farmer Tuffley not to take advantage, for he's as sly as they come, and when you've to watch every penny, you can't be too careful.'

Following in her wake as she led the way, Nell had found these artless disclosures intensely aggravating to her burning curiosity. It was with difficulty that she prevented herself from pelting the housekeeper with questions. While the elder lady prepared, she seated herself out of the way to wait, smoothing the petticoats of her working gown of dyed calico—one of several that she had fashioned in the modest style befitting her station, with sleeves to the wrist and a wrapover bodice made high to the neck. This one was of dull bronze, but its cut, Nell flattered herself, was yet fashionable, the waist riding below her bosom.

Her discretion was rewarded once Mrs Whyte had supplied her with a generous meal. Carving several slices from a fine ham, she had thrown them to warm on to a griddle placed across the great range that spread heat throughout the kitchen quarters. Apologising for the lack of eggs—a supply of which were to be fetched today from the farm—the housekeeper instead produced newly made oatcakes, which had come off the griddle that very morning.

'And there's a seed cake I made only yesterday, which will come up fresh again. I've only to warm it on the griddle with the ham.'

Nell had accepted the offer with grace, although she was by no means as hungry as the meal warranted. For no consideration would she risk offending the housekeeper, whose friendliness and good will were doing a great deal to reconcile her to the difficult future she faced. When she at last sat down—in an adjacent room that evidently served as a pantry for Mrs Whyte and the butler—Nell was gratified that the housekeeper chose to join her and partake of a cup of coffee from the pot she had made.

'I've much to do, but it'll keep, and we can enjoy a little cose.'

'That will be most agreeable,' said Nell warmly.

The mob cap rippled as the housekeeper nodded with vehemence. 'Nothing more uncomfortable than to come among strangers, that's what I say. And worse, to find yourself in a place such as this, where you couldn't be blamed if you was to tease yourself with thoughts of ghosts and such.'

Nell laughed. 'Very true. It is certainly intimidating, but I hope I am not such a ninny as to suppose that it is truly haunted.'

A little to her surprise, Mrs Whyte appeared to be more troubled than amused. The plumpness in her countenance became creased and her mild eyes took on a look of distress. Nell laid down her fork.

'Why, what is it, Mrs Whyte?'

The woman's voice was tense. 'It isn't ghosts, Miss Faraday. But I won't say as there wouldn't be naught to frighten you. An unhappy household is this, and if you ask me, there's those as would keep it so.'

Those? Who in the world could she mean? At a loss for an answer, Nell hesitated a moment too long. It might be a cue. On the other hand, it ill behoved the governess to be indulging her curiosity in a gossip with the housekeeper. But perhaps it had been a slip of the tongue, after all, for Mrs Whyte's manner changed as she nodded towards Nell's plate.

'Don't let it go cold, Miss Faraday.'

Resuming her meal, Nell sought for an innocuous way to re-introduce a discussion of the household. She might with propriety ask about her charge—without touching upon the hateful fears expressed by her employer. Digging into the butter, she carefully kept her tone light as she coated a second oatcake.

'Is Henrietta a pretty child?'

Mrs Whyte's face softened visibly. 'She's a little beauty. Was so, from the cradle.' A reminiscent look crept into her eyes. *'Hair as black as a raven, and eyes like a velvet night.* That's what his lordship said, first time he saw her. Grew up as near a mirror image of the mistress as makes no odds. Though I'd swear her eyes are darker than her ladyship's.'

Into Nell's mind leaped a memory. That picture she had seen. The question was impulsive, out before she could think twice.

'Is that a portrait of Lady Jarrow in the parlour? If Henrietta resembles her so very much, she must indeed be beautiful.'

'Yes, poor soul.'

Was that for Henrietta, or her mother? Nell's thirst for knowledge got the better of her. 'How did she die, Mrs Whyte?'

Clouds gathered in the woman's face. 'Terrible it was. I'm not saying it wasn't a mercy, considering everything, but the manner of it was hideous. My poor mistress was murdered.'

Chapter Three

Despite the warmth exuding from the kitchen next door, a sensation of clammy cold swept through Nell's veins. How could Lady Jarrow's death have been a mercy? And a murder! A vision of Lord Jarrow's haunted countenance, suffering etched into its hollows, swam into her mind. Her heart went out to him.

'Heavens, what a tragedy!'

Mrs Whyte nodded. 'That it was. And all for the curse of a miserable footpad!'

Nell jumped. 'What did you say?'

'Shot her in cold blood!' pursued the housekeeper, a note in her voice that gave echo of the shock she must originally have experienced. 'Folk say it was that wretch Lord Nobody, but there's none to witness it. All that's known is there were a tussle with a masked rider and his gun went off. But he must have meant to kill her. Who'd cock a gun on an unarmed female?'

The instant image of the highwayman Nell had seen was fading in her mind, overlaid instead with the dread features of Papa. So pale, but for the red ooze that seeped steadily past his sightless eyes and ran in a rivulet down his cheek. Pale, and deathly still, until the weight of his lifeless body had toppled him, and he slumped sideways, a heap upon the cushioned seat, ungainly and unmoving.

Unaware that she sat as she had done then, as if petrified, unable to speak or move as the terror bubbled up, Nell was only conscious of a resurgence of that same sensation of faintness that had attacked her at the sight.

She became aware of a voice of concern in her immediate vicinity. 'Oh, dearie me, how pale you look! Miss Faraday! *Miss Faraday!'*

With an effort, Nell pulled herself out of the memory. She blinked upon the plump face peering into hers. She summoned a response. 'I am all right.'

'You don't look it,' said Mrs Whyte frankly. 'Wait. I'll fetch you a glass of water.'

She was gone only a moment, but the sensations were fading with the memory, and Nell was able to take the proffered glass into her own hand. The housekeeper fretted as she sipped.

'I shouldn't have said anything. I'm that sorry, my dear. I'd no call to shock you so deeply. Only I never thought how it might appear to a stranger. I've become used to it, I suppose, like the rest.'

Nell laid down the glass with fingers that shook slightly, and managed to smile. 'It makes no matter. You do not know—'

She broke off, unwilling to shatter her self-imposed silence. Let the woman think her a poor creature. She could bear that better than the inevitable expressions of sympathy—which she had never been able to endure. But she must make some amends.

'Pray do not blame yourself, Mrs Whyte. I am glad you told me. It explains a good deal, and I had rather know than make a slip and distress anyone through ignorance.'

The housekeeper conceded that she had a point, but she was greatly discomposed and not only insisted upon Nell remaining quietly in the kitchen until she should feel fully recovered, but went off to prepare some tea. A luxury in this household, Nell had no doubt, but she refrained from protest. Truth to tell, she was much in need of a cup of the sustaining beverage.

The tea did indeed revive her, and she was able to reassure the housekeeper, who was inclined to blame herself.

'I am not prone to fainting, Mrs Whyte. I suspect it has been rather an accumulation of surprises. There have been several—shall we say unexpected?—aspects to this post that were only to be learned on arrival.'

The housekeeper set her mob cap aflutter. 'I don't doubt it for a moment. The wonder is that you're still here, Miss Faraday.'

Nell thought so too, but it was scarcely politic to say so. 'I hope I have a little more gumption than to run away, however difficult the situation may be.'

'Well, I wouldn't blame you,' declared the house-keeper stoutly. 'No more than I blamed young Liza, hoity-toity madam though she was.'

Upon enquiry, Mrs Whyte explained that Liza had been the last kitchen maid who had left a few weeks back. 'We've not yet replaced her, but then kitchen maids are so hard to come by these days.'

Nell was glad of the change of subject. 'How in the world do you manage?'

'Grig does most of the heavy work. Only he's got so little up top that it has me fair rattled sometimes. I'd rather cope with a sour-faced kitchen maid any day!'

The inconsequent chatter did much to bring Nell back to her usual composure. At length she set down her cup. 'I am sure I have wasted enough of your time, Mrs Whyte.'

'Don't think of it, ma'am. Count upon me at any time, Miss Faraday. There's no denying you've an ordeal ahead of you. I will do all I can to support you through it.'

Nell reached out to press her hand. 'That is kind. I could wish Lord Jarrow had been as forthcoming.'

'That's ever the master's way.' Mrs Whyte sighed. 'He's had a lot to put up with, that I will say. But it's probably best he don't tell you it all. You'll find out soon enough.'

Nell felt again the irritation this comment had created in her before. 'Yes, that is what his lordship says, but I prefer to confront problems head on.'

The older woman clicked her tongue. 'I can't think that's best. You're a deal too young to be taking the troubles of this house on your shoulders, and that's a fact.'

'Pray don't say so. You sound just like his lordship. I am a good deal more resilient than either of you suppose.'

But the housekeeper remained unconvinced. 'Why, look at how you almost fainted clean away but a moment ago!'

Nell frowned. 'That was different. I assure you I will not in general be found to be such a poor creature.' She rose resolutely. 'Perhaps it is time I faced the future and met Henrietta. Will you tell me how to find the schoolroom?'

Looking about, Nell could only be glad no one had thought to inform her that the schoolroom was set into the top of one of the towers. It could only have added to the matters upon which she had brooded last night. As it was, she came upon it with no expectations and found it surprisingly pleasing, apart from the approach, which necessarily took her up a horrid stone stair in one of the towers. She had entered with misgiving through a studded doorway in the curved corner nearest the parlour, feeling relieved that Mrs Whyte had opted to lead her in person.

It would not have been so bad if the inner wall had not been broken in places, with gaps through which one was able to glimpse the blackness of the hollow within. A dank odour pervaded, and the atmosphere was chilly. Chinks that had once been windows had been bricked in, and oil lamps set instead into the recesses. The result produced in Nell a sensation of stifling, and she was glad to come out upon a round room flooded with brightness.

The turret had been roofed, and windows set into each of its wall spaces. An outer door led to a walkway about the castle battlements. A splendid view was to be had from the windows at the outside edge, and every advantage of the sun's rays could be felt. Nell thought the heat might prove overwhelming in summer. She had said as much to Mrs Whyte, but that lady had sensibly suggested that the inner windows might then be opened. Urging Nell to make herself at home, she had departed in search of Miss Jarrow.

There was a large desk for the governess's use, in the drawers of which Nell found all the books and implements she might require. In the school desk provided for the child, there were a slate and chalks, a variety of counters and games, and a small wooden doll with hair painted yellow. There could be no doubt that Henrietta had introduced those items she considered essential to her well-being. A little attention that gave Nell her first ray of hope. The child could not be as abnormal as she had been led to believe.

A clatter of feet upon the stairs below signalled the arrival of her charge. It was followed almost immediately by the banging of the door against the wall, and the tempestuous entrance into the room of the

Honourable Henrietta Jarrow. She was accompanied, but Nell's attention held at first upon the little girl.

She was as lovely as report had made her. Under a cluster of rolling curls of darkest hue, two black eyes appraised Nell in a wide stare. The rosebud of a mouth was pert, the plump cheeks flushed, and a pointed chin gave promise of a determined will. Her figure was rounded, and she was dressed most unsuitably in an old-fashioned waisted gown of blue taffeta, with a wide sash, and a profusion of braid and ribbon.

Before Nell could open her mouth to greet the child, she was forestalled. The woman who had come in with Henrietta put a hand to the girl's back and pushed her forward, her voice a blend of scolding and persuasion.

'Well, here we are, miss, all ready for lessons. Make your curtsy, Miss Hetty. We're in a good mood this morning, I'm happy to say, though it's odds on that won't last. We're ready to do Papa's bidding, aren't we, Miss Hetty? Time and past we had some sense knocked into our head and no mistake!'

Nell was already bristling, but she fought down the hot words that choked her. She fixed the creature with a steady eye and spoke repressively. 'You must be Duggan. How do you do?'

Her tone was without effect. The nurse continued in the same fashion.

'Joyce Duggan, miss. And I'm well enough, though that's a wonder after the dance I was led last night. A right paddy we were in, weren't we, Miss Hetty? As

I hear it, our new governess won't put up with none of our nonsense. Isn't that right, miss?'

Nell pointedly did not answer. She was taking an immediate dislike to the woman, and not because her manner was wholly lacking the deference due to the governess, who was her senior in station. It was the patronising attitude she adopted towards the child, coupling herself with her nurseling as if she spoke for her. Making a mental vow to treat the little girl with respect, Nell watched her thrust the silent Henrietta into the chair of her small desk.

The nurse was quite young—four or five and twenty perhaps?—and well looking in a blowsy sort of way. Although she wore the correct attire of a long linen frock of dark stuff over a black taminy petticoat, the ensemble was surprisingly fashionable, its waistline high. She wore no apron, and her cap was all over lacc. She was decidedly above herself. Nell gathered her forces.

'Thank you for bringing her, Duggan. I will not keep you, for I am sure you have a great deal to do.'

'True enough.' The nurse gave her a significant look. 'Only the master thought you might have need of me this first morning.'

The meaning of this was plain. Nell longed to send the woman to the rightabout, for she was sure she would make no headway with Henrietta in her presence. But it would be impolitic to dismiss her without first discussing the matter with Lord Jarrow. She temporised.

'Very well, but be so good as to seat yourself in the background while Henrietta and I become acquainted.'

She glanced at the child as she spoke, and found her still staring, her expression unchanged. It occurred to Nell that she had not reacted in the least to anything the nurse had said to her. Nor did she turn as Duggan took up a position behind her in a recess supplied by one of the battlemented windows. Was it possible that the wide stare was not, as she had thought, a critical examination? The girl's eyes were unblinking, her gaze fixed. A faint stirring of apprehension awoke in Nell's veins. Were there thoughts revolving behind those lustrous eyes? Or were both mind and stare quite vacant?

With deliberation, Nell smiled at her. 'Hello, Hetty.'

The child's gaze did not waver. But her mouth opened, and a deep little voice came out. 'Why have you gold hair? Are you a princess?'

A laugh was surprised out of Nell. 'A princess! No, indeed. Have you never seen anyone with gold hair before?'

Hetty shook her head, her eyes fixed upon Nell's face.

'Well, I assure you, it is quite common. I am not a princess, Hetty, but a governess.'

'I am six,' announced the girl.

It was a *non sequitur*, but Nell took it up at once. 'Yes, so I understand. You are quite grown up, are you not?'

'Papa give me a doll.'

'For your birthday?'

The child remained silent. Was she incapable of playing her part in a conversation? Nell tried again, using one of the tricks she had been taught at the Seminary to introduce the alphabet. There were several, but this one fitted the occasion.

'Do you know that your name starts with the same letter as mine?' Not a flicker of interest! 'Your name is Henrietta and mine is Helen. So you see, both our names begin with the letter H.'

No response. She would have to try another tack. Hark back to something the child could identify with. 'Do you like fairy stories? With princesses in them?'

A solemn nod, then a return to the old theme. 'Princess have gold hair.'

'Like mine? Yes, they often do. But I am not a princess, Hetty. Do you know what a governess is?'

To her relief, the child's answer was fully appropriate. 'Guv'ness come teach me. Papa said.'

Come, this was more encouraging. 'And did your papa tell you what I am going to teach you?'

The smile was so sudden that Nell was startled. It lit the chubby features, and the eyes were all alive! 'Reading, writing and 'rithmetic.'

She had chanted the words, a litany learned by heart. But Nell warmed to the change. Her pulse beat a little faster at this evidence that there was after all some hope. The child was intense, but she was not wholly buried in a world of her own.

* * *

Restless, Nell left the schoolroom for the roof and wandered along the battlements. The day was fine enough, the sun warming and the fresh air welcome. For a while, she looked out upon the vast acreage of the forest. The sense of isolation was strong, and she recalled the words of the old retainer, Detling: 'Nothing to be seen but forest nigh on mile an' mile.' Indeed, Nell felt as if she lived in a world that was all forest. And within it, there was little but frustration. She turned to walk again.

She had scarcely made headway in the brief time that had been granted to her with Henrietta. All she had accomplished was a smattering of exchanges—hardly conversation!—in which she had herself talked much and learned little.

She had made no attempt to teach the child beyond introducing her to the implements she must use. Upon being shown her slate, Hetty had immediately taken a piece of chalk and proceeded to scrawl pictures upon it that were largely unrecognisable. Nell had instantly praised her efforts, and moved to the blackboard where she drew a crude representation of a castle. When Hetty left her desk and came to join her, she had hopes that the child might attempt to copy her drawing. To her disappointment, her pupil merely took the opportunity to scribble her own hieroglyphics upon a larger canvas.

Nell stood back and left her to it, now and then putting a question that might encourage the girl to identify what she had drawn. She was ignored.

Shortly thereafter, Duggan had announced that it was time for Hetty's luncheon. When Nell had asked what time she might expect the child back in the schoolroom, she learned that Henrietta always took a nap in the afternoon, after which she was permitted to play. In other words, Nell had realised irately, she was expected to accomplish the child's education in a couple of hours each day!

It would not do. It was going to be uphill work as it was. Besides, what in the world was she to do for the rest of the day? Perhaps Lord Jarrow expected her to make up the hours with household tasks! If so, he would soon learn his mistake. Except that she might well be driven to offer her help to Mrs Whyte out of sheer boredom.

Discovering that she had reached the other end of the roof walkway, Nell swished about and began to stroll back again. She had gone but a few steps when she was attacked by an eerie sensation that she was not alone. Halting, she turned.

In a doorway to the turret she had just passed stood Lord Jarrow, watching her.

She had seen him. Not that he had been at pains to conceal his presence, but he had not meant to disturb her. Too late. There was nothing for it but to speak.

Miss Faraday had halted, but she made no attempt to approach him. Jarrow gave an inward sigh and made towards her. He had known her but a few short hours, but already he could tell at once that she was in an uncertain mood. As he neared, he tried to read her face. She was eyeing him with complete assurance, but there was stiffness in her carriage. He plunged straight in.

'Are you wishing to leave?'

Her brows rose. Such hauteur! It could not but amuse him, no matter how misplaced. But then Miss Faraday was no ordinary governess. That much he had deduced at the outset.

'Why should you think so, sir? Nothing has occurred since I saw you last to change my intention.'

Jarrow smiled. 'I am glad to hear it. But you will not persuade me that there has been nothing to disturb you.'

She hesitated, but only for a moment. She gave a decisive nod. 'Since you have guessed it, sir, let me not beat about the bush.'

'I am all ears, Miss Faraday.'

Nell was almost betrayed into a laugh, but she stifled it. She had been excessively annoyed, and here was the opportunity to unburden herself.

'This morning I was privileged to have Henrietta in my schoolroom for the better part of an hour, and no more. Admittedly we began late, for I overslept. But even taking that into account, it is absurd to expect me to make any progress if the child is not to have lessons in the afternoon at all.'

To her further annoyance, Lord Jarrow did not even respond to her complaint. His brows had drawn together.

'How did you get on?'

'We cannot be said to have got on at all!' retorted Nell. 'That is what I am trying to tell you. Is it not possible for—'

Jarrow interrupted her without ceremony. 'Miss Faraday, you are the child's governess. If you wish her to come back to you after her nap—I gather that is where she is now?—then that is what she will do. There is no necessity to drag me into the business.'

It gave him a curious sense of satisfaction to see her nonplussed. She said nothing for a moment, but he could almost see thoughts revolving in her head.

'This,' she said at last, 'becomes interesting, sir.'

He bit back a laugh. 'Indeed? How so?'

Nell gathered her forces. Let them establish this immediately, for it would make her life a good deal easier.

'The nurse Duggan, my lord, gave me the impression that she is the arbiter of what Henrietta may do. Now you tell me that I must decide. Were I in the nurse's place, I should certainly resent interference from one who necessarily knows less than I, particularly in a case such as this. I should expect her to take my advice. On the other hand, it is unlikely that Nurse Duggan and myself will easily reach agreement upon any point.'

She thought there was a good deal of comprehension in his eyes. Yet there was also a gleam suspiciously ironic.

'Tactfully put, Miss Faraday. Let us find a compromise. I will tell Duggan that Hetty is to attend school at your pleasure. After all, she is no longer a baby, and some change in her routine is to be expected.'

'But?'

He noted the returning stiffness. She was no fool! He could not help a rueful note from creeping into his voice. 'I confess my reliance is a great deal upon Duggan. The arrangement is not ideal, but frankly, Miss Faraday, I don't know what I would do without her.'

'The matter is now perfectly plain, sir.'

Jarrow frowned. 'You are angry.'

Disconcerted, Nell looked quickly away. He saw too much! Abruptly recollecting his distressing bereavement, with all that Mrs Whyte had let fall, she felt immediately guilty. Who was she to be causing him difficulties? Naturally he must value Duggan above herself, for she had done nothing yet to demonstrate her usefulness. Besides, she was perfectly capable of dealing with the nurse herself. She forced a brief smile.

'Not at all, sir. I quite understand. It was perhaps a little disappointing to have done nothing to further Henrietta's education.'

'It is early days, Miss Faraday. You have barely begun.' He wondered if it was too soon to ask, but anxiety got the better of him. 'What did you think of her?'

The forest eyes instantly clouded and his heart sank. Then she had seen it too! He could not bring himself to speak, and waited in a species of torture for what she might say.

Nell saw the withdrawal, and sympathy stirred her response. 'The truth, Lord Jarrow, is that I do not know. I found her a trifle unnerving at first—she stared so. But then I was a little heartened when she answered me with sense.' She saw a quick frown, and hastened to elaborate. 'I do not mean to imply that she talked nonsense. Far from it. Only her responses were out of place to start with. That is not uncommon in young children, and certainly she did find some apt answers. But I will not conceal from you that the task of teaching her is not likely to be an easy one.'

He was looking a little less tense, Nell thought with relief. In the broad light of day, the lean features were decidedly less worn and his true age was more apparent. His voice sounded easier.

'I had anticipated as much. She will no doubt prove a handful.'

'I suspect the problem will be to get her attention to remain for long enough upon one thing.' Nell gave him a smile she hoped was reassuring. 'There are ways to counteract it, my lord.'

'Such as?'

Was he interested? Or did that dry note betoken scepticism?

'It is best with a butterfly mind to engage in a frequent change of subject. The moment one detects inattention, it is time to turn to something else.' His aspect did not change, and Nell felt compelled to offer more. 'If that does not work, one may allow the child's interest to lead, introducing several possibilities and letting her choose. Or else there is the tried and tested method of endless repetition, which I do not favour. It is much more productive to go over something a second time on another occasion rather than to bore the poor child into a stupor by going over and over the same thing.' Warming to her theme, she found various precepts she had been taught flooding into her mind. 'And if all else fails, one may set aside the primer and teach through fairy stories. Which, since your daughter mistook me for a princess, might well work in her case. Otherwise—'

Jarrow threw up a hand in laughing protest. 'No more, I beg of you! It is clear that your head has been stuffed to bursting at your Seminary with endless schemes for a pathway to success.'

Her features lightened in a smile of such warmth that he almost lost track of her answer. His mind caught on something she had said earlier. Henrietta had thought she was a princess—due to the hair, no doubt. It glowed in the sunlight, a very halo about her head. She was not beautiful in the conventional sense. Not like Julietta, whose lush enchantment had made his senses swim on that far-off accursed day of their first meeting. But the hair, together with her unusual eyes, had a quality of making this girl appear almost angelic. An epithet that could not have been less apt!

Miss Faraday had far too strong a personality to be mistaken for an angel.

Jarrow became aware that she had ceased speaking, and was regarding him with question in her face. He brushed away the stray thoughts. But the words that came out of his mouth had no volition.

'You are such an innocent! Why in the world are you here? Why are you not looking after some innocuous young females in a country mansion where your comfort would be assured? Is it the challenge, or what?'

Utterly taken aback, Nell could only gaze at him. He had read her so accurately! Yet they were scarce more than strangers. It did not occur to her to deny it. Indeed it felt natural to confide her fears to him.

'Am I too ambitious? Last night when I arrived, I thought I had been taken at fault. My stupid pride! Only now that I have met her—'

'You have changed your mind?' he broke in swiftly.

'Oh, no, Lord Jarrow. The reverse! I want to help her—if I can.'

He found the little smile she gave unbearably touching. 'But you don't know that you can.'

She shook her head. 'If only your fears may be unfounded! She is so very beautiful. How shocking it would be if her mind is indeed disordered!'

'Only because she is beautiful.'

Startled at the sudden harshness, Nell's eyes flew to his. 'Of course not.'

There was a spark in the dark gaze. 'But her beauty makes it the more shocking, does it not? Don't I know it!'

Bitterness was rife in his voice and the furrows deepened in his countenance. Dismayed, Nell withdrew a step or two. What intimacy they had briefly shared was shattered. How changeable a man he was! And she had allowed herself to forget it. Although she was at a loss to know how she was to guess what careless remark of hers might set him off. Best to leave him now, before she laid more coals on the fire. She dropped a curtsy and turned away.

'Miss Faraday!'

Nell checked, looking back. 'Yes, Lord Jarrow?'

He brooded for a moment, his eyes hard and unyielding. What now? Nell waited, conscious of a faint motion in her veins that she did her best to ignore.

The breath sighed out of him, and his gaze dropped. 'Nothing.' Curt, and dismissive. 'I should not have engaged you.'

Indignation rose like thunder in her breast, all but choking her. She watched him walk away, the door to the turret closing behind him with the snap of finality.

There was tension in the dining room. To Nell's consternation and—to her shame!—her secret relief, Toly Beresford was absent. Lord Jarrow had given the brief explanation that he was dining out with nearby acquaintances. His tone had been stiff. With resentment? Nell could not judge.

'I trust it will not discompose you to be dining tête-à-tête?'

'You trust wrong, sir,' said Nell instantly. 'It is excessively improper.'

He had shot her a look that might indeed have discomposed a woman of lesser nerve. Nell had thrust down on the flutter at her stomach. Lord Jarrow had become acid.

'Your virtue is in no danger, ma'am. But, if you wish for it, I shall ask Keston to have Mrs Whyte come up.'

Nell was immediately ashamed of herself. There was no question of troubling the housekeeper, who must be at her wit's end down in the kitchens. She lifted her gaze and looked her employer in the eye.

'That will not be necessary. Your butler's presence will afford protection enough.'

She was treated to one of his ironic glances. 'Let us hope he will prove able to curb my unnatural desires.'

Silence reigned through the first course. But by the time Keston had removed what remained of the fresh beef roast, along with a selection of plain boiled vegetables that had been served alongside, Nell had become acutely conscious. Her conduct was disgraceful! What the Duck would say she dared not think. The wonder was that his lordship had not thrown her out on her ear!

While the butler passed from the table to the door, collecting the next set of dishes from whoever it was outside—the unfortunate Grig, Nell supposed—she debated what she should say to Lord Jarrow. An apology was certainly in order. She had thoroughly overstepped the mark, and he had every right to be as surly as a bear. Merely because he had pokered up this afternoon—leaving her, it had to be admitted, positively fuming!—was no reason for Nell to forget her manners.

From the array of fruits offered, she selected an apple, taking time over peeling the skin. She saw that his lordship ate nothing from the second course, instead brooding darkly over his wine. Nell's guilt increased. What was she about to be adding to his distresses in that shabby way?

She waited for the butler to withdraw into the background. Then she took a breath, trying to quiet the faint tattoo that would keep erupting in her veins.

'Lord Jarrow?'

Over the rim of his glass, his eyes looked towards her. They wore a sombre expression. He did not speak, and Nell's courage almost failed her. The apology was hovering on her tongue. Why could she not say it?

He was waiting. She must say something! Her usual calm had deserted her. Her mind swung wildly this way and that, catching at some point of observation. She chose at random, the first thing that entered her head.

'It—it struck me today—when I was walking by your battlements...'

She faltered to a stop. Heavens, what a ninny she had become! To be so tongue-tied was wholly un-characteristic. The gathering frown impelled her to continue—to say anything, as long as it broke the dreadful impasse. Inspiration came.

'I was thinking of your ancestors. However inconvenient this place may be now, it must once have spelled security. I should doubt if the most determined siege could have succeeded against it.' There was no mistaking the puzzlement at his brow. Nell blundered on. 'I had looked for signs of a moat. Surely the entrance must once have held a drawbridge?'

Jarrow responded automatically, his attention not at all upon what he said. 'There never was a moat.' What in the world possessed the girl to bring up such a subject? Was she trying to dissipate the constraint that had arisen this afternoon, when he had been about to confide in her more than he should, and then stopped? He spoke almost at random.

'The height of Hog Hill and the surrounding forest afforded protection enough. I believe there was at one time a heavy wooden gate, however.' She was regarding him with an expression of interest. Spurious, surely? She could not truly wish for information upon such a subject. 'There used at one time to be ramparts around the hill. But little remains of their ruins today. You may glimpse broken walls here and there among the gaps in the trees.'

Contrary to her expectation, the beat of Nell's pulses had increased. She felt the conversation to be absurd, but he was talking. Was there a diminution of the tightness in his features?

'How old is the castle?'

'It was built in the eleventh century. It has lasted this long only because it has continued to be lived in.'

Nell became abruptly interested. 'Always?'

Jarrow nodded, surprised to be affected by the spark of real question. 'There have been Jarrows here continuously. Only during Queen Anne's day did the fellow who held the title leave here. But he allowed his relative—a cousin, I think it was—to live in the place in his stead.'

'Where did he go?'

He answered with constraint. Of course it had to lead to that question! 'Collier Row. He built a house near there. Padnall Place.'

The name rang an immediate bell. 'We passed it on the way here. I am sure Detling pointed it out to me. I wondered why he did so.' Her tongue was too quick for her mind. 'Why in the world do you not remove there?'

Too late, Nell saw the blackness enter Lord Jarrow's face. Heavens, what a fool! The answer was obvious. And now she had alienated him again. In a bid to avert the inevitable, she tried to retract. 'I should not have asked. I must suppose it to have been sold long since.'

Without surprise, but with a sinking at her stomach, she heard the bitterness return to his voice. 'No, I do own it. Only I cannot afford to live in it.' His eyes were bleak. 'The curse of the Jarrows, Miss Faraday, is bad judgement—to be ever on the wrong side. In King Stephen's day, we sided with Matilda. In Elizabeth's, we supported Essex. And Charles II could not be expected to reward one of Cromwell's fellows. The Jarrows, therefore, lacked preferment. We have no riches, and our peerage is yet a barony.'

Nell could not bear his self-disgust. 'I should rather call it unlucky than bad judgement, sir. Has there been no possibility of restoring your fortunes?'

The question proved disastrous. Lord Jarrow fingered his wine glass and his lips curled in a travesty of a smile.

'There is always a circumspect marriage. Many a Jarrow tried that path, but the luck, as I have said, is never with us.'

'Is that what you did?'

His eyes blazed as he looked across at her. Nell could have cursed herself. What had possessed her to say that? 'Oh, my wretched tongue! Forget I said it, my lord, if you please.'

A mirthless laugh escaped him, an ugly sound. 'Forget? If only I could!'

He lifted his glass and tossed off the wine. Setting it down, he grasped the decanter. Nell watched him with a feeling of hopelessness. She could feel the depths of his unhappiness. He began to pour and then paused, the decanter poised over his glass. He looked up and their eyes met.

'No, Miss Faraday, my marriage was neither circumspect nor fortuitous. I was too much of a deluded fool to be choosing for the sake of a fortune.'

Within a week, much against her expectation, a pattern had begun to form in Nell's days. Within two, she had established an almost invariable routine, broken only on mornings when Henrietta unaccountably arrived in the schoolroom yawning and distrait. On being questioned, Duggan said only that the child was a bad sleeper, and the change of routine was the cause. By the time May arrived, bringing with it a spell of weather unusually warm for the time of year, the child appeared to have settled down. Contrary to Mr Beresford's information, there had been no sudden screaming in the night, and she had seen no evidence of either tantrums or dementia.

Lord Jarrow, when she mentioned this, had reiterated that it was early days.

'It is likely that the novelty of what you are doing with her is holding her interest. Experience leads me to warn you not to let yourself be lulled into thinking that it will last.'

Nell had felt both irritated and disappointed. She had dared to believe that the regime upon which she had embarked was having an effect, and her life here had begun to take on an aspect of normality. Each morning she rose betimes, and went immediately up to the turret schoolroom to get ready for the day's lessons. By nine, she knew that Mrs Whyte had likely completed preparing breakfast, and Keston would be serving the gentlemen in the dining-parlour. Nell then repaired to the kitchen, where the housekeeper, anticipating her arrival, would be setting out her meal. Mrs Whyte broke her fast along with the rest of the staff a good deal earlier, but she nevertheless sat with Nell and enjoyed a cup of coffee.

It amused Nell that the good woman, having readily taken to the habit, found it necessary to give herself the justification of an excuse.

'It does a body good to have a little break now and then. Besides, I'd not wish you to eat alone, Miss Faraday.'

Mrs Whyte's little break conveniently lasted until the governess had finished and it was time for her to meet her charge in the schoolroom. Nell had no fault to find with this arrangement, for the housekeeper's company afforded her a welcome period of rare relaxation, and it helped to discuss her daily progress. Her regime was not arduous, although it taxed her ingenuity to make headway with Henrietta. There had been no outbursts in her presence, nothing unnatural beyond the child's odd unblinking stare.

On the other hand, there was a tension in the household that was almost tangible. Nell could not sit at the dinner table with either one or both of the gentlemen—for Mr Beresford had been several times absent—without feeling the brooding undercurrents that surrounded the unknown secrets of Lord Jarrow's past and his present fears.

Added to this, the arrogance—and sometimes outright insolence!—of the nurse Duggan was an incessant thorn. Nell had come off triumphant in a battle to have the child more suitably dressed. A threat to inform his lordship if her wishes remained unregarded had resulted in Henrietta's appearance thereafter in a round gown of blue dimity with a white cotton apron atop. But the nurse was unforgiving of this change.

She was more often present than not during Hetty's lessons, and Nell was at all times conscious of her supercilious eye in the background. She tried not to allow it to weigh with her, and it was an irritant that she did not succeed. Yet it was increasingly evident that, whatever her mental state, Henrietta was possessed of a sharp intelligence that only needed channelling.

Nell had opted to use the scheme involving fairy tales to interest her charge, Mr Perrault's rendering of 'The Sleeping Beauty' proving by experiment to be Hetty's favourite. Nell took immediate advantage in discovering the letters of the alphabet within the story. The princess most fortuitously rejoiced in the name Aurora, which gave Nell the opportunity to begin. By dint of writing the letter A upon the blackboard, and showing Hetty where it appeared in printed form on the written page, she scored an instant victory. Henrietta even consented to try to recreate the figure.

But she astonished Nell by recognising the smaller 'a' at the end of Aurora's name the moment Nell wrote it on the board.

'Yes, that is exactly right, Hetty. How clever you are!'

The child beamed. Nell was about to encourage her to write the small letter when a daring thought occurred to her. Instead she returned to the board.

'This one follows A, Hetty.' She wrote B on the blackboard. 'Can you see a letter like that in the story?'

Interested, Henrietta pored over the text. With a squeal of triumph, she suddenly pointed to the B for Beauty in the title. Nell's heart quickened with excitement, but she curbed it. Could it be that the child had already learned the alphabet?

'Do you know how to find a C, Hetty?'

The dark brows drew closer together, and the red lips pouted. She kicked in a petulant way at the footrest of her desk.

'There we go,' muttered the nurse in the background. 'We'll be throwing things in a minute, miss, if you ain't careful.'

Nell hastily retracted. 'Never mind, my dear. It doesn't matter in the least.' She pointed at the board again. 'Come, let us try to write this B for Beauty.'

'*Sleeping* Beauty,' corrected the child, brightening again.

Clearly she had not yet grasped that the B belonged only to the one word. Yet her ability to pick out the letter was remarkable. It became a simple task to devise a game where Nell wrote the next letter, in both capitals and small, and waited for Hetty to find them.

The child became absorbed in the hunt, and by this means they had so far arrived as far as F for Prince Florimond.

It was another matter getting the pupil to copy the letters more than a couple of times. Nell was obliged to make it a point of competition to write all the letters they had learned so far before she would introduce another one. The list, which Nell kept permanently on the blackboard, was growing steadily, and she felt she had reason to feel pleased with Henrietta's progress.

She was chagrined to find that Duggan greeted each failure with the smugness of one who had foretold exactly how it would be, and each success with prognostications that it would not last. Worse, these were addressed directly to the child, in that hateful manner of possession.

'All new to us, ain't it, Miss Hetty?' she said of the alphabet letters. 'Which is why we're keeping our temper. But we know how it'll be the moment we get bored. We won't never make it to the letter Z without screaming, I'll warrant!'

It was true that letters palled quickly. Once the child became bored, there was no keeping her attention on the dull work of copying. Wisely, Nell made no attempt to do so, and instead put together a timetable that covered a variety of subjects each day. Nor did she try to make the child give up her doll, which Henrietta was prone to take out of the desk at any time that suited her.

Counting was accomplished with the girl's own wooden bricks—when she could be persuaded to leave off building to find out how many she had used.

'There now,' said the nurse when three requests had been ignored one day. 'We're deaf and blind when we want to be, ain't we? Oh, when we don't want to learn nothing, there ain't nobody going to make us, is there, Miss Hetty?'

Nell could have slapped her. Not that Henrietta paid the woman the slightest heed. It seemed that she was indeed deaf and blind to Duggan's little digs. Or perhaps she was so used to the woman's nagging words that she had become adept at ignoring them. Nell elected to follow the child's lead, refusing to become discomposed by Duggan's frequent interruptions.

A set of toy soldiers that had belonged to Henrietta's father in his childhood were found to be another means of counting, together with learning to sing. Nell made the soldiers march to the song, so that Hetty began to copy her. She used the doll to introduce the child to dance, and had recently taken the little girl on to the roof walkway to try out some steps for herself. Mrs Whyte had found, upon request, some braid and ribbons, with which Nell began Hetty upon the art of weaving as a preliminary to sewing and knotting a fringe.

When all else failed, Nell read to the little girl from Mr Perrault's collection of fairy tales, and found that Henrietta knew all the stories so well that she would frequently interrupt in order to interpolate the next bit.

Wondering who had read to her in the past, and reluctant to ask anything at all of Duggan, Nell questioned the housekeeper.

'Is it Duggan?'

Mrs Whyte set down her teacup. 'Joyce? Bless you, no, ma'am! Why, she can't read, not with any great fluency. She's a country girl is Joyce. No, no, Miss Faraday. She might tell the child a story or two, but she wouldn't think to read one.'

Not altogether surprised, Nell tried not to be satisfied by this intelligence. 'Then it must have been Lady Jarrow.'

The housekeeper looked dubious. 'I suppose she might. Though it weren't my notion that her ladyship took time nor trouble with the babe.'

'But she must have given her some attention. She could not have ignored her own daughter.'

Mrs Whyte became distressed and, to Nell's eye a little uncomfortable. 'She weren't in a state of mind to think of anyone but herself, ma'am.'

Nell's instinct was to probe, but she withheld it. She would not put the housekeeper in the unhappy position of betraying what she had rather not. Yet those few hints that had been thrown out could not but pique her interest, particularly in light of Lord Jarrow's troubled words. It was clear that his marriage had been disappointing, if not downright unhappy, but nothing more concrete had been revealed in the period since Nell's arrival.

Only one circumstance had given her further evidence of the deep-seated rancour that drove him. The first Sunday had arrived with no mention of prayers or church, and Nell—brought up to correct Christian conduct at the Seminary—had been forced to enquire about it.

Lord Jarrow had looked blank. 'Church?'

'Surely, sir, you keep some form of worship?'

His lip had curled. 'For what purpose?'

It had been Nell's turn to stare. 'To keep faith with your Maker, my lord. For Henrietta's sake, if not your own.'

He had uttered a harsh laugh. 'You suppose it will make a difference?'

'It must always make a difference, sir!'

At which, his eyes had flashed fire. 'Don't preach at me, Miss Faraday! If you choose to genuflect and mutter for the benefit of the Almighty, you may do so at your leisure. But you will not inflict your meaningless prattle upon a creature who has enough to endure without looking for salvation to a merciless God who has long since abandoned the Jarrows!'

He had stalked away on the words, leaving Nell torn between shock and dismay. Thereafter, when she had seen his lordship at dinner, conversation with him had been strictly neutral. When Mr Beresford was present, he hardly spoke at all, allowing his brother-in-law to maintain the burden of conversation, which did nothing to alleviate the heavy atmosphere generated by the brooding silence at the head of the table.

Even during the day when she was in the school-room, Nell was oddly aware of his lordship, although she saw nothing of him. But she knew from Mrs Whyte that he spent the better part of his time inhabiting that room in the adjacent turret, from which he had emerged the first day. The knowledge kept her from too frequently walking alone on the roof, but the need—either from frustration or a desire for fresh air—sometimes outweighed caution. The roof, moreover, afforded a degree of release from the sense of being shut in. Despite the isolation, it gave her an illusion of space not to be found in the castle rooms. Yet the knowledge of Lord Jarrow's presence not far away was a deterrent. Nell welcomed her sessions with the housekeeper.

From Mrs Whyte she had learned that the Jarrows had been traditionally Catholic, another cause of disfavour in the eyes of the ruling Royal house. The Baron of Queen Anne's day, the same that had purchased Padnall Place, had converted to Protestantism, but religious fervour had never afterwards been a strong point. The household, revealed Mrs Whyte, had fallen out of the way of attending Sunday Service at Collier Row a short time after the Jarrows had returned from London for good.

Against her employer's express command, Nell was left with no choice but to introduce Christian precepts indirectly, only to improve her pupil's behaviour. Deciding that the task of bringing Lord Jarrow back to God lay outside her province, Nell contented herself with her own weekly prayers—for the present. She could not help but be intrigued by the notion that his troubles had been of a nature dreadful enough to cause him to eschew religion altogether.

It was not, Nell insisted to a niggling conscience, vulgar curiosity that had led her lately to dropping into the kitchen a second time, when lessons finished for the afternoon. The housekeeper downed tools in her preparation of the evening meal, dismissing the handyman Grig without ceremony.

The fellow was a large man, with an expression of amiable vacancy, who took no exception to the manner of Mrs Whyte's address.

'Be off with you, now! I don't want you shambling about the kitchen and fidgeting Miss Faraday.'

Favouring Nell with a grin and a touch of his forelock, Grig withdrew, leaving the housekeeper to settle down with Nell for a refreshing cup of tea. She baked only once a week, but she always produced a cake or biscuit from her store for Nell's delectation, and would not hear of it being refused.

'There's precious little luxury in this barrack of a place, ma'am, so you'd best take it where you find it.'

Nell protested in vain that she did not come for the treat. 'I come for your company, Mrs Whyte, and I am only grateful that you allow me to disturb you.'

'Bless you, my dear, 'tis a pleasure! A body can do with another female for company, and you may believe it's as much my comfort as your own, for I've no one else bar Joyce, and I can't say as I relish—I mean, I can't say we've a deal in common.'

Noting the slip, Nell's curiosity almost got the better of her discretion. Did Mrs Whyte dislike the nurse as much as she did herself? Nell knew she could not support a discussion about Duggan without betraying how she felt. She had best withdraw.

Leaving the housekeeper to resume her cooking, she returned by way of the hall and climbed back up to the schoolroom. It had become her habit to return there after tea to tidy the place and make preparations towards future lessons.

Entering the turret room, she was brought up short by the sight of Henrietta lying at full stretch in the middle of the floor, apparently unconscious.

Chapter Four

After a brief moment of shock, Nell's first care was to move quickly to kneel beside the motionless figure, feeling her hands and face. Her skin was warm, and a trifle damp. With perspiration? Nell took up the little wrist, pushing back the band and feeling for her pulse. It proved tumultuous and her concern grew.

Where in the world was the nurse when she was needed? Should not the child have been abed by now? To allow for extra time at lessons, Hetty's nap was now a short one after luncheon, with the result that a further couple of hours—if the child could be induced to remain in the schoolroom without becoming fretful!—was spent with Nell. After which, she was usually so tired, Duggan averred, that she went straight off to sleep. She usually woke for an hour or so later in the evening, when she partook of a light dinner and a glass of warm milk before settling back to bed for the night.

Why in the world, then, had she been permitted to wander back into the schoolroom? Nell supposed that must be what had happened, although the girl was clad still in her blue school frock, but without the apron. Only why had she collapsed?

Searching the lovely features, Nell discovered them to be pale and without animation. The pert little mouth was open, and her breath came in long drags, as if she laboured to breathe at all. Nell became alarmed. The child was ill!

Her priority must be to get Hetty back to bed. Even as she slipped her arms underneath the girl, intending to lift her, Nell recalled the peculiarities of which Lord Jarrow had warned her, and wondered if perhaps this was a regular occurrence. Was there some certain method of dealing with it? It might be that she should not be moved. Nell recalled instances where the visiting doctor at the Seminary had deprecated any shifting of patients in some circumstances until he should have seen them. On the other hand, it could not be good for her to lie upon the cold stone floor.

Seizing up an old shawl, which she had taken to leaving in the schoolroom for those occasions when the spring weather proved uncertain, Nell tucked it under the child's head and about her young shoulders. Then she darted through the outer doorway, and raced across the roof to hammer frantically on the door to Lord Jarrow's study, calling for him.

'My lord! My lord, pray come out!'

She heard movement within and stepped back as the door was tugged inward. Lord Jarrow's features appeared, his brow black.

'What the devil is the matter?'

He must have seen the trouble in her face, for his look changed and he stepped through the doorway. His voice sharpened. 'What is it, Miss Faraday? Has something happened to Hetty?'

Nell breathlessly explained. 'I found her unconscious on the floor in the schoolroom, sir. She feels as if she has a fever and her breathing is tumultuous.' Lord Jarrow was already on the move, and Nell sped to keep up with him. 'I would have taken her down to her bed, only I feared to move her in case this had happened before.'

His voice spat, but Nell heard the tinge of fear beneath. 'God send she has not had another of her fits!'

She said no more, but followed him as he hurtled through the schoolroom door, which Nell had left open in her haste. Almost she cannoned into Lord Jarrow as he stopped short. There was an instant of silence, and then he turned on her.

'Where is she?'

Was he blind? 'There, between the desks.'

Jarrow stepped to one side, and gestured angrily. 'The room is empty, Miss Faraday!'

Nell pushed rudely past him, and stared blankly at the place where she had left Henrietta. 'But she was right here!' Her glance swept the room, and caught on her shawl. It was back in its usual place upon the back of her chair. 'Impossible!'

'What is impossible? What the devil do you mean by this?'

Her confusion found expression in a spurt of temper. 'Do you suppose I would call you for nothing? I tell you, the child was here!' Worriedly, she shifted to the inner door. 'She must have woken and wandered off again, only—'

She stopped short, her eyes straying to the tidy shawl.

'Only what?'

Nell shook off the puzzlement. It must be left for later. 'Nothing.' She pulled open the door. 'Will you go first, sir, or shall I?'

Lord Jarrow gave her a narrow look, but elected to precede her, running lightly down the stairs. Nell could not negotiate them without a stirring of dislike, but she followed as fast as she could, entering Henrietta's bedchamber a bare moment after her employer, only to discover the little girl lying on her side in the bed, a down coverlet laid over her.

Confusion wrought at Nell's mind again, as she watched his lordship step up to the bed and place a hand on the child's brow. Could the girl have got herself down here in that state? And how in the world had she covered herself over—or even thought to do so?

'She is warm,' murmured Lord Jarrow, 'but I do not think she has a fever. She looks to be sleeping peacefully.'

Nell tried to curb a rising indignation, but she was not wholly successful. 'She was anything but peaceful a few moments since, I assure you, sir!' She came to the bed and pressed in close, forcing her employer to give way. She leaned over the child, listening to her breathing. It sounded less heavy perhaps, and more even, but it was still a little laboured. She straightened.

'She is a degree easier, thank heaven! But how in the world—?' A solution presented itself to her questing mind, and her eyes flew to Lord Jarrow's. 'Could she have been sleepwalking, do you suppose?'

A grim look settled upon his features. 'She had better not have been!'

Nell saw with dismay that his eyes had begun to smoulder. More to placate him than to stifle her own questions, she seized at the next explanation that offered.

'Could Duggan have been searching for her and found her there?'

'We shall soon find out!'

Lord Jarrow moved to the bell-pull and tugged it. Even as it crossed Nell's mind that the nurse could not be far enough away to heed a bell that rang only in the domestic quarters, she noted her employer heading for the door. He almost collided in the doorway with Duggan herself, who was bearing a covered tray.

'My lord!'

'What the devil is going on?' The question was nonetheless fierce for the undertone in which it was addressed.

The nurse, however, looked taken aback. 'Sir?'

'Miss Faraday found Hetty lying on the schoolroom floor not a few moments since. How could you be so careless as to let her wander?'

Duggan blinked at him in a manner that brought back Nell's confusion. Her puzzled gaze shifted to Nell's face. 'In the schoolroom, miss? I think you must be mistook.'

'I am not mistaken! Do you take me for a fool?'

'No, miss. Only Miss Hetty has been all the while in this room since her lessons finished, and asleep for the most part.'

'But I saw her on the floor up there!'

The nurse turned to Lord Jarrow. 'Did you see her, my lord?'

'I did not.'

'Then miss must be mistook, as I said.'

'Do you suggest I imagined it?' Nell demanded angrily. 'Or perhaps you will tell his lordship that I made it up?'

Jarrow intervened. 'Hush, Miss Faraday! You will wake Hetty.'

He eyed the flushed features of his daughter's governess. No, she most definitely was not a fool. But he was at a loss to account for the discrepancy. The nurse was placing the tray on a table by the window.

'Duggan, are you certain? If Hetty has been sleep-walking again—'

The nurse shook her head with vehemence. 'That she has not, sir. I'd have told you if she had, as you bade me.'

'But can you be sure she has not left this room today? After all, you were absent when we came in.'

Her manner was as respectful as ever, but Jarrow noted that inflexible look the woman always wore when she knew herself to be in the right.

'I was gone but a moment, my lord. Her tray was on the table by the dining-parlour where Keston always sets it. I shouldn't think two minutes could have passed since I left her side, sir.'

He was ready to accept this, but he had reckoned without the governess. Miss Faraday's attractive eyes were sparkling and her features were tight. He could only admire the cool quality of her voice, although it was the deeper for the held down emotion he could hear beneath it.

'I am neither fanciful nor stupid, Duggan. I would not have run to his lordship for assistance had there been no occasion for it. I tell you again, despite your explanation, that Miss Hetty was lying on the floor in the schoolroom. I had almost carried her down myself, but that I bethought me of her peculiar condition.'

'Well, I don't know how that may be, miss, but her condition has been comfortable enough for my money.'

Jarrow left them to it, and crossed back to the bed. His daughter was certainly unmoving, but if her breathing had earlier been arduous, there was little sign of it now. He felt her limbs. They were warm to his touch, but nothing to be alarmed about. If she became any worse, he would despatch Detling to Collier

Row for the local doctor. The worst aspect of the matter was the resemblance of this occurrence to those involving Julietta. He had found her several times in odd places, and in just such a condition.

He found that the argument, which had murmured on in the background, had dulled. He turned. 'If she is feverish, call me at once. I will reserve sending for the doctor until tomorrow. If she is still warm to the touch, or she does not wake betimes, I shall despatch Detling for him. You had best remain with her tonight, Duggan.'

The nurse curtsied her acquiescence, and Jarrow did not doubt of being obeyed. With Miss Faraday, however, he had no such comforting reflection. She was looking like a thundercloud! He must make an effort to forestall further pointless discussion.

'This incident had best be forgotten. No one knows the truth of it save Henrietta herself, and since she has been asleep throughout, that is unlikely to help us.'

Nell bridled. Best forgotten? Not if she had anything to do with it! The smug look on the features of the nurse could not but infuriate her further, but it was no use talking. The woman clearly believed her own version of events. Lord Jarrow, on the other hand, was another matter. For some reason, it was unbearable to allow him to think anything but that she had spoken the truth.

She followed him out of the room, and waited as he shut the door. The light was poor, but she felt his impatience as she detained him.

'My lord, will you give me a moment of your time—in private, if you please?'

'Is there any point?'

His tone was clipped, but Nell refused to be deterred.

'For my part, sir, there is every point!'

She thought he sighed, but his face was inscrutable.

'Very well, Miss Faraday.'

The parlour felt alien, and Nell guessed that it was rarely used. Certainly she had only entered it once before, upon the occasion of her arrival. And just as Lord Jarrow had stated, there had been no visitors, not to her knowledge at any rate. It was chilly, despite the warmer atmosphere outside, and there was no light beyond that which came in at the window.

'Well, Miss Faraday?'

It was curtly said, and Nell was hard put to it to keep her temper. She held down the rising distress and spoke as calmly as she could.

'Unlike my friend Kitty, my lord, I am not a person of lively imagination, prone to see things that do not exist. On the contrary, I pride myself upon being level-headed, and if I am to continue here, I expect at least to be given credit for my common sense.'

Lord Jarrow said nothing for a moment, and the silence felt as if it closed in upon Nell. By tacit consent, the confrontation was taking place by the table near the window, so that one side of his lordship's face was in shadow. With the black clothes below, Nell received the disquieting impression of half a countenance, strangely disembodied. Like a portrait sketch, etched in charcoal—and singularly attractive. Her upset gave way to a feeling to which she could not immediately put a name.

'Is that a threat?'

The tone was quiet, and very grave. Nell's pulses gave an unruly jump. 'What do you mean, sir?'

'Do you intend to leave if I fail to credit you with common sense?'

He had moved a little as he spoke, and the oddity of his appearance vanished, leaving Nell vulnerable to consciousness that she had been taken at fault. She had no intention of walking out! She was glad of the shadows in the room for her own sake now. She floundered over a reply.

'No! At least—no, I had no thought of—' She broke off, unaccountably annoyed. 'Do you wish to put me at a disadvantage, my lord? I have been here three weeks without incident, and I am not to be frightened away by this! I meant no such thing.'

His eyes narrowed. 'You said it, however.'

'I believe you are trying to evade the issue!' declared Nell hotly.

A faint smile creased his lips. 'Well, yes, I am rather. I wish you will not allow the incident to distress you.'

Nell was a trifle mollified, but it would not do. 'How can I help but do so, sir? My integrity has been called in question.'

'Not by me, Miss Faraday.'

'Then you do believe me?'

Jarrow knew not how to answer this. While he could not see any reason why the governess should have made up such a thing, it was her word against that of Duggan. Unless the nurse was herself mistaken. He hesitated too long.

'I am answered,' the girl said dully.

He put out a hand. 'No, you are not. Only consider my position, Miss Faraday. I am loath to dispute what you saw, but where is the evidence? It is possible that Duggan's notions of time leave something to be desired, and that Hetty did indeed wander while she was absent from the bedchamber. But—'

Nell interrupted him without ceremony. She had remembered the shawl. 'If it is evidence you want, sir, consider this. Before I left Hetty, I took my own shawl from my chair and placed it under her head. When we got back to the schoolroom, it had been put back upon my chair.'

Lord Jarrow was frowning. 'You said nothing of this before.'

'In the light of subsequent events, I forgot it. I remarked it at the time, but we were in too much of a hurry to discover Hetty's whereabouts for me to be troubling over it then. But it came to mind when you spoke of evidence. You cannot suppose, my lord, that the child woke from her stupor in such a sensible frame of mind as to be thinking about replacing a shawl!'

'Indeed, no.' The ghost of a laugh escaped him. 'Nor that Hetty would think of tidying it, even were she in full possession of her senses.'

'There you are, then.'

Jarrow took a turn about the room, walking into the darkness and out again. 'What do you mean to imply by this, Miss Faraday? Am I to take it that Duggan is lying? Or that someone else is involved?'

'I have no notion!'

'Then what would you wish me to do?'

Defeated, Nell sank into a chair by the table. 'I do not know, sir.'

At least he seemed inclined to believe her. Curiously, although this gave her satisfaction, it did little to settle the disorder of her mind. He had asked the very questions she was asking of herself, and Nell had no answers.

'I have disturbed you for nothing, it appears,' she said at last. 'I am sorry for that at least.'

'Don't be,' he returned. 'I would prefer to be disturbed a thousand times than be ignorant of any of my daughter's oddities of conduct.'

Nell looked up at that. 'My lord, if she was indeed sleepwalking, there is no harm in it, I assure you.'

His voice was dry. 'Is there not, indeed?'

'I assure you,' she repeated. 'We had several girls who did so at the Seminary, and nothing dreadful happened to them at all.'

He did not pursue the subject, but Nell felt as if he withdrew into himself. He was facing her, standing in the light. The worn look had returned to his features, and she saw again the clefts beneath his eyes and below his cheekbones. Guilt traced a hazy path into her bosom, and the rhythm within it stepped up.

'I will leave you, my lord. I thank you for listening with patience.'

Rising from the chair, she made as if to pass him. Lord Jarrow caught at her arm.

'Wait!'

Her flesh burned under the thin fabric of her sleeve, and she felt a quiver inside. Dismayed by this unprecedented reaction to his touch, she concentrated all her attention to prevent his noticing it.

Jarrow saw the change in her face, but he did not release her. She was stiff, he thought, but let that pass. She had insisted upon this interview, and there were things that he wished to know.

'I have not troubled you, Miss Faraday, as you will have noticed. But my anxieties are as they were. Can you add anything now to what you told me that first day?'

She was either unable or unwilling to understand him! Why the puzzled look?

'I am talking of Henrietta. How is she doing?'

Beset by too many sensations to be able to think straight, Nell could no longer refrain from pulling away. 'Pray let go of me, Lord Jarrow!'

He snapped back as if stung, snatching his hand away. 'I beg your pardon.'

The curtness was back, and Nell's heart sank. He must think she suspected his motives. Better that, perhaps, than he should guess that her thoughts were quite otherwise. She felt unequal to managing any further conversation with him.

'It must be near time for dinner, sir. May we discuss this on some other occasion?'

His bow was ironic, she thought. 'By all means, ma'am.'

Nell fled the room in disorder.

The silence of night had a muffled feel, as if it was covered over with a heavy cloth. Nell lay in the darkness of the curtained bed, her ears stretched to catch the slightest sound. She had no notion what had woken her, but its impact had thrust sleep from her, peeling it away. There was nothing to be heard beyond the pounding of her own heart, yet the conviction grew upon Nell that she was not alone in the room.

Gathering herself, she sat up in one swift movement and dragged back the curtain. Thanks to her habit of leaving the windows unshuttered and the drapes undrawn, a faint spill of moonlight showed her the figure standing by the side of her bed.

'Henrietta! Great heavens, what a start you gave me!'

The child said nothing. Nor had she reacted to the sudden movement. Nell peered closely towards the gleam of the girl's pale face. Her eyes were open, staring straight ahead, and her breathing was both long and regular. She was in her nightgown, dark curls tumbling over the shoulders, with her feet bare. There could be no doubt of it. This time the child was definitely sleepwalking!

Nell eased herself out of bed. Hetty remained standing just where she had found her, even as Nell reached to the hook behind the door for her dressing robe. She slipped it on, and thrust her feet into a pair of slippers.

Without speaking, she took the little girl's hand in hers. She was cold, poor child, and no wonder! Then she gently turned Henrietta about and led her from the room.

It was not a great distance to the girl's bedchamber, but there was no light in the corridors bar that which came in at the windows. Nell had necessarily to proceed slowly. Besides, the child must not be rushed, despite Nell's anxiety to get her back into the warmth of her bed. Passing Duggan's door, she paused to listen. The nurse was likely asleep, for the contretemps over Hetty's unexpected appearance in the schoolroom had occurred on Tuesday, two days ago. Duggan had slept with her that one night, and although Henrietta had been drowsy on the Wednesday morning, she had been none the worse. And now this!

There was nothing to be heard within the room, and Nell moved on. The child's docility was unsurprising. None of the girls who had sleepwalked at the Seminary had ever attempted to defend themselves from being returned to bed. Indeed, just this factor had given Kitty away when she had pretended to sleepwalk so that she might effect an entry to the forbidden area of the pantry in order to abstract a delicacy or two. She had fought off her would-be rescuers, and the deception had cost her several hours of solitary confinement on a diet of milk and dry biscuits.

Reaching Henrietta's room, Nell found the door open. Once inside, the little girl needed no urging to move straight to the large bed and climb up to settle quietly between the sheets. Nell tucked the covers close about her and bent to listen to her breathing. It was even, but laboured, as it had been the other day. She eyed the child's features, pallid in the creeping moonlight.

What did this betoken? Perhaps she ought to request Lord Jarrow to send for the doctor he had mentioned. There was no need to wake him tonight. What could he do, after all? There had been no special treatment mentioned before. Nevertheless, Nell was loath to leave the child. She perched on the edge of the bed.

'And what might this mean, miss, if I may make so bold?'

Nell jumped, turning her head. Duggan—a silhouette merely, but Nell could not mistake her!—was standing at the foot of the bed, arms akimbo. She had spoken in an undervoice, but the tone was as insolent as the words. Nell rose to face her.

'I woke to find Henrietta beside my bed, Duggan. She was sleepwalking.'

She saw the woman's head toss. 'Oh, was she? And I suppose you wouldn't think to wake me for it?'

Nell felt her temper rising. She moved away from the bed, fearful of waking Hetty. 'As it happens, I did stop at your door. But as I heard no sound within, I did not trouble you. I judged it of more moment to get the child back to bed.'

'Yes, if she had been walking, which is by no means certain.'

This was not to be borne! 'Do you again suggest that I am making it up?'

The nurse's face was in shadow, but her voice held an unmistakable note of contempt. 'I wouldn't know why you'd do that, miss. Less it were to curry favour in a certain quarter.'

It was a moment before the implication hit Nell. Astounded, she could only stare at the woman's silhouette. Could Duggan seriously suppose that she would put the child at risk in order to gain an interest with Lord Jarrow? Unless she had entirely misread what the creature meant, Duggan was either jealous of her position or fundamentally stupid. Or there was a more sinister reason, at which Nell could not yet hazard the haziest guess. She opted for an attack direct.

'I do not know what your motive may be, Duggan, in attempting to give me the lie, but you may believe me when I tell you that whatever it is, I am not easily to be vanquished in a battle of wills!'

She then stalked past the woman and walked out of the room, inwardly seething.

It was long before she slept again, her mind roving. And not, as might have been expected, over the astonishing vagaries of the nurse. To her chagrin, Nell found herself obstinately returning to the extraordinary effect upon her senses of Lord Jarrow's grasp upon her arm the other day. Try as she would, she could not shake off the memory. Yet until the incident tonight, her obstinate brain had obeyed her insistent refusal to think about it. Why must it come upon her now, torturing her with the same racing pulse, the churning at her stomach, and the feel of intense heat in her arm where his fingers had held it?

The answer stared her in the face, and a damping cold rolled through her at the thought, sweeping it all away. She stood accused tonight! And the knowledge that she was innocent of any attempt to engage her employer's interest did nothing to assuage a hideous feeling of guilt. Could those dreadful sensations mean that she was susceptible to his attraction?

The very word caused her to groan and turn her face into the pillows. Heavens, but there was something in it! Even on the day of her arrival, her interest had been caught by the signs of that distress to which he had now and then given voice. Her fingers seized the edges of her pillow and clutched them painfully.

Where had her wits gone begging? Such self-deception, Helen Faraday! The Duck would frown upon her, and with good reason. Clever Nell! Priding herself upon her self-control, upon her cool head, and her management. And she was incapable of managing her own feelings!

She flung herself about, turning in the bed and staring up into the dark reaches of the unseen tester. Enough! She would not give in. She would conquer this. Come, the first step was taken. She had recognised her fault. Belatedly, but at least before any damage had been done. She could not have betrayed herself to Lord Jarrow. She had that comfort. And there was always the advice of her revered preceptress.

'You will be tempted, make no mistake about it. You are young, and desire is a natural thing. God made us to be subject to it, and with good reason. It is His way of continuing the species. Sadly, my dears, in your case it is not to be. But that does not mean that you will not encounter someone who evokes in you those sorts of feelings. I tell you this for your own protection. When it happens—notice that I do not say if!—*when*, I say, it happens to you, *you must take control.*'

There was ever a fluttering of sighs among the girls, Nell remembered, when it came to that point. She had heard the speech a number of times, for Mrs Duxford made it a regular feature of her teaching. Kitty had been used to clap her hands over her ears, refusing to listen. But Prue had nodded in solemn agreement. Not on account of her own future, recalled Nell smiling a little, for Miss Prudence Hursley had thought there could be no occasion to fear on her own account. Nor had Nell believed that she could fall victim herself.

Victim? No, that was putting it too strongly. She was no victim, for she had caught it in time. She could with advantage pursue that remedy advocated by Mrs Duxford.

'To fight against the feeling is the worst thing you can do, for you will only occasion in yourself an obsessive conflict that will take up all your attention. No, my dears, do not make that mistake. Acknowledge to yourself that the feeling is there, or has been there. And then concentrate your attention upon your duties. And, most importantly, avoid the object of your interest as much as you can. Fortunately, your circumstances are such that it is likely to be an easy course to pursue. The gentlemen of the house are in general far too occupied to have any interest in the whereabouts of the governess.'

In general, yes. Only the Duck had not bargained for a household where the governess daily supped with these gentry. Nevertheless, it was sound advice, and Nell determined to follow it. She began to plan a campaign of avoidance, which became strangely involved. Her last coherent thought was of the portrait in the parlour, of Julietta Jarrow.

When she woke in the morning, she was horrified to realise that all her dreams had been of her employer. Thankfully, she could remember none of the circumstances.

The problem was relegated to the back of her mind, however, within a short time of her charge's arrival in the schoolroom. Hetty was in a black mood. Just as his lordship had predicted, the halcyon period was over.

The child began with a heavy sulk, dark brows lowering and a pout upon her rosebud mouth. Recalcitrant, she objected to Nell's every effort to introduce lessons.

'Where had we got to? Ah, yes, we have done the letter G. Now look at this, Hetty.'

'Don't want to!' came the deep little voice as Nell began to write on the board.

She turned to find the child had buried her face in her arms upon the desk. Nell touched her gently.

'Hetty, look at me, please.'

The girl flinched away. 'Don't want to.'

'What is the matter?'

'Don't want to.'

Nell drew a breath. 'Very well. Shall I read to you instead?'

The child sat up with a bang. *'Noooooooo!'*

Her hair was wild, her eyes fierce. For the first time, Nell felt the want of Duggan's presence. However much she disliked the creature, at least she was used to dealing with the child. Nell had no notion how to proceed. It would be today that the woman chose to absent herself! For a brief moment, Nell toyed with the notion of seeking Lord Jarrow's help. But only for a moment. After last night, that was the last thing she wished to do.

'Hetty, what is it?'

She thought the gentle note might help, but the child positively glared at her. Her small fists clenched on the desk, and the pale features had all the brooding intensity of her father. Nell was conscious of a sliver of alarm in her breast. Was this a prelude to one of those shrieking tantrums? She tried another tack.

'Well, if you do not wish to do anything, we will simply sit here.'

With which, Nell seated herself at her own desk and folded her arms upon it, meeting the violent black eyes with an assumption of cool indifference.

The little girl's expression altered a trifle. Was her interest caught with the unexpected? Deliberately, Nell looked away and began to hum a simple tune—one that she had introduced with the toy soldiers. Her glance went about the schoolroom, but she managed not to include Henrietta. For a few moments, this treatment was productive of a profound silence. Nell longed to check, but she contented herself with what she could see in the periphery of her vision. Hetty remained unmoving, but Nell could swear the scowl on her face had worsened.

A low growl emanated from the child. Startled, Nell's eyes turned towards her. Had she truly heard what she thought? It had sounded like the threatening menace of an animal! She broke the silence.

'I beg your pardon?'

The growl was repeated, louder this time.

Nell raised her brows, and cast a swift look about the room. 'Heavens, is there a cat in here?'

A stifled giggle rewarded her. Pursuing her advantage, Nell pretended to look under the desk. 'Puss, puss! Where are you? Dear me, now where is the creature hiding?'

Next moment, Henrietta had dropped to the floor. Crawling about, she assumed the mien of a kitten, yowling and growling by turns. Nell sprang up, and at once made a game of it, scolding the 'kitten' and asking if it was hungry. The child allowed her head to be stroked, and by degrees was coaxed into laughter.

Nell's relief proved to be short-lived. The moment she attempted to resume lessons, the little girl withdrew into her sulk. She would not co-operate, and complained bitterly throughout the morning—albeit in a variety of unintelligible noises rather than words! It would have been tempting to allow her the afternoon off, but Nell knew this would set an undesirable precedent. The Duck had been clear. One did not reward bad conduct. That was only to reinforce the notion that the pupil could get her own way by this means.

Accordingly, Nell suffered through a wearing afternoon session as well. She would not allow the child to escape lessons altogether, and indeed taught each subject scheduled without regard to the fact that Henrietta participated not at all and achieved no results. Equally, she received no praise, and Nell made her feelings clear when Duggan came to fetch her and they parted.

'This has not been a good day, Hetty. I trust that you will do better tomorrow.'

To which, the little girl had only one response uttered in a frenzied manner that was typical of the passion she had exhibited all day.

'I hate you! I hate you!'

Nell watched her slam out of the room and listened to the clatter of her footsteps down the stairs. It was a sentiment Nell might well have reciprocated! She felt battered, and it was only by force of will that she remained standing. For no consideration would she show Duggan how she had been affected.

The nurse was eyeing her with an ill-concealed smirk upon her face. 'Given you a hard time, has she, miss? You should've taken a stick to her.'

Nell gave the woman a cold stare. 'Is that what you do?'

Duggan shrugged. 'Only language she understands at times.'

'Indeed? It is not a language I choose to adopt. Nor, if I have anything to say to it, shall it be used by anyone else while I am here!'

There was no mistaking the light of triumph in the creature's eyes. 'Then you'd best tell the master so, or he'll be speaking it hisself before the night's out.'

Upon which, she flounced out of the room, leaving Nell furious. She did not know whether she was angrier at the implied threat or the idea that Lord Jarrow could be guilty of such cruelty. Not that there was anything unusual about the habit of beating the young.

Only it was not a remedy that the Duck had recommended. Nor, to Nell's knowledge, had Mrs Duxford once resorted to it in the entire period she had been at the Seminary.

'If one cannot reason with a child, one had better think again. No child has ever been brought to reason with the rod.'

Not that Mrs Duxford had been against punishment. But she held to it that a period of incarceration and deprivation was a much more useful tool. The time might be spent in thinking it over, hopefully to arrive at the conclusion that the bad conduct was not appropriate. The Duck's methods had been almost uniformly successful at the Seminary, with a few notable exceptions—Miss Katherine Merrick for one!

Henrietta, however, was a special case. How Nell wished she had not fooled herself into believing in her success. Today's conduct was not that of a mischievous or volatile temperament. Nell wished she knew its origin. Was it a result, as Lord Jarrow feared, of a disorder of the mind? There was a possible reason, she remembered—today at least. The sleepwalking. Hetty may merely have been excessively tired. Only she had been more than bad-tempered. She had been actively hostile.

It had been a question with Nell whether she ought to tell her employer the whole. In the event, she had no need to do so. When they met at dinner, he appeared to be well informed.

'I gather you were treated to one of Hetty's temperamental moods today, Miss Faraday?'

Before she could reply, Mr Beresford butted in, his utterance preceded by his usual hearty laugh. 'What, has she been in a tantrum again? Knew that saintly conduct wouldn't last. Gad, ma'am, rather you than me who has to deal with it!'

'She was not in a tantrum.' Nell heard the reproof in her voice and made an effort to amend it. With a little difficulty, she forced herself to meet Lord Jarrow's dark gaze at the head of the table. 'She was sulky and scarcely manageable, sir, and I encountered a good deal of hostility from her. I would not allow her to abandon her lessons, however.'

'Bravo, Miss Faraday! Don't let the little devil win, that's my advice.'

'Toly, do hold your tongue!'

Nell cut in quickly. 'My suspicion, Lord Jarrow, is that Hetty was overtired. She was sleepwalking last night.'

'Was she, by Gad?' Mr Beresford whistled his concern.

Too late, Nell recalled his lordship's earlier remarks upon the possibility. And then she remembered the nurse's refusal to believe her. 'Perhaps Duggan mentioned it?'

'She did not.' Lord Jarrow's features had tightened. 'What happened?'

Nell tried to make light of it. 'Nothing much. I woke and found her standing by my bed. She did not move upon hearing my voice, but when I led her back to her own room, she came willingly. I tucked her up, and then—'

She checked herself, realising that she did not wish to disclose the snatch of argument she'd had with the nurse. The uncomfortable reflections engendered by that had best be kept to herself!

'Hell and the devil!' It was softly uttered, but it was clear that Lord Jarrow was upset.

'Funny, that,' commented the other man.

His brother-in-law turned to look at him. 'What is funny?'

'Well, it appears she didn't fight Miss Faraday. Unusual. But a good sign, don't you think?'

'They never do, sir,' Nell broke in. 'Sleepwalkers, I mean. They are usually perfectly docile.'

Another of his irritating guffaws erupted. 'Docile? Not Hetty, I'll be bound. Been known to batter at anyone who said her nay.'

'Not while she was sleepwalking,' argued Lord Jarrow.

'That's not what Duggan says.'

There was a silence. His lordship eyed his brother-in-law in a manner that sent a chill down Nell's spine. What in the world did this mean? There was an edge to his voice.

'What does Duggan say, Toly?'

Toly Beresford appeared a trifle conscious. He fidgeted with his utensils, and then laid them down and made a play of sipping his wine.

'Well?'

There was almost menace in the one word. Nell had stopped eating. She hardly dared breathe, her eyes riveted upon the man's handsome features. She watched him lift a hand and thrust back that unruly lock that had once more slipped over his brow.

'Well, you must know, old fellow,' he brought out at length. 'Woman talks to you more than she does to me.'

'I doubt it.'

Nell had never heard his lordship as dry. What did it betoken? An incredible supposition leaped into her mind. Could there be something between Mr Beresford and the nurse? It was not unknown—and the proximity in this place must make it tempting.

'What I wish to know,' pursued Lord Jarrow, 'is what Duggan may have said about Hetty's sleepwalking. She did not report it to me.'

'Dash it, Eden, I'm not privy to the child's activities! She may have mentioned it once, that's all. I'm sure she said Hetty fought her tooth and nail once when she tried to steer her back to bed. For all I know, the brat wasn't sleepwalking at all. May have got up out of bed and started to wander. No saying what she'll do, and you know it!'

'Alas, yes.'

Lord Jarrow resumed his meal, relapsing into the brooding silence that was habitual to him. Casting a glance across the table, Nell caught a shrugging look of appeal from Toly Beresford. He grimaced comically, casting his eyes to heaven and jerking his head slightly to indicate his brother-in-law. Nell kept her gaze steady, refusing to be drawn into complicity against Lord Jarrow.

Wrath crept into her breast. Did he imagine she would show herself either amused or insolently intolerant of her employer? She was evidently meant to understand that his lordship's moods were as unpredictable as his daughter's had been today. It was not for her to censure the man, but she could not prevent the reproof showing in her eyes. He saw it, for his expression changed to one of rueful apology. He gave her a shrug and a grin, and took up his knife and fork again.

Nell followed suit, wishing she might have something concrete she could offer to assuage Lord Jarrow's troubled fancy. From what she had seen, she had no reason to suppose Henrietta to be even marginally deranged. On the other hand, there was evidently a good deal she had not been privileged to see, and she had little knowledge of insanity.

She retired immediately after dinner, but she could not sleep. She felt decidedly on edge, and prey to a feeling of failure. At last she gave in, and got up, pulling on her dressing robe. Where to go? She needed air, and the moon was well out tonight. Slipping on her shoes, she dug out her cloak from the clothes press and slipped out of the room to steal along the corridor and into the turret that led to the schoolroom.

The familiar shapes looked eerie in the semi-darkness. But Nell slipped out onto the battlements, and sighed in immediate relief. The world was motionless, bathed in a silver glow, and a measure of peace began to seep into Nell's soul. She wound her cloak about her, and strolled gently along the roof walkway.

The change in her life was enormous, but it felt now as if she had been here forever. She had expected to feel unfamiliarity for a good length of time. She had adapted all too readily. Was it because everything at Castle Jarrow was so intense that she hardly missed her previous existence? If it was not true to say that she had not thought of Kitty or Prue very much, at least she had not felt the want of their company. She had Mrs Whyte to thank for that, perhaps. And, truth to tell, there was a more cogent reason. But Nell refused to give it voice. Yet for that alone, she found herself wondering for the first time in an age why she could not have chosen to go elsewhere.

'Are you thinking that you should not have come here?'

Lord Jarrow's voice jangled into her thoughts so that she leaped with shock, turning to find him standing almost immediately behind her. The uncanny perspicacity of his question slipped through her mind, and was gone. She let fly.

'Must you do that? You made me jump half out of my skin!'

Was there a look of amusement in his face? It was the more visible for the melting of his black clothes into the darkness. Pale in the moonlight, he looked curiously young, the troubled clefts smoothed out. He did not apologise.

'From the look of you, I would suppose you to be already in a state of unnatural agitation.'

'On the contrary, my lord, I was just beginning to achieve some much needed peace.'

The tartness in her tone was not lost on Jarrow. 'A commodity in short supply here, I grant you.'

She did not answer. His gaze roved her face. It was softened by the light, the halo of her fair locks gleaming silver. A riffle disturbed his senses. Involuntarily he shifted, looking quickly away. He would not go one step down that road. She was too good a creature to be lured into his accursed destiny. Even if only obliquely.

His tongue gave voice to the tenor of his thoughts. 'I could wish you had not come here, Helen Faraday.'

'No one calls me Helen.'

The utterance had a husky quality. Without volition, he turned his head. 'What do they call you?'

'Nell, sir.'

The instant it was out of her mouth, she knew it was a mistake. His gaze became intimate, probing hers. She wanted, needed, to look away. She could not. What had possessed her to speak of her name she could not imagine. Except that his expressed wish so closely mirrored her own. It should have distanced her

that he said it. Instead it had created the opposite effect. As if a kinship had sprung up between them.

His voice came softly. 'If I were not an honourable
man, Nell, I might well be carried away by the romance of the occasion.' A wisp of a smile curled his
lip. 'Moonlight and a pretty girl—balm to ease a troubled heart. It is almost unbearably tempting.'

Chapter Five

In that instant, cut to her own heart by the sadness in his face, Nell was tempted to offer up her own honour—if it might ease him. Common sense tapped a reminder on the walls of her conscience, and the Duck's sage words popped conveniently into her mouth.

'I am all too aware of the disadvantages of my situation, Lord Jarrow. Let me assure you that I have every intention of protecting my virtue.'

Jarrow snapped instantly out of the dangerous mood. He withdrew a step. 'You are very frank, Miss Faraday. Is that a warning?'

The dry note was back. Nell thrust down the immediate rise of disappointment. She backed to the battlemented wall, putting distance between them. 'You may take it as you choose, sir.'

'And if I choose to be insulted?'

'That is between you and your conscience, my lord.'

A burning sense of injustice threw Jarrow into attack. 'If that is your considered opinion, it was foolish of you to invite me to make free with your name.'

Nell hit back. 'Did I so invite you?'

'You know you did! A dangerous game, Miss Faraday, were I any other man.'

Her conscience stung and she sighed. 'You are right, Lord Jarrow. I had no intention of it. I assure you it was accidental. And I am persuaded you are too much the gentleman to take advantage.'

'I could though, Nell, very easily.'

What had she done? He no longer sounded angry, but there was something in his tone that both alarmed and thrilled her. Had she awakened it by what she had said and done, or had it been there already, if dormant? Heavens, but this could not be! She summoned all her resolution.

'Sir, this is altogether absurd. Recollect that I am your daughter's governess. This conversation had better not have taken place.'

A wry look was cast at her. 'Backing down, Miss Faraday?'

'I am trying to be sensible, Lord Jarrow!'

Jarrow felt obliged to relent. Why he had persisted in the face of her apology, he did not know. The interlude had somehow lightened the blackness of his life for a few moments. Truth to tell, he had been more anxious since the girl had arrived here than before. The reason flashed into his head. Had he been so certain that she would not stay? The thought thrust him into speech.

'Forgive me, Miss Faraday. The last thing I want is to provide you with any added incentive to leave. Your coming has been a godsend. I believe you must be doing Hetty a great deal of good, for she has been much calmer of late.'

Nell held her tongue on the urgent wish to assure him that leaving was the last thing on her mind. The mild words of praise warmed her, more for the ammunition they provided against the uncomfortable pricks from the nurse.

'I thank you, my lord. I only hope time will prove that your fears are unfounded.'

The reminder served to blacken his mood. 'You hope, Miss Faraday, for I cannot. Hetty follows closely in those footsteps I can all too easily recognise. Goodnight.'

The episode had not helped to ease Nell's path into sleep. She lay wakeful for some time, unable to banish the image of Lord Jarrow's features in the forgiving rays of the moon. Her own conduct upset her. She had provoked that intimacy—and he had known it! Yet instead of the shame she knew she ought to feel, Nell could not forbear a disgraceful exultance at having discovered in herself the power to attract him. It was abhorrent to be so much at the mercy of her desires. Mrs Duxford had not sufficiently warned her. How lowering it was to find herself so out of control of her own emotions!

And to know, too, that she truly had to thank Lord Jarrow's sense of honour that nothing had come of it. Nell was guiltily aware that she would not have fought him had he attempted to kiss her. Indeed, the thought of such a proceeding so wrought upon her physically that she groaned aloud.

The sound mingled with some other noise, outside her making. Instantly alert, Nell twitched back the curtains of the bed, half expecting to find Hetty there. There was no one else in her room, but the sound increased in volume. Nell got up and went first to the door, pulling it slightly open.

Voices, unmistakably male, were raised somewhere down the corridor. They were receding, however, accompanied by clattering footsteps. Nell strained to hear as they died away. Then a distant bang indicated the slam of a door. She closed her own door, and retreated into the bedchamber. Almost immediately the sounds of altercation came again. Nell crossed quickly to the window and looked out.

In the courtyard below stood two men, evidently in hot argument. A third held a horse, a great restless stallion, sidling on the gravel. Detling? It must be. And there could be no doubt that the two in altercation were Jarrow and his brother-in-law, although Nell could not judge in this light which was which. They were much of a height, and dressed alike in dark clothing. She saw one of them pull away and mount up.

The other stepped up to the horse to say something more. But the rider gathered up the reins.

'Stand aside!'

She heard it clearly, but could not recognise the voice. Next moment, the horse was clattering forward and the image sliced into Nell's mind. The footpad? Then she had seen him here! He was not wearing a mask, but the outfit was so similar as to beg the question. Was one of the gentlemen playing at highwayman? If so, one of them must be Lord Nobody. She watched transfixed as the rider passed out of her sight into the arched entrance below her window.

In a daze, she saw the one who was left watch him ride out, exchange a brief word with Detling—if the other was he—and turn for the main doors of the castle. She was nettled to think that the aged groom had deceived her. The wretch knew the identity of the fellow perfectly well!

Which of them had it been on the horse? Not Jarrow! A horrible sensation of nausea rose up. By his own admission, he was purse-pinched. Had he sought this means of mending his fortunes? And if it was he, her whole judgement of him was mistaken. For had not Lord Nobody shown himself to be affected by her that first day? Had he not spoken as if he knew her destination? What had he said—that he envied Lord Jarrow? Her heartbeat speeded up. Then it must be the other! Lord Jarrow had never until tonight given her any reason to suppose that he thought her anything out of the ordinary. And that had been due to her mismanagement. Or had it all been an act?

Nell became aware of cold and realised that she was standing in her nightgown, fully exposed to the night air. She returned to the bed and snuggled under the covers, still warm from where her body had been lying before. Yet the chilling sensation would not leave her, and the sickness grew in her stomach.

She had remembered the words of Mrs Whyte. Had it not been the fell hand of Lord Nobody who was thought to have murdered Julietta Jarrow?

Henrietta was late. Nell glanced impatiently at her pocket watch, which she always set upon her desk. It was near fifteen minutes past the hour. It did not help that the day was overcast, threatening rain, in keeping with Nell's mood. Herself in a state of near exhaustion from lack of sleep, she wondered whether the child had been disturbed by the activities of the night. Should she perhaps go down to the bedchamber and find out what was keeping her? She had scant faith that Duggan would trouble herself to come up and let her know what was going forward. Before she could make a decision, the outer door opened and Lord Jarrow entered from the roof walkway.

Nell rose from her place at the desk, damping down upon the upbeat of motion in her pulses. 'My lord?'

He looked heavy-eyed, the clefts more firmly etched into his features. He was holding out a package as he came across to the desk.

'Detling went to the Receiving Office yesterday. This came for you, Miss Faraday. I had meant to give it to you at dinner, but what with one thing and another, I'm afraid I forgot it until I saw it lying on my desk this morning.'

Nell took the package and read the inscription, realising that it was the first she had received since coming here. 'This is Mrs Duxford's hand. I had expected her to have written before this.'

Jarrow felt compelled to apologise. 'It has likely been lying in Rumford some days. We collect perhaps once or twice a month, and I have insufficient correspondence to justify the expense of having it delivered.'

She looked up quickly, and he warmed to the swift smile. 'It makes no matter, sir. I cannot think there will be anything in it of the least importance.'

To his own surprise, this answer made him feel worse. She looked a little wan. Was she a trifle out of sorts? Or had last night's contretemps upset her more than she had allowed him to believe? He found a neutral response.

'It is pleasant, nevertheless, to hear from one's friends. It lessens the sense of isolation.'

He noted the fleeting touch of sympathy in the forest eyes, and stiffened involuntarily. She had taken the idea as his. Which it undoubtedly was. The girl was decidedly too intelligent for his comfort. He turned to go.

'Stay a moment, Lord Jarrow, if you please.'

Was there a hint of censure in her voice? He checked on the threshold and looked back. There was a pause. She appeared to deliberate within herself, but that bold gaze did not waver.

'What is it, Miss Faraday?'

'About last night, sir—' He made an involuntary gesture as if to silence her, but Nell hurried on. 'I don't mean when we met out there, but later. I heard voices—yours and Mr Beresford's, as it turned out. And then I saw you in the courtyard.'

'What of it?'

His eyes had turned hard as steel, but Nell met them with challenge in her own.

'One of you—I could not tell which—rode out.'

'And?'

She ignored his obvious anger. 'Nothing, Lord Jarrow. I am merely informing you that I heard it. If there is some circumstance that links the episode with a certain highwayman, I will bear witness—if I have to.'

'Is that a threat, or merely a warning?'

'Neither, sir. It is an attempt at plain dealing, and I think you have deserved that of me at least.'

The anger died out of his eyes, but it left them hard. His jaw was tight and he spoke in that old clipped tone. Nell discovered with a sinking heart that it now had the power to hurt her.

'I am not sure that I understand you. However, let that pass. For your information, I did indeed quarrel with my brother-in-law—and not for the first time. He rode out as he often does. I can say no more than that at this present. Pray believe that the less you know the better!'

Nell watched him walk out, and the door shut quietly behind him. She knew neither what she had expected from him, nor what devil had urged her to speak out. A small voice prompted her honesty. If Lord Nobody did live in this house, she did not wish to identify him as her employer. She could not bear to think that he might have been responsible for the death of his own wife.

But he had not ridden out! Or so he said. She was annoyed to find that she could not trust his word. Could not? Or would not? He had done nothing to afford her the right to doubt him. Nothing, that was, but to cause her to lose her senses over him!

She discovered that she was holding the package he had brought her, and sat down at once to break the seals. The distraction was welcome, although she was unlikely to have leisure to read anything now. Henrietta must be here at any moment.

As she unwrapped the paper, a trifle of excitement stirred her after all. The abnormality of her existence here had come to seem the norm. It would be good to read of something that she could readily relate to. Perhaps it might serve to set her feet firmly back on the ground.

In the event, there was only a short letter from Mrs Duxford, wishing her well and enclosing three others—one from Kitty and two from Prue. The second had followed so fast upon the first that it had arrived before the Duck had a chance to forward the one.

'You will be astounded, my dear, at the good fortune that has overtaken our dear Prudence. Utterly unexpected, as I am sure you will agree. But I will let you read her news for yourself. We continue here as ever…'

Discovering the rest of the page to be concerned with the various little crises of the Seminary with which she was all too familiar, Nell discarded it in favour of the letters from Prue. What in the world could be so momentous? Prue had not been altogether happy in her employment at Rookham Hall—that much Nell had gathered from her earlier correspondence—and it had been but a temporary position. Perhaps she had secured a remarkably good post at some other establishment?

Scarcely had she ripped open the letters and checked the dates to find the later one, than the turret door opened to admit both Duggan and Henrietta. Depressing her frustration, Nell greeted her charge, and refolded the letters. The girl was in one of her better moods, for she actually smiled. Relieved, Nell slipped the package and its contents into the top drawer of her desk and began upon the first of the day's lessons.

When Hetty retired with her nurse for her luncheon, Nell meant to seize the opportunity to snatch a look at Prue's letters, but prevention came in the person of Mr Bartholomew Beresford.

He entered close upon a tentative knock, putting his head round the door to the roof. A deprecating expression invited her rejection.

'Pray don't hesitate to hurl me forth if I am disturbing you, Miss Faraday.'

Nell perforce disclaimed, but she eyed him with no little distrust as he shut the door upon the spitting rain and advanced into the room, brushing at his black coat.

'Just beginning to come down. Shame, after all the sun we've been having. Let's hope it won't last long.'

Too intent upon the reason for his unprecedented visit, Nell made no reply. She could not think but that it must have to do with last night. Nor was she mistaken.

'Eden gave my head a washing not a moment ago. He says you heard us last night, and he's afraid of your leaving us.'

Having made no such intimation to his lordship, Nell could not help being sceptical. Was the man making it up? She gave him a bland look.

'Indeed? I would ask you to sit down, sir, but as you see there is only Henrietta's chair.'

He broke out into his irritating guffaw. 'Ain't likely to afford me much comfort! Never fear, I'll make do with this.' So saying, he placed himself in one of the seats formed by the battlemented windows.

'How can I serve you, Mr Beresford?'

The eyes widened to their fullest extent. 'You can't!
I mean there's no occasion for it. What I came for,
Miss Faraday, was to reassure you that there's nothing
havey-cavey going on.'

Nell saw that some response was called for. Was
she supposed to believe him? She opted for a neutral
note, refusing to assist him.

'Indeed?'

He grinned in a manner that she could not but admit
to be engaging. 'Well, it's what you supposed, ain't
it?'

'Well, yes,' agreed Nell, capitulating. 'Only because I had heard something of Lord Nobody's exploits.'

A shout of laughter greeted this. 'I'll wager you're
imagining one or other of us to be none other than
that wayward gentleman.'

Curiously, this assertion had the opposite effect
from that which Nell supposed he intended. She debated whether to make her suspicions real to him.
Instinct prompted her to speak plainly, but caution
won. She tried for a smile, hoping that she did not
look as dismayed as she felt.

'I confess that had occurred to me.'

He shook his head and tutted. 'Miss Faraday, you
surprise me. Gad, but I wish I had thought of it! The
wretched fellow is forever nabbing gewgaws from the
gentry roundabout. I believe most of the ladies take
care these days to venture out without 'em.'

'A sensible precaution.'

Nell watched him carefully. Was it her imagination, or was there a calculating look in his eyes, as if he noted the effect upon her of each of his utterances? He wanted to know how his story was working with her. She determined to keep him guessing. Heavens, how she loathed pretence! Infinitely did she prefer Lord Jarrow's clipped wrath. Pain her it might, but its effect was to invite her belief in him.

'But you did quarrel with his lordship?' She gave a little shrug. 'Not that it is in the least my affair. Only I woke up, you see, and I should hate my employer to suppose that I was spying upon him.'

'Ah, so that's why you mentioned it.' Mr Beresford nodded his understanding. 'Thought it odd myself, but now I get the picture. Difficult position for you, Miss Faraday, I appreciate that.' He fetched a heavy sigh. 'Yes, we quarrelled. Not surprising, y'know. On top of each other the way we are. And he's moody is Eden. Quite as bad as Hetty. Got to get away now and then. Can't blame him, and I don't think he blames me.'

Trying to follow the gist of this, Nell became thoroughly confused. 'But is it Lord Jarrow you mean? Did he ride out in the middle of the night? I thought it was you!'

He looked blank. 'Did Eden say so? Gad, no knowing what he's going to come out with! Been the same all along—since the accident, I mean.'

A chill crept over Nell. 'Accident?'

Beresford frowned. 'Of course, you don't know, do you? M'sister was killed by a stray bullet. That's where the highwayman business comes in. At least, that's the way Eden told it.'

Startled, Nell forgot caution. 'But was he there?'

The wide eyes were briefly chagrined, but the look was so quickly gone that Nell could not be sure she had seen it. Now he looked merely puzzled.

'You've heard something of it, then?'

Ah, so that was what had surprised him. Annoyed him, perhaps? Useless to prevaricate. Nell opted for a head on challenge.

'Mrs Whyte hinted at something of the sort. Only she spoke of murder.'

His features crumpled, and he threw a hand to his face. 'Don't say it!'

Nell was stricken by remorse. 'Forgive me, Mr Beresford. That was stupid of me.'

Without looking up, he shook his head, throwing out one hand in a gesture that begged her silence. As if in sympathy, the rain stepped up, tapping at the windows. In a moment or two, Mr Beresford had apparently mastered his emotion. But when he lowered his hand, there was wetness at his eyes. Against her will, Nell could not help feeling sorry for him. The words came unbidden from her mouth.

'Why in the world do you stay, Mr Beresford, in a place so full of memories? Surely you would do better to go elsewhere. Pray do not fob me off with that tale your brother gave. I have no doubt he could be persuaded to give you pecuniary assistance.'

A heavy sigh greeted this. 'I would not ask it of him. There are Beresfords enough upon whom I could call. But how can I leave him? Were I to go, who would give the lie to the rumours? I am Julietta's brother. As long as I stand by him, no one dare accuse him outright.'

The sense of this was clear, but Nell's heart refused it. She would not give it credence. She would not even acknowledge that he had said it!

'Then why don't you ask your family for help?' she said, ignoring the entirety of the remainder of his speech.

An understanding smile was directed upon her. 'I see what you are at, and I don't blame you. Do you suppose that I believe it? Don't you think that, despite all the evidence to the contrary, I hold Eden entirely innocent?'

There was lead in Nell's chest. The drip of waters upon the roof walkway outside increased in volume, and somewhere inside her, a scream was forming. She wanted to hurl his words back at him, forcing him to unsay them. She wanted to curl her fingers into claws and scratch his face until he admitted that it was a lie. She did none of these things. She sat perfectly still, and kept her gaze steady on the man's handsome face.

But she could do nothing about the tremor in her voice, and its husky quality echoed in her own ears. 'What possible motive could he have?'

The sadness increased in the abruptly hateful features across the room. 'Why, have you not guessed it, Miss Faraday? Have you not both seen and heard the fear in his expressions every day?'

An inkling was creeping into Nell's mind, despite the fog suffusing it. Now she thought herself a fool not to have realised before. 'Henrietta?'

'Is following so closely in her mother's footsteps that poor Eden dreads the sight and sound of every symptom.'

Mr Beresford rose from the window seat, pacing to the desk. He placed his hands upon it, leaning over her. Nell stared up into his features, and saw in them for the first time the portrait of Julietta Jarrow. His eyes met hers, wide and fierce with a species of agony.

'Yes, Miss Faraday. My poor sister was demented. She led Jarrow a life so hideous that I doubt any stranger could imagine it. Which of us who knew of it could blame him if he could not endure it? If he wished at last to be rid of her.'

The housekeeper's round cheeks were flushed, her kind eyes uncharacteristically ablaze. 'He'd no call to say such a thing, he as was brother to the poor mistress and all! Wicked young wastrel he always was. Leading her astray, if you was to ask me the truth of it!'

Nell had not meant to stir up such a storm, in keeping though it was with the protests in her bosom and the lashing rain outside. Contrite, she laid down her cup. 'I should not have told you.'

'Begging your pardon, Miss Faraday, you should! You need someone to tell you what's what, if you're to be fed a pack of lies.'

Longing to beg for reassurance that it was indeed a pack of lies, Nell banished the question from her lips. Bad enough that she should have roused Mrs Whyte to this extent, only because she could not contain her own distress. She put it down to the frustrating necessity to keep her emotions festering inside while she took Henrietta through her lessons for the afternoon. The result was that instead of questioning the housekeeper obliquely about the late mistress of Castle Jarrow—which was what she had intended—she had spilled the whole tale within moments of the housekeeper serving her with a dish of tea. She hastened to amend the situation.

'Mrs Whyte, pray don't upset yourself. It is not as if Mr Beresford said it was so, but only that rumour had got about.'

'Don't tell me! There is naught so wicked as those with gossiping tongues.' A great sigh escaped the other woman, and she stirred sugar into her tea with a moody hand. 'It's the master I'm sorry for. It ain't as if he hadn't enough on his hands with the mistress murdered and the place full of constables and magistrates, but some noddy must needs go and start a tale that says he pulled the trigger. Never heard such a nonsense in my life!'

How can you be sure? But Nell could not say it. She was not even certain she could endure to hear the full account of what had happened upon the fatal night. Not merely for its own horrors, but because she knew it could not fail to remind her of that dread image in her past. Better to stick to the other matter upon which she sought enlightenment.

'What is most important at this present, Mrs Whyte—at least for my purposes—is what you can tell me of Lady Jarrow's condition.' The housekeeper's features sagged, and her eyes clouded. 'It distresses you, I know, but—'

'Yes, it does, ma'am, and I'll tell you for why.'

Nell waited. Mrs Whyte fidgeted a moment or two with her cup, picking it up and putting it down again without, Nell was persuaded, noticing what she was doing. She shook her head, setting the mob cap dancing, and gave forth another gusty sigh.

'You see, my dear, while there was conduct as made it certain my poor mistress wasn't in full possession of her wits, it ain't that sort as you see in Miss Hetty.'

'I don't understand you.'

The housekeeper fortified herself with a gulp of tea. 'She'd fall into unaccountable rages, yes. Tantrums you'd call it in the young'un. Then there was fits of shaking and muttering, moaning fit to frighten the whole household. After such times it was almost worse, ma'am. Flat out calm she'd be, sleeping for hours and looking like the dead.'

A tattoo started up in Nell's chest, and the battering rain sounded loud in her eardrums. 'And her breathing? Was it laboured?'

The housekeeper shot her a questioning look. 'Heavy it was, yes. Used to frighten me horrible.'

'Did she walk in her sleep?' Was not that one of his lordship's worst fears?

Mrs Whyte looked dubious. 'Well, she was used to walk the corridors of a night. Whether she were asleep or no I can't rightly say. Nor anyone else, for the matter of that. Excepting his lordship perhaps.' A tinge of colour stole into the lady's cheeks. 'They slept separate mostly.'

This intelligence had the oddest effect upon Nell, for a sliver of heat shot through her and her mouth went dry. She was glad to be spared having to speak, for the housekeeper had not completed her disclosures. They proved more and more unsettling.

'Her chamber was next to his. Times you'd go in and find her gone. Only you couldn't be sure she was walking, for she'd go in to him on occasion. For comfort, I think, though it can't be gainsaid she'd her—' darkly, with a hand flipping quickly beside her mouth to indicate secrecy '—*other* needs. And he'd not repudiate her, not his lordship. On either count, I'd guess.'

Nell could readily believe it. Lord Jarrow had ever struck her as a man with a sense of duty. And he must have loved his wife. The thought caused a flicker of hurt to which she refused to give acknowledgement.

Yet though he loved her, she must have tested him to the utmost. She recalled where the housekeeper had begun.

'You mentioned at the start, Mrs Whyte, that Henrietta is not quite following in her mother's footsteps. Or have I misunderstood you?'

The frill of the mob cap emphasised her denial. 'I think you understand me very well, Miss Faraday. You've seen something of all that in Hetty. And it's my belief there are those as want it seen.'

Nell stared. 'Now you have lost me.'

The housekeeper pursed her lips. 'Shouldn't have said that. Pay me no mind, ma'am.'

'Yes, but I don't think I can,' said Nell frankly.

'Best I keep my suspicions to myself.'

Her curiosity thoroughly aroused, it was all Nell could do to agree to this. 'Yes, but you were going to tell me something more of your mistress, weren't you?'

Mrs Whyte fiddled with her spoon again. 'I don't know as I ought. It ain't that I don't trust you, ma'am, for I can see for myself as you're a sensible female. Only there's no saying who might hear me, and a body can't be too careful.'

Could there possibly be room for such fears? It argued a certain desperation on the part of those who might be supposed to hear. Nell felt thoroughly discomposed. However, the Duck had always said that more knowledge, and not less, was the key to overcoming apprehension. She tried again.

'Mrs Whyte, I don't know what may be occurring here in Castle Jarrow, but I have already been subject to certain peculiarities. The more you can tell me, the easier it will be for me to judge of the rightness of anyone's actions. Ignorance can only leave me open to—well, to whatever it may be that is being played out here.'

The housekeeper sighed again. 'Well, I can't argue with that.'

Nevertheless, she got up out of her chair and stepped softly to the pantry door, opened it and listened intently. Evidently, she was satisfied with what she heard—or did not hear—for she nodded, quietly closed the door, and returned to her seat, gesturing to the splatter of water upon the casement behind Nell.

'No one won't hear us, I dare say, above that racket.' She leaned forward, nevertheless, lowering her voice in a conspiratorial fashion so that Nell had to strain to hear her above the rain.

'What you've seen in Miss Hetty, my dear, is only a tithe of what the mistress put him through. I was that fond of her, but it can't be gainsaid that she would have tried the patience of a saint.' She leaned even closer, dropping almost to a whisper. 'It weren't the tantrums, nor yet the fits and such. It was the *men*, Miss Faraday. She couldn't help it. It was like a sickness. The gambling was another. Though there I blame her brother, for he encouraged her. It seems as there was one too many scandals, for at last his lordship brought her home. I think it was that sent her over the edge, if anything did. She never forgave him, and she led him such a dance as it's a wonder it wasn't his lordship as was driven crazy!'

Appalled, Nell could only gaze at her. Was this sordid history intended to relieve her fears? It was having just the opposite effect. The housekeeper had as well say exactly what Mr Beresford had said. Who indeed could blame Lord Jarrow for ridding himself of such a burden? She could not keep the words from tumbling out of her mouth.

'But you spoke as if you championed him, Mrs Whyte. You called Mr Beresford wicked for making the same accusation. You paint a portrait of a man at the end of his tether. Yet you claim he could not have pulled the trigger!'

'Nor he couldn't!' stated the woman, red with indignation. 'Upon my word, ma'am, you take me up wrong, indeed you do!'

Nell made haste to apologise. 'I was shocked by what you told me, Mrs Whyte. Pray go on with your tale.'

A trifle huffily, the housekeeper sniffed. 'What I was about to come to, Miss Faraday, is that I don't believe as the mistress was mad. Or if she was, it weren't that which gave her fits and tantrums. Nor I don't know what it was, to say truth, only why didn't she throw them when she was here at the first?'

Arrested, Nell caught her breath. 'You mean when they were first married?'

Mrs Whyte nodded, her offended manner deserting her. 'You never saw nothing like that with her at the start. Admittedly, she only stayed the summers, for she couldn't bear the place. One winter was enough, she said, and his lordship couldn't blame her for that. Mostly they was in London, staying at the Beresford house. Or winters they'd go to her family's estates. In the north they was—and I wish as he would up sticks and go there now!'

'Lord Jarrow?' But Nell realised as she spoke that it was wrong. She had been too caught up in the tale to think clearly. 'No, you mean Mr Beresford, of course. When was it that they came back to live here then?'

'Near three years now. And it weren't a month or two before he followed. And he's been here ever since, more's the pity.'

That this bitter reference was to Toly Beresford, Nell could not doubt. What grounds had the house-keeper for her extreme distrust of the man? Her own dislike made it imperative that she did not allow herself to be ruled by prejudice. *Facts*. Never judge but upon facts, had said Mrs Duxford, time and again. She did not hold with intuition, feminine or otherwise. But it was difficult not to be swayed by personal feeling— or was it intuition?

'Yes, I have observed that even Lord Jarrow is not overly fond of his brother-in-law.'

'Fond? He detests him!'

Nell would not have gone as far as that. 'How can you know, Mrs Whyte?'

But the housekeeper's confidences were at an end, for she stood up. 'I've a liking for you, Miss Faraday, and that's a fact. But there's some things a body should keep to herself! I've said too much already, I don't doubt. Only it's a relief to have it out, I'll say that. I've my suspicions, and I know who I'd point the finger at. But I'm not saying nothing more on that score.'

On impulse, Nell rose from her chair and went around the table, seizing the housekeeper's hands. 'I have made you betray yourself, and I'm sorry for it. I can only promise you that your trust is justified. I will say nothing of this.'

Her hands were squeezed by the pudgy ones she held. 'Not even to his lordship?'

Nell released her, attempting to quell the instant flutter at her breast. 'Least of all to his lordship!'

To her consternation, Mrs Whyte's gaze became a trifle smug. 'We'll see that in due course. But I can see I'm too previous there, so I'll hold my tongue.'

Upon which, Nell made haste to leave her to her cooking, her emotions in disarray.

The events of Saturday having given her food for much thought, it was not until Nell went to her bed-chamber after breakfast upon the following morning—for the dutiful purpose of reading a page or two from the Bible since she could not go to church—that she remembered the letters from her friends. Feeling horribly guilty, she ran up to the schoolroom and retrieved them from the desk. The rain had ceased, but the day was dull and a trifle chilly. Nell left the schoolroom and returned to her chamber, where she wrapped a warm shawl about her shoulders and settled comfortably upon the bed to read the letters.

But when she spread open the sheet that had been written from Rookham Hall some three weeks ago, its contents threatened to plunge her into instant flight from Castle Jarrow.

Prue was to be married! And to her employer, Mr Rookham! Heavens, was it possible? Could she have read it aright? It was a love match, her friend wrote, unlikely as it seemed. Nell's mind was reeling so that she hardly took in the effusion that followed, detailing some of the circumstances that had led up to Prue's extraordinary fortune.

Try as she would, Nell could not prevent the foolish rise of hope—nay, expectation even!—that immediately overtook her on her own account. Why must she be so absurd? That fatal Faraday pride! Merely because Prudence Hursley had achieved the impossible, was she to suppose that her own future could be no less dazzling? *Dazzling.* A choice of word that must prove her descent into idiocy! Dazzling, to be tied forever to this dreadful castle and a man so broodingly bitter that the slightest word was liable to throw him into gloom? It was laughable. Or it would be, were it not so tragic.

Wake up, Helen Faraday! The man was in mourning, grieving for a murdered wife—or riddled with guilt for having done the deed. A circumstance so truly Gothic as must have sent even the romantic Kitty screaming into the night!

She read swiftly through the preceding letter from Prue, and was further disgusted at the leap of interest that she felt upon recognising from the contents that her friend's path had been proverbially rough. Very different in tone was this first letter from the second, which bubbled over with happiness and explained the doubts expressed earlier. Doubts that had been happily resolved—in Prue's case.

Nell was obliged to remind herself several times that there was an unbridgeable gulf between Mr Rookham having doubts of his feelings being sufficiently strong to enable him to engage in a matrimonial tie, and the extreme unlikelihood of Lord Jarrow stepping a second time into a contract that had all but ruined his life upon the first occasion.

But worse was to come. Throwing Prue's letters aside, Nell turned with relief to Kitty's. The feeling was short-lived. The first few lines were dedicated to reminding Nell that her other friend had been the only one to predict the future correctly. The next sentences almost threw Nell into strong hysterics.

'I do hope you have not neglected any opportunity to attract Lord Jarrow's attentions. Has he yet fallen in love with you? My dearest Nell, you positively must marry him. If you do not, I shall never forgive you for not letting me go to his horrid castle in your stead.'

Nell crumpled the sheet into a ball and flung it across the room. Kitty, foolish Kitty! How little she knew! If only she had an inkling of the effect of her words! Nell dashed a hand across her eyes. She would not weep. Why must her dearest friends be the innocent means of sending her into despair?

She must be glad for Prue's sake. She *was* glad. No one deserved her happiness more. Dearest Prue. Small wonder her soft heart had won another for her. Who could help loving Prue? As for Kitty...!

Nell drew a steadying breath and shut out further thought. With deliberation, she got up from the bed and went to pick up her friend's unfortunate letter. She smoothed it out with shaking fingers, but she could not read it to the end. Not yet awhile. She would have to write back—to both of them. Only she must allow time for her abominably stupid feelings to be conquered. Or at least subdued. How long that might take she dared not even guess at. The music, though, was soothing.

A flash of recognition brought her up short. Music?

She stood still, listening. Sure enough, she could hear the strain of some melody. Was it played upon a spinet? It had not the rounder tone of a pianoforte, but rather the tinny sound of an older instrument. Only who could possibly be playing?

Setting aside her letter, she crossed to the door and opened it. The music increased in volume. It was near at hand, perhaps a little way down the corridor, in the opposite direction from her usual route past Henrietta's room. Nell drew her shawl tidily about her, closed the door behind her and followed the sound.

It was a light little dance tune—of Mozart? Yes, it had his distinctive rhythm. The player was inexpert, but was managing well enough. Nell had judged of so many fingers that she could readily guess at the level of skill. She rounded the tower and saw in a moment that the first door stood open. Without hesitation, she hurried towards it and entered the room, which proved to be a bedchamber.

A swift glance round showed her that it was empty. Then she spotted the instrument set against one wall. The lid was open, but the keys were silent now. Whoever had been playing was no longer there.

Chapter Six

For a space that felt an age, Nell remained motionless. She could feel the hairs on the back of her neck rising and a prickle of cold crept across her skin. Gradually the suspension of thought began to ease, and a moment's reflection convinced her that this was not a supernatural manifestation. Someone had been here. Was still, perhaps?

She darted to the bed and ducked down to peer beneath it. No hiding body rewarded her. Feeling foolish, Nell rose up and looked quickly about. The four-poster dominated the room, but its curtains of dull gold velvet were open. Upon the matching cover, spread across the pillows, lay a cloth of black gauze centred with a long-dead rose.

A dreadful premonition seized Nell. This must be Lady Jarrow's room!

Her glance travelled across other furnishings, similarly decked with black gauze. Heavens, it was like a shrine! Only the clavichord—Nell recognised it now—had been left unadorned in this manner. Or had the perpetrator of this shocking trick removed it?

There could be no doubt that it was a trick. They had made a swift exit, but someone had certainly been here. She could see nowhere for anyone to hide, for the dresser and the commode were close against the wall, and there were only shutters to the windows. They were open, flooding light into the room.

She stepped softly to the head of the bed and checked behind the fall of curtain. Nothing! Had there been time for someone to leave the room before she entered? Nell tried to recall just when the music had stopped, but she could not place the exact instant. She was sure she had heard it as she came in, but it might have ceased a few seconds before. Only how had they been able to get out?

A horrid thought made her turn quickly towards the door. Had they hidden behind it, and slipped away as she halted? That must have been it. A clever ruse, but not quite clever enough! Whoever did this had reckoned without the inculcation of Mrs Duxford's common sense into her least susceptible pupil. Nell had ever been far too prosaic to believe in ghosts.

Nevertheless, the episode had unpleasant repercussions. She took an aimless turn about the room, fetching up beside the clavichord and staring at the keys with unseeing eyes. She could not doubt but that the music had been intended for her. Who else would be about on a Sunday at this hour? Hetty was permitted to play in her room, and Duggan would be with her there. Lord Jarrow, who took no account of the Lord's Day, would be in his study as usual, and Mr Beresford generally spent the day visiting friends—or so she understood. Which left whom?

Mrs Whyte? Hardly. And it was the height of stupidity to suppose that either Keston or Detling—both elderly—could have made the necessary dash between ceasing to play and getting to the door. Nor could Nell imagine the slightest reason for their doing so. And the fellow Grig was never permitted within the area of the house given over to the use of the gentry, except when he brought the dinner dishes from the kitchen to the dining-room door.

Without thinking, she sat down on the stool before the instrument and spread her fingers over the keys. Someone had wanted her to enter this room. She was evidently supposed to indulge in the absurd supposition that the ghost of Lady Jarrow had been playing! But for what reason? What purpose could be served by the deception?

Recalling the housekeeper's dire warnings, Nell was dismayed to feel a resurgence of the apprehension that had attacked her earlier. Was there devilry afoot? But how should it concern her?

Then she remembered the episode of the unexplained shawl that time Henrietta had been left asleep in the schoolroom. Left? The significance hit her abruptly. The child had not wandered. Someone had placed her there! Just as they had lured Nell here and then disappeared without trace. She was *meant* to fall into confusion. Were they—whomever it might be—bent upon frightening her? To what purpose?

But that was obvious. So that she would leave. How foolish not to have realised it at once! Whatever they were engaged upon, the governess was in the way.

The logical progression from there sent a chill racing down her spine. If that was the case, then the matter must concern Henrietta. *What could they want with the child?*

Hardly knowing what she did, Nell began to drum upon the keys. Notes pattered on the air, half startling her, and she pulled her fingers away. Her breath had shortened, and her mind felt distressingly blank.

'Miss Faraday!'

Nell leaped where she sat, her nerves jangling violently. Her startled eyes fell upon the figure of her employer standing in the doorway, his hand upon the edge of the open door.

'What the devil do you think you are doing?'

Both face and voice were irate, and Nell's heart sprang into life. She got up quickly, her thoughts darting this way and that as she sought for a plausible explanation. Would he credit the truth? Only how else was she to account for her presence in his dead wife's bedchamber?

'It looks odd, I know,' she began.

'Excessively,' he agreed curtly. 'What occasion had you for entering this room? You can see it is disused. What should bring you here?'

Nell's churning emotions got the better of her. 'If you will allow me to speak, sir, I will tell you!'

Jarrow hesitated. He had heard with disbelief the jangle of the clavichord keys as he was walking in the direction of his own room. Hastening past his door, he had discovered Julietta's to be open. Shock had thrown him into fury. The last person he had expected to find was Miss Helen Faraday.

He entered the room, and absently shut the door. 'Well?'

The governess sighed and sank down again onto the stool. Her gaze dropped from his. 'It will sound quite mad, sir, but therein lies the problem.'

Jarrow eyed the bent head, the honey-gold hair uncovered. But then she never did wear a cap, he thought inconsequentially. She should do. Those locks were far too disturbing. He quelled the thought.

'Go on, Miss Faraday.'

She looked up and the frank gaze caught at him. 'I heard music playing and followed it. The door was open to this room, but even as I entered the music stopped.'

Yes, it did sound mad. But he could dismiss no oddity out of hand with his brother-in-law in the house. 'And so?'

He watched the gathering frown upon her brow. 'I was nonplussed for a moment.' Her warm smile brightened her face for an instant. 'No, let us be truthful. I was briefly terrified! However, it was soon borne in upon me that it must be a trick. You will laugh, I dare say, but I looked under the bed and even behind it before I realised that someone could well have exited through the door while I was standing transfixed.'

Jarrow glanced back at the door. It opened inwards from the corner. Yes, a convenient hiding place. He moved to the bed and grasped one of the posts, staring down at the covers. He should have locked this room and kept the key on his person. Not that he had left anything of value in here, which was all that could draw Toly to make a search through Julietta's belongings—and who else would come in here? But why target Miss Faraday?

'Where were you when you heard the music?'

'In my room, sir.'

He looked at her and saw his own concern mirrored in her face. 'I should be sorry to think that a person in my household was making it their business to spy upon you.'

'In order to become aware of my movements? I confess it is not a thought that fills me with unmixed pleasure!'

Jarrow bit back a laugh. 'You take it coolly, ma'am.'

That swift little smile captured him again. 'There is little point in succumbing to the vapours, or some such absurdity. Besides, I have ever been known for my lack of sensibility.' A tiny spurt of laughter escaped her. 'Berated sometimes. My friend Kitty found me sadly deficient in that area.'

This was too close to home for amusement. 'You have my sympathy. I know too well the frustration of being thought callous when one cannot enter into the emotional whirlpool that surrounds one.'

The harsh note jarred in the confines of this particular chamber. Nell eyed his darkening features, a catch at her breast. He sank down onto the bed, reaching out a hand to grasp at the black gauze, dragging it out of shape so that it formed into ripples and folds, dislodging the dead rose. Nell's heart twisted at the guttural bitterness of his tone.

'God knows I tried! But I loathe and detest these scenes. They make me ill. It was not her fault, for she had no control. Like a spoilt child, demanding and wayward by turns, flying into rages without rhyme or reason, and then falling into pretty contrition so that one must have been a monster to reject her pleas.'

With a gesture of distaste, he released his clutch upon the gauze and smoothed it away from him. 'Poor Julietta.'

His gaze came up, and Nell saw with pain the clouding at his eyes. She did not speak, although she wondered at his openness. She watched his lip curl, and the dryness entered his voice.

'You should thank your stars for your position, Nell Faraday.'

Her answer was a murmur. 'Why so?'

'You have been spared the eyes of society. The deceits and petty gossip that thrive in it to take advantage of the misfortunes of others.' A species of passion became rife in his tone. 'And so indulge the perfidy of a creature who had always an unanswerable excuse. She did not know what she was doing!'

Nell did not flinch from the haunting agony in the brown eyes. 'She must have hurt you very much.'

'Enough to justify her early demise? There can be no doubt it was a mercy.' His gaze roved the chamber. 'One would suppose that I am heartbroken. All this welter of black is of Mrs Whyte's doing. She was fond of Julietta.' There was a pause, and his hand clenched. 'I detest the place!'

Searing doubt struck at Nell. He had as well have said that he detested his wife! Did he wish her to believe him capable of murder? Here was all the motive one could desire. Yet all she could feel was the violent pull of compassion that urged her to go to him and offer the comfort of her arms.

Instead, she got up, automatically shaking out the bronze petticoats and gathering her shawl about her. 'I will leave you, sir. Perhaps it will be the better for both of us if we forget what has been said in this room.'

Lord Jarrow neither spoke nor moved, and Nell quietly crossed the room and left him.

Dinner was interminable. Barred from bringing up the subject of today's episode in Lady Jarrow's room, Nell found it difficult to maintain any semblance of normality. Whether it was the presence of Toly Beresford—who, she was persuaded, eyed her narrowly now and then—or the relapse of his lordship into his usual moody withdrawal, she could not say with any certainty. Lord Jarrow's frankness had made her privy to his secrets, throwing her into a few moments of intimacy from where there was nowhere to go. Neither backward to her proper status, nor forward. A destination from forward she did not care to contemplate.

Even Mr Beresford was abnormally subdued. His jests were sparing, and for the most part he confined himself to partaking of the viands on offer. The menu had once more reverted to pork, for the quarter of beef purchased from the adjacent farm had come to an end. That the gentleman made no cutting references to it only increased Nell's conviction that almost everything he said and did was an act. Her distrust of him was growing, and she could no longer conceal from herself that she thoroughly disliked him, which made it the more difficult to pass judgement upon him as against his brother-in-law. Her personal feelings must inevitably interfere. Yet if she was to narrow down the suspects in the matter of the tricks to which she was being subjected, Mr Beresford came high on the list.

She excused herself early, leaving the gentlemen to their port. But instead of going directly to her chamber, she headed for the turret that led to the schoolroom. She had not changed for dinner after that first evening, and the bronze calico was sturdy enough to withstand a short walk upon the roof. It had been misty all day and the stars were obscured by cloud.

Nell's candle flame danced in the uneven air and she was obliged to cup her hand about it to keep it from going out.

Avoiding the route that led to Lord Jarrow's study, she took a path around the turret and down towards the front of the castle. Halfway along that side, she set her candlestick down in one of the recesses of the battlements and shifting to the next, leaned out a little into the night.

It must be a month since she had entered the castle courtyard, and she had not once set foot outside. Indeed, she reflected, recalling the date, tomorrow it would be exactly one month. She felt like one of those princesses of the fairy tale, immured in a tower until the prince came to rescue her. Only the prince in this case was himself caught fast. It was tempting to think she might turn the fairy tale on its head and rescue him. From the torments of the past? Nell did not think she had that power. A waste of energy even to think of it. She had a deal better bend her mind to that question she had come up here to solve. Should she stay?

Someone wanted to be rid of her, although the motive was not yet fathomable. If she gave in, who would benefit? Not Hetty, for the child was involved, though Nell could not see how. Lord Jarrow? Nell could not suppose he would be affected either way, so wrapped up as he was in his own despair. She dared not flatter herself that he could be brought to forget only through her agency. The servants? Only Mrs Whyte might miss her a trifle, though that would soon be mended. Which left Nell herself.

Had she a brain in her head she would escape as fast as she could! What purpose did it serve for her to remain in a place where her sanity was threatened by weird manifestations? Where her heart was rendered bleak through proximity to a man for whom she could never be more than a—what? Her thoughts suffered a check. Was she merely the governess to him? No, it was more than that. A companion? A friend? Both were possible, and either would leave her prey to a gnawing emptiness that must destroy her if she stayed.

No, the only safe course was to leave. Which certainty instantly swung her back into wretchedness, for of course she could not leave. If Henrietta was in danger, there could be no question of walking away— which conveniently permitted her to ignore the added incentive. Heavens, what a self-deceiver she had become!

There was room for no more. A sudden grip upon her shoulders made her jump with shock. And then she was being tugged back, and a man's arms were encircling her, holding her hard against a firm chest. She could feel warm breath upon her neck, and a voice spoke intimately close to her ear.

'Can it be that you are intent upon suicide, Miss Faraday?'

The soft tones were far from those she had half expected to hear. Next instant, a coarse guffaw nearly shattered her eardrum. She grasped at the encircling arms and tried to wrench them away.

'How dare you, Mr Beresford? Let me go!'

But his grip rather tightened. 'By no means, m'dear. Leave off such a cosy armful? I'd prefer to be shot!'

Nell twisted her head away from the heat of his cheek, which he was trying to lay against her own. She wasted no more words, but releasing her hold on his arms, she instead clutched her petticoats, lifting them to free her foot. Then she kicked hard with her heel, backwards against his shin.

His yelp gave her a good deal of satisfaction, and his hold loosened sufficiently to enable Nell to tear herself away. She turned on him in fury.

'You chose the wrong woman for your advances, Mr Beresford! I have been well trained in prevention.'

He laughed wildly, the glitter of his wide-eyed stare visible even in the half-light. 'I should say you have, by Jove! Fairly broke my leg.'

One hand went down to rub at his shin, and Nell was torn between triumph and a sliver of guilt. 'I am sorry if I hurt you, sir, but it is your own fault. What in the world possessed you to seize hold of me in that fashion?'

A flash of teeth showed as he gave out another of his odd laughs. 'Thought you were meaning to do away with yourself.'

Nell dismissed this out of hand. 'Don't be absurd! Why should I do anything so extremely foolish?'

'I could hazard a guess, only I don't want to draw your fire again.'

'Keep your distance, sir, and you won't.'

But he shifted a step closer. Nell drew back, noting the disorder of his white cravat and the undone buttons at the top of his grey waistcoat. She wondered briefly if he had been drinking to excess. His words effectually drove the thought out of her head.

'Eden's a lost cause, y'know. Can't help feeling sorry for the fellow, but I know you females. A man's only got to exhibit a thorny past and you're all over him!'

Nell stiffened. 'I beg you will not jump to conclusions, Mr Beresford. Remember that I am the governess.'

'I don't forget it. But you're a comely piece for all that. I'd try my luck given half a chance.' He must have seen Nell's reaction for he threw up his hands in surrender. 'Never fear, I've got the message. Trouble is, Miss Faraday, we've both been starved of feminine company for so long, you can't truly blame us.'

'On the contrary, sir, I blame you very much indeed. An honourable man would not attempt to compromise a female in my situation.'

Again he laughed, but the sound was ugly. There was a twist to his features, not wholly a smile. Nell found it excessively unpleasant.

'I'll warrant you wouldn't say so if it were Eden standing here!'

Nell closed her lips firmly. She could neither rebut him nor confound him. Better to hold her peace.

The sneer increased, shifting into his voice. 'I hope it's set down somewhere that I did try to warn you. M'sister ruined the poor fellow for any other woman. He won't forget and he can't forgive. You won't change him, so don't think it. You might say he's cursed. Add to that the suspicion of murder, and there you have Eden Jarrow. If you take my advice, Miss Faraday, you'll get yourself out of his clutches before it's too late.'

The horror that was seeping into Nell's brain held her silent for a moment. She could no longer doubt what her senses had been telling her. The Duck's teachings were overthrown. She had no hard facts, no evidence. But nothing in the world would induce her to believe otherwise than that Mr Bartholomew Beresford wanted her out of Castle Jarrow. And he would go to any lengths to achieve his objective.

She had no words. The man radiated so much danger that her tongue cleaved to the roof of her mouth. Her eyes never left him, and she kept her back to the battlements as she gathered up her candlestick. Edging past him, she made steadily for the turret, keeping him in her sights. He made no move to follow her, and Nell turned, walking as quickly as she could without putting out the light of her candle. Reaching the turret door, she opened it thankfully and stepped inside—and almost into emptiness.

By a miracle, she managed to fling herself back against the wall. Her breath caught in her throat as she took in that she had mistaken the way. She was in the wrong tower!

She had retained her clutch on the candlestick, but the flame was shifting madly from the trembling of her hand. Nell tried to hold it steadier, peering about. She was on a stone stairway, but the central wall had long since crumbled away. There was no possible way she could descend! She must go back.

Even as she turned to find the door that had closed behind her, she heard the scrape of a key turning in the lock. The implication frozc her to the wall. Terror gave her voice.

'Mr Beresford! Open the door!'

Pushing her numb legs upwards, she managed the two steps. Then she hammered on the door with one clenched fist.

'Mr Beresford! Mr Beresford!'

There was no response. Only silence. She listened, one ear glued to the door. Was he still there? Had he heard her, and was capable of standing there, listening to her frantic cries and refusing to help her? Heavens, was the man mad? How could he serve her so?

A series of little images, like the clues of a puzzle, came flittering into her mind and coalesced into a horrid certainty. The Beresford taint! It was in the wide-eyed stare, the senseless guffaws, and the cunning of his conversation. And it was the more dangerous for being hidden under the plausible exterior.

Nell softened her voice. 'Mr Beresford? Are you there? Pray let me out! This is beyond a joke, sir. Come, that is enough now. Open the door, if you please.'

No response. She tried the door, and the latch gave. Her heart jumping, she pulled it cautiously inwards. Then she stepped out again into the night.

There was no sign of Toly Beresford. Thankfully, Nell shut the turret door, and moved quickly away to lean against the battlements, catching her breath. The oddity of the event beat at her brain. Had she imagined that locked door? Now that it was over, she could no longer be sure that she had truly heard the scrape of a key. Nor was she any longer certain of her conviction that Mr Beresford was a trifle mad.

What was certain was the disorder of her nerves! If he had done it, it must be in an attempt to hasten her departure. Yes, that much must be true. He wanted her out, and it must then have been he who had lured her into Lady Jarrow's room with a tune on the clavichord. Which meant that he was indeed spying upon her. Had he not followed her up on to the roof? How many times had she been the object of his unseen eyes, watching where she might go? Could he have listened to enough of her conversations with Lord Jarrow to be accusing her of having developed a *tendre*? For that was what he had meant.

Nell could not accuse herself of showing her partiality in Mr Beresford's company. So he must have learned of it by other means. Only how? He had not been in the castle that night when she had encountered Lord Jarrow on the roof. Honesty compelled her to admit that, had he seen and heard her then, he could have room for his suspicion.

And today, in Lady Jarrow's bedchamber—if it was indeed he who had brought her there—what should stop him returning to listen to what passed within the room? Heavens, there must have been endless opportunity!

Distressed, she hurried along the roof walkway, seeing with relief the windows in the schoolroom turret spaces. How could she have been so foolish as to enter the wrong tower? So much for Helen Faraday's famous sang-froid!

Thoroughly ruffled, she hastened to her bedchamber and prepared herself for bed with fingers that were far from steady. Before getting into the big four-poster, she took the precaution of locking her bedchamber door. But she had only been between sheets for a few moments when she remembered Henrietta. If the child walked in her sleep again, she must not find the way to her governess barred.

She slept only fitfully, waking in spurts to the conviction that someone stood without the chamber, listening to her breathing. No amount of self-chiding served to lessen her fear, and she welcomed the grey light of morning with heartfelt relief.

So bizarre had been the happenings of yesterday and last night that Nell felt distinctly out of place to be teaching her charge just as if nothing had occurred. Hetty was in a malleable frame of mind for once, behaving quite like a normal child. Even Duggan, who remained only a short time in the morning, was bent upon being pleasant. She greeted Nell with a modicum of unusual warmth, and had a word of praise for Henrietta.

'We're all bright and shining today, miss. We've had a good breakfast, and we're ready to get some learning into our tricksy head, aren't we, Miss Hetty?'

Nell began to feel disorientated, as if she was out of step with the world. So much so that doubt about what had happened last night set in. Had she dreamed the whole?

She waited only until Henrietta had been taken away by her nurse before stepping out on to the roof. A weak sun had succeeded the dull aftermath of the rain, and the air felt a degree less penetrating. Nell was relieved, for in the oddity of her mood she had forgotten her shawl.

With deliberation—and not a little trepidation—she made her way down the same walkway, heading for the tower at the front. The whole aspect was different by daylight. The walkway seemed wider, and the squat tower bore no threat. She gained the door in a matter of moments.

Her fingers quivered as she reached for the handle, grasping the fullness of her brown petticoats in one hand to hold them out of the way. Nell drew a breath. Come, there could be nothing to frighten her now. She had half expected to find the door locked, but it opened readily.

Within, she could now see that the winding stair was intact. It was only the inner wall that was severely eroded. The black hole down the centre of the tower yawned wide. Nell wondered what its use could have been in the old days. A chimney? Or perhaps a more gruesome purpose—the disposal of one's enemies. Had she fallen last night, would anyone ever have found her down there?

Hasty footsteps behind her impinged upon her consciousness. Next instant, her wrist was seized and she was pulled sharply back. The door slammed shut, and Lord Jarrow released her. The dark eyes were fierce. But not, she noted with a leap at her pulse, with anger.

'What the devil are you doing, Nell? This stair is dangerous!'

She nodded. 'Yes, so I had ascertained.'

He was passing a hand over the keyhole. 'We keep it locked. Who opened the damned thing?' His glance came back to her. 'Was it you?'

Nell uttered a startled laugh. 'Why would I do such a thing?'

'For the same impossible reason, I imagine, that you were examining it with interest.'

'You are mistaken, sir.' She debated what she should tell him, and shrunk from the complication of the truth. She prevaricated. 'The case is that I was up here last night and lost my bearings. I went in through that door by mistake, and nearly lost my footing.'

His features paled. 'You could have been killed!'

There was a rough quality to his voice that could not but send a thrill down her veins. It was a balm that she had the utmost difficulty in seeing for what it was. A natural reaction to the thought of one of his dependents coming to grief in such a fashion. She forced a smile.

'Well, thankfully I was able to stop myself in time.'

Jarrow could not take this light view of the matter. His mouth was dry, and a burden of dread sat heavily in his chest. He ought to send her packing! Not, the Lord knew, because he wanted her gone, but for her own safety. Why she had become a target, he could not fathom. Unless the same inconsequential mind that plagued his existence sought its strange pleasures in her discomposure. He became aware of a question in her face.

'I wish I knew what to do for the best.'

'In what regard, my lord?'

He had been unaware of speaking aloud, but the answer came readily. 'About you, Miss Faraday.'

Her eyes shadowed. 'Why should you do anything?'

Jarrow noted the deepening voice and knew he had distressed her. He put out a hand. 'It is not for what you have done. Far from it. I believe I could not have chosen better. Only I am not sure I can reconcile it with my conscience to allow you to stay.'

She did not flinch, but a spark flickered in her eye and her head came up. 'And what will you do if I go? Hire another governess? *If* you can find one who will tolerate the peculiar habits obtaining in this household.'

He was obliged to smile. 'There you have me.'

Nell was conscious of a sensation of melting within, and had to turn away. She shifted to the battlements and looked out through a recess, gazing upon the vast expanse of the forest, seeing it but vaguely. For the most part, it lay out of the way of the struggling sun, presenting a dark mass. She tried to speak coolly.

'Believe me, I have seriously considered the question. Indeed, it was for that I came up here last night.'

'To think? Yes, there is a sense of tranquillity here that one finds nowhere else, I grant you.' She did not reply, and Jarrow felt compelled to probe further. 'What was the result of your deliberations?'

Her head turned, and a shaft of sunlight, escaping from the clouds, caught at the golden tresses piled up behind. Jarrow experienced an abrupt longing to see them loose, tumbling about her shoulders. His fingers itched to touch the stray strands that escaped unbidden from confinement.

She was watching him, and he hastily thrust the thoughts away.

'You were saying?'

'I did not speak.'

Jarrow cleared his throat of an unaccountable obstruction. 'You were going to answer me, I thought.'

'Was I?'

There was vagueness to her tone, as if she had lost the thread of the conversation. To tell the truth, Jarrow could not immediately recall it himself. He broke the contact, moving to stare unseeingly from the battlements a little way to one side of her. She was speaking, and he had to concentrate to make sense of her words.

'I wish you will not encourage me to leave. I cannot but agree that it is the course a sensible woman should pursue. But there is Henrietta. And there is—'

She broke off, and Lord Jarrow's eyes turned quickly towards her. Heavens, what a slip! She had been about to say *you*. Hastily searching her mind, she grabbed the first substitute that came to her.

'There is my duty. At the Seminary we were taught the importance of duty so that we would not lightly abandon a promising post.'

'Promising!'

Nell smiled involuntarily. 'It is not perhaps the most congenial one, but it has the merit of—shall we say unpredictability?'

'You may so describe it if you wish, Miss Faraday. I could think of half a dozen more appropriate terms. And none of them remotely flattering.'

He warmed to her laughter. She was the most extraordinary girl. And, no, he could not easily part with her. He held out his hand.

'Come, let us make a pact.'

She put her fingers into his and he could feel a faint tremor. She was not as much at ease as she would have him suppose. He drew her towards him, and cupped the hand within both his own. Her gaze met his with that frank appraisal that he so much admired.

'I will engage not to wish you otherwhere, if you will promise a degree of circumspection. Your common sense is admirable, but you are prone to impulse—and that is risky. What do you say?'

'Impulse?' Nell snatched her hand away, glad of the excuse. 'What, pray, could I possibly have done to earn this from you?'

Irritation sounded in his voice. 'What else was it that sent you stumbling through that doorway? You have been here long enough not to mistake the way.'

Nell had nothing to say in her own defence. How was she to complain of Mr Beresford's conduct? She was loath to tell tales, nor would she create trouble between them by doing so. Had they not already quarrelled? She took refuge in umbrage.

'Is that all your evidence, sir? Since you were not present, you cannot know how it was that I missed my way. But setting that aside, I beg you will enlighten me as to what you consider to be impulsive.'

Jarrow threw his eyes to heaven. 'Pray come down off your high ropes, Miss Faraday! Perhaps I should have said impetuous rather than impulsive. You do tend to spring into action, do you not? An admirable trait in certain circumstances, but not uniformly happy in its outcomes.'

Resentment showed in her eyes, and he almost regretted having begun upon this. What could he say to mitigate it?

But Nell was before him. 'You are thinking of my having called you when I found Hetty in the schoolroom that day.'

'When you thought you found her,' he corrected gently.

Her eyes flashed. 'I now see the worth of your compliments, my lord! No doubt I also imagined the playing of the clavichord in Lady Jarrow's room! Not to mention Hetty's sleepwalking. Obviously you are at one with Duggan upon that episode!'

'Miss Faraday—'

'Pray don't trouble yourself, sir! It is no more than I should have expected, had I thought the matter through. You are, after all, no mean exponent of the art of subterfuge—if all I have been privileged to hear is true. I should have known better than to imagine you had respect enough for my—'

'Will you be silent?'

Nell caught herself up with a gasp, her hot temper abruptly arrested. Lord Jarrow's features were pale with wrath, eyes hard as agates. A hollow opened up inside Nell, and she almost cried aloud. How had she let her tongue run away with her? She backed an involuntary step, clasping her hands tightly together to still their sudden trembling. Her throat ached, and she strove to suppress the rise of tears. She could barely manage a whisper.

'I beg your pardon! I don't know what came over me.'

He did not soften, and Nell knew she had offended beyond forgiveness. He spoke at his most clipped, the held-in rage vibrant under every word.

'If there was one person whom I would have trusted not to be swayed by rumour, it was you. It is evident that we have both been mistaken in each other's characters.'

Despair gripped Nell as she watched him turn away from her. She wanted to call him back, to throw herself upon his mercy, crying that she had not meant it. And she had not! How could she have said such a thing to him? As well accuse him outright!

He had gone half the distance down the walkway already. If she was to intercept him, it must be immediately. Nell could neither move nor speak. Her heart cried out to him, but an insistent voice within told her it was better this way. She had come perilously close to betraying herself.

Nell was thankful for the necessity to pursue her calling. She had gone blindly back to the schoolroom, her thoughts in turmoil, fighting the welling tears. Her intention had been to go straight on to her bedchamber, there to indulge in a hearty bout of weeping. But circumstance, in the person of Henrietta, had intervened.

The child was sitting upon her desk, nursing her doll and swinging her legs as she hummed one of the tunes she had been taught. She stopped as Nell checked in the doorway and, jumping off the desk, came skipping up to her governess.

'I give Duggy the slip and come up myself.'

It had been all Nell could do to thrust down upon the hideous upset and give the child her attention. Long habit reasserted itself swiftly, however, and she was soon behaving as if the world had not been turned on its head. The effort to maintain her calm gave her a headache, but it was salutary in removing the immediate necessity to plunge herself into gloom.

The nurse either knew or did not care that her charge had absented herself, for she did not appear. A circumstance that gave Nell occasion to be glad, for Henrietta proved to be in confiding mood.

'Miss Fallyday,' she piped up, interrupting Nell's reading of one of the child's favoured fairy tales. Fallyday was the name she had adopted for want of being able to say the correct one. Nell looked up from the book.

'What is it, Hetty?'

'D'you know where the treasure is?'

Nell had become used to having non sequiturs thrown at her. She paid it little heed. 'We are reading a story now, Hetty.'

'But do you know?'

'I'm afraid I don't know what you're talking about. Do you mean Aladdin's treasure?' They had read the Chinese tale only a few days since.

Henrietta gave a scornful snort. 'Mama's treasure.'

A faint sense of unease pulled at Nell's attention. It was the first time the child had mentioned her mother. Yet she looked to be unaffected by it. She was waiting, black eyes impatient, for Nell's response.

'What treasure is that?'

'I told you, Mama's treasure. It secret. Mama showed me.'

Excitement sparkled in those expressive orbs, and her plump cheeks glowed. Nell's unease deepened. With Henrietta, one never knew what might be real and what imagined. She must tread warily—and lightly.

'She showed you? That was lucky for you. What did the treasure look like?'

'Gold,' said the girl without hesitation. 'Green bits too, glass ones.' She cocked her head on one side. 'Like a princess.'

Everything gold was like a princess for Hetty. It sounded as if the child was talking of some jewel that her mother possessed. Likely she had shown it to her. Little girls were notoriously interested in the contents of their mother's dressing-cases. Nell had like memories from those far-off days when her mother had been alive.

'Well, that is most interesting, Hetty, but wouldn't you like me to go on reading the story now? We are just about to get Cinderella to the ball, you know.'

It was plain that Henrietta had lost interest in Cinderella. She scowled. 'Don't care.' Opening her desk, she flung the doll inside and shut it again with a bang. 'Want to find the treasure.'

'I don't think that will be possible, Hetty,' began Nell firmly.

'Mama want me to find it.'

How in the world was she to deal with this? She knew so little of the relationship that might have existed between the girl and her mother. From what Mrs Whyte had said, Lady Jarrow had paid her little attention. Nell opted to humour the child. She was in no condition to cope with a tantrum! She rose from the desk.

'Very well, let us go and look for it. Where is it?'

But Hetty remained seated, her features slumping into gloom. 'Can't tell.'

'Won't, you mean,' muttered Nell under her breath. The child had heard her. *'Can't.'*

'Why can't you?'

'Can't 'member.'

'You can't remember where the treasure is?'

'No, I told you!'

Nell sat down again. 'There is no need to get cross.'

The little girl banged her small fists on the desk. 'Can't 'member! Can't 'member! Mama want me to find it. Mama get cross acos I can't 'member.'

A riffle of alarm shot through Nell. This was scarcely the product of a balanced mind! The child knew her mother was dead, that much she had ascertained. Now she was speaking as if Lady Jarrow were alive. Nell spoke soothingly.

'All right, Hetty, never mind. Tell me all about it. Have you looked for the treasure?'

'I looked and looked and *looked*,' stated the child dismally. 'Want to find it so's I don't have to drink the nasty milk no more.'

Nell's mind reeled. What in the world had it to do with milk? Was this a manifestation of the girl's disordered thoughts? Only something in the manner of her telling rang true. There was logic to it, in Hetty's mind at least. Nell determined to find it.

'When do you have to drink the milk?'

'In the night.'

'Every night?'

The child shook her head, dark eyes fixed upon Nell's face in that unnerving stare. She reiterated her complaint. 'It nasty. Don't like it.'

Nell reverted to the treasure. 'Where have you searched for the treasure?'

Hetty glumped, shifting her shoulders and fidgeting. 'All over.'

'Where is all over?'

'All over!'

'What, all over the castle?'

Henrietta nodded, pushing out her lips in a pout. 'Don't want to. Mama make me.'

'But your mama is not in the castle, Hetty,' uttered Nell despairingly. 'How can she make you?'

The chubby cheeks became suffused. 'Mama is in the castle!'

Nell looked pitifully at the child, and gentled her voice. 'Dear Hetty, it cannot be your mama. You know that your mama died.'

Hetty let fly. 'She didn't, she didn't! She is in the castle, I telled you. She comed back. She comed back to the castle, and she come in the night.'

Chapter Seven

Nell stared at the child, bemused. Henrietta's insistence was all too convincing. Only it could not be—the girl must be mistaken. Or was this a manifestation of grief? She wanted her mother to be there, and therefore she saw her. There was another possibility.

'My dear child, are you sure you did not dream it?'

The question was ill judged. Hetty kicked violently at the footrest on her desk.

'*Nooooo!* I told you and *telled* you! Mama send me milk and she come in the night and she make me look for the treasure and I look and look and look and *I can't 'member*!'

The distraught squeal of the final words had Nell up and swiftly around her desk to catch at the small shoulders. 'Quiet, Hetty! That will do! I believe you. Do you understand me, Hetty? I believe what you say.'

But Henrietta had dissolved into noisy sobs. These were not the shrieks of a temper tantrum. Nell recognised the desperate sound of a child in suppressed

191

terror. Without further ado, she drew her up from the desk and gathered her into a close embrace.

'There, now, my little one,' she crooned, rocking Hetty back and forth in a rhythmic way as she had done often and often with some poor orphaned girl cast adrift in the alien confines of the Paddington Seminary. 'There, there, my dear. Nell is here. Nell will keep you safe. Never fear, my dear, never fear.'

It was some little time before Henrietta's gulping sobs settled into quiet. Even then, she caught them on her breath now and then as she lay quiescent in Nell's arms, her own chubby arms clutching tightly about her governess's neck.

As she soothed, Nell began to suspect—with strong indignation!—that there was no one in this household who cuddled the little girl. Duggan was abrasive. Her father, with the spectre of his dead wife's alleged madness in his sight, could evidently hardly bring himself to partake of her company, let alone caress her. And there was no one else. Mrs Whyte was sorry for her, but Nell had yet to see her take time to show it in person—not that the housekeeper had time. With the result that the poor child was left to confront the demons of her mind quite alone.

And, if what she had just been told was to be believed, they were horrid demons for a little girl of six to bear. Guilt swamped Nell. So wrapped up had she been in fighting her growing feelings for Lord Jarrow that she had positively neglected her duty to the child. How the Duck would scold her! Even today she had been blind and deaf to Henrietta's troubled soul. And all on account of an absurd argument with her employer. An argument, moreover, that she had no right to have engaged in at all. She ought to be thoroughly ashamed!

At least she had the wit to recognise her fault—and the chance to amend it. There was nothing for it. She must swallow her pride and go to his lordship. This matter must be put before him without loss of time.

And then she realised that Hetty had fallen asleep. The thought of carrying her down that dreadful winding stair did not recommend itself. Better to wait until Duggan returned to fetch her. She made herself as comfortable as she could without disturbing the little girl, and ran over in her mind what the child had told her.

It was fantastic! She refused to believe that Lady Jarrow's ghost walked. But Hetty evidently thought that she did. The memory slipped into her mind of the music that had lured her to Lady Jarrow's bedchamber. A chill crept through her. She had supposed it to be a trick. Could there be a more sinister aspect? Were such tricks being perpetrated upon Henrietta herself? But what in the world could Mr Beresford hope to gain? If indeed it was he who played them.

The child had spoken of treasure. Her mama wanted her to search for the treasure. Could it be possible that there really was something of value in the castle? But then why should not Mr Beresford search for it himself? He had access everywhere. No, it was too absurd.

There must be some other explanation. That, or the child had been having nightmares and confused them with some random memory. Which was altogether more likely.

By the time the nurse came to fetch Hetty, Nell's mind had settled. She still thought of approaching Lord Jarrow. But perhaps she need not seek him out just yet. If there was a hope at the back of her mind that his anger might cool if she left it awhile, Nell refused to acknowledge it. She told herself that nothing would be gained by rushing headlong into explanations, which could not be other than awkward to make. What had he called her? Impulsive and impetuous. Let her not warrant that accusation a second time.

Nell's appetite was poor. She had known the atmosphere must be strained, but she had not bargained for the dreadful thumping that had attacked her in the chest as she had made her way to the dining-parlour. She had entered to find Lord Jarrow already occupying his place. He had risen at her entrance, but Nell had contrived to avoid his eye as she took her seat.

The absence of Mr Beresford made it worse, for she might have brought herself to converse with him more easily than with her employer—despite the man's suspect conduct of the previous night. Her brush with Lord Jarrow had superseded the power of that encounter to affect her. Yet the fact that his brother-in-law was not there opened the way for Nell to broach the subject of Hetty.

She was so much dismayed by the errant behaviour of her pulses that she was unable to say anything at all at first. She stirred aimlessly at the steaming soup, at length drawing Lord Jarrow's attention.

'You are not eating.'

Nell glanced at him, and found concern in his features. His eyes were more bleak than angry, and her heart twisted. She slipped her spoon into the pottage and hurried into speech, aware that her voice was gruff.

'I have a great deal on my mind.'

He was silent. Nell stole another look at him, and found him watching her still. Their eyes met, and her heartbeat increased. A faint smile creased his mouth.

'I would ask, were I not apprehensive of your answer.'

A tiny laugh escaped her. 'Not more so than I, be sure.'

He frowned, reaching out for his wine glass. 'Don't be. You must by now have recognised that my bark is worse than my bite.'

Nell watched him sip at the ruby liquid. 'I believe you have reason.'

'You are generous, Miss Faraday.'

'Only realistic, sir.'

Jarrow drank again, eyeing the pale cast of her countenance. Had he been a coxcomb to suppose her unease was wholly to be set to his account? He waited while Keston removed the soup bowl and replaced it with a platter. His own dismay at the outcome of the encounter had been intense. He had found himself furious at the implication that she had been discussing him with someone. Rationally, he knew it was inevitable—unavoidable in so small a household. Yet his resentment knew no bounds. It did not need much imagination to realise what gossip had been fed to her. Somehow it mattered intensely to discover that Nell Faraday had been capable of coming to the worst conclusion. A little reflection, however, had shown him that he had possibly misjudged her. Miss Faraday had lost her temper, and he had taken her words to heart.

The butler set about laying out the main course. Jarrow set down his glass, leaned his elbows on the table and clasped his hands together.

'What is troubling you, Miss Faraday?'

The green eyes flicked a look at him, and then turned away again. 'Henrietta.'

Jarrow's chest went hollow. 'What about her?'

'I believe—I believe she is having nightmares.'

He would have been relieved had it not been for the slight hesitation. Nightmares were almost a normal feature of his daughter's condition. Miss Faraday was sharp enough to have realised that much. A child did not wake screaming in the night for no reason. No, there was more to it. He tried for a neutral note, despite his rising apprehension.

'Of what nature?'

There was a shade of reserve in her voice, but she turned her frank gaze upon him. 'Of her mother, sir.'

Jarrow felt a sharp stab at his breast. 'The accident! Hell and the devil, who told her?'

'No, my lord, it is not the accident. As far as I am aware, she knows nothing of it. Although I had gathered that she was told of her mama's demise?'

'That she had died, yes, but of some sickness. I lied, what would you? I could not have told her the truth!'

Under the harsh tone, Nell detected a measure of pain. He was gripping his fingers together so that the knuckles whitened. She hastened to deflect his thoughts.

'No one could blame you there, sir, but the fact is that Henrietta thinks her mother has come back, that she is in the castle.'

He turned to her, eyes grown haggard, the blue shade beneath pronounced. 'Then she is indeed losing her wits!'

Nell became irate. 'Why should you assume so? I have given you but the gist, Lord Jarrow, and already you are jumping to conclusions.'

'What else am I to think?' he returned sharply. 'If she is seeing things—'

'I did not say so. Nor, if she were, would it necessarily show her to be witless. What if she was being tricked into believing it? Have you thought of that?'

He looked sceptical. 'An unlikely contingency.'

'As unlikely as my having been drawn into your late wife's room? Or finding Hetty herself on the floor of the schoolroom?'

Arrested, Jarrow stared at her. The spark in her eyes reproached him. He spread his hands. 'You leave me without a word to say.' She did not answer, but the flush in her cheeks died down. He picked up the decanter and poured her a measure of wine. 'I find claret excellent for the restoration of an even temper.' He was rewarded with a laugh.

'I do not know how it is, my lord, but you have a knack of inviting my worst side to reveal itself. It is a great deal too bad of you.'

He signed to Keston to begin serving. 'Console yourself, Miss Faraday. Your temperament is equable compared with my own. But pray let us return to the matter of Hetty's nightmares.'

Nell allowed the butler to lay several thin scollops of veal upon her plate, and accepted a spoon or two of succulent gravy, which proved to contain a concoction of mushrooms, truffles, sweetbreads and artichoke bottoms, together with forcemeat balls and bacon. A delicious aroma emanated from the dish, and her appetite quickened.

'What a pity Mr Beresford has chosen to be absent,' she remarked. 'I believe Mrs Whyte has excelled herself.'

'Keston, pray convey both my own and Miss Faraday's compliments to Mrs Whyte.'

The butler looked gratified as he murmured assent. Nell began upon the food with enjoyment, and it was with a much more natural tone that she resumed the discussion.

'About Hetty, sir.'

Lord Jarrow nodded as he disposed of a mouthful of veal. 'I was going to ask you to give me the substance of these nightmares.'

Nell did not beat about the bush. 'She believes that her mother wants her to search the castle for what she calls *treasure*. She asked me if I knew where it was. She is frustrated because she says that she has looked and looked and cannot find it.'

She paused, caught by a particularly intent look in the brown eyes. Nell thought that Lord Jarrow looked through her rather than at her. Was he even listening? She partook of another mouthful, but he did not speak.

'Hetty says that her mama sends her milk and then comes in the night. Apparently she dislikes milk, for the burden of her complaint was that she must find the treasure so that she need not drink it any more.'

For some little while, Lord Jarrow ate in silence, his gaze directed upon Nell, although she would swear that it was involuntary. He was lost in thought. She could not help feeling a little indignant. Had he nothing to say to this history?

'My lord?'

He blinked quickly. 'Yes?'

'Have you any idea what treasure it could be? Henrietta described it as gold, with green glass.'

Lord Jarrow's dark gaze became arrested again, but this time it was fully concentrated upon Nell's face. 'What did you say?'

'The treasure. Hetty says it is gold, with green glass. I assume she is talking of some jewel? She says her mother showed it to her, but I do not know when that might have been.'

His features darkened, and the taut closed-in expression that Nell had begun to dread came over them. 'Long since. And she will never find it, if she looks 'til Domesday.'

Nell's heart sank. Must he turn back into that enigmatic and unapproachable creature that pulled so upon her heartstrings? Yet he knew just what Henrietta had meant. Frustration gnawed at her, but she had no chance to express it, or even to enquire further. Mr Beresford, all smiles and apologies for his tardy arrival, bustled into the dining parlour.

Constraint returned, and Nell was left to lend a spurious ear to the newcomer's high praise coupled with laughing suppositions about the housekeeper's sudden excellence in the kitchens.

Nell was in a ferment of speculation. Desperately as she wanted to tackle his lordship again, she knew that to do so would inevitably encourage that brooding intensity which so much dismayed her. Yet he had confided in her now and then. If she could catch him in the right frame of mind, she might find him forthcoming. That he knew something of this treasure she could not doubt after last night's conversation. Whether it would help her to solve the mystery of Henrietta's nightmares was another matter. But there might be a surer way to put a stop to them, if the alarming suspicion that had flown into her head in the night had any foundation.

The housekeeper, however, was less than sympathetic. 'If I were to pay any heed to that complaint, Miss Faraday, I'd have abandoned sending up milk for Hetty long ago.'

'But if she does not like it, Mrs Whyte—'

'I can't help that. The master thinks she needs it to build her up, and that's that.'

Nell tried to keep the annoyance out of her voice, but she could not do other than protest. 'The child is scarcely undernourished!'

The housekeeper tutted. 'It ain't that at all. She eats well enough, and she's still got her baby fat on her. But her sleep is bad, Miss Faraday, and that you'll not deny.'

'No, but—'

'Well, the milk is to help her to sleep. When she drinks it down like a good girl, she usually sleeps like a log.'

Like one dead, Nell might have said. Only she could not yet voice her suspicions to Mrs Whyte. Until she was sure of her ground, she dared not speak of them to anyone. Certainly not her employer, who had not, she was persuaded, even been listening when she mentioned the milk. Nell was glad of it now. For the notion with which she was toying was a wild one, that would put the cat among the pigeons—if it proved true. There was much it might explain. And raise a good many questions into the bargain. She must tread warily.

'How does the milk reach Henrietta, Mrs Whyte?'

The housekeeper eyed her frowningly. 'What's in your head, my dear?'

Nell smiled faintly. 'Humour me, pray.'

'There's something to this,' stated the other bluntly. 'Why don't you want the little 'un to have it?'

'Beyond the fact that she doesn't like it?'

Mrs Whyte ruminated in silence for a moment. Then she sighed. 'Well, I won't ask no more. Only a body can't but wonder. I don't see how it helps, but I warm the milk for her of a night, and Duggan fetches it.'

'At what time does Henrietta have it, if you please?'

'Late. She'll sleep an hour or two after her meal at seven or thereabouts, and then she wakes again. Without the milk, she'd be wakeful to midnight.'

'So she has it when—around eight or nine?'

The housekeeper set her arms akimbo. 'What was you meaning to do, Miss Faraday? Do you wish to fetch the milk yourself? Don't come before nine if that's the case. Only I'd not answer for Joyce taking it tamely, and that's a fact!'

Nell reassured her. 'I should not dream of interfering with the routine. I am merely trying to establish things in my mind, Mrs Whyte.'

'Yes, and I'm as much of a noddy as Grig!'

Nell laughed and begged her pardon. But she refused to say more. It would not do to involve the housekeeper. If the burgeoning idea came to nothing, no harm would come of it. At least, not beyond an entanglement with the nurse on her part, but that was already past praying for. She fully expected to encounter opposition from that quarter. But she intended to take the nurse by surprise—and succeeded.

Walking into Henrietta's bedchamber a few moments after nine the same evening, Nell found Duggan in the act of handing a glass of milk to the child, who was sitting up in bed. The candles in the wall-sconce to one side were alight. Nell knew they were always left to burn down into the early hours, for there was no knowing when Henrietta might need attention.

The little girl greeted her with surprise. 'Miss Fallyday!'

Duggan turned sharply, and a little of the milk splashed upon the covers.

'You spilled it, Duggy,' protested Hetty at once.

The nurse laid the glass upon the bedside table, and Nell found herself confronted before she could reach the bed.

'You've no business here at this hour, miss,' she hissed angrily.

'I beg your pardon, but there is no hour when I have no business about Henrietta's concerns.' Her haughty demeanour had the effect of fanning the flames.

'Highty-tighty! And what might you be wanting? We're all but asleep already, and won't want to be disturbed.'

Oh, won't we! Nell brushed past her and went to the bed. 'I came to say goodnight, Hetty.'

'Stay with me,' commanded the child. 'Duggy can go 'way.'

The nurse bridled. 'She can, can she? We'll see that. I ain't going nowhere 'til we've drunk our milk, young lady, and so I tell you.'

Henrietta looked mutinous, but Nell seized the chance to take up the glass. 'Yes, you must have your milk, Hetty.'

A reproachful look was directed at her from the wide black gaze. 'Don't want it. Don't like it. It nasty.'

Duggan bustled to the other side of the bed. 'I'll give you don't like it! We're a naughty little girl, aren't we? Just you drink it up and no nonsense!'

Hetty shot her a dagger look and Nell hastily intervened. 'Allow me, Duggan, if you please.'

Ignoring the nurse's darkling glance, she lifted the glass to her own lips and sipped at it. To her relief, the milk tasted normal. She noted the little girl's incredulous expression and smiled, holding out the glass.

'Try it, Hetty. It doesn't taste nasty to me.'

Henrietta looked from the glass to her face. 'Duggy don't taste it.'

Nell cast a quick glance at the nurse and found the woman regarding her narrowly. Heavens, had she given herself away? Deliberately, she raised her brows.

'Now I wonder why? Perhaps Duggan doesn't like milk.'

'*I* don't like milk,' insisted the child, pouting.

The nurse said nothing, and Nell was further disconcerted by the woman's unwavering stare from across the bed. Either she had betrayed herself, or Duggan had guessed at her suspicion. Which could only mean that there was a reason for it. On impulse, she dismissed the creature, knowing she could not be gainsaid.

'You may go, Duggan. I will make sure Hetty drinks the milk.'

Henrietta glowered at her. 'Won't drink it.'

The nurse turned on her. 'We're very free with our won'ts tonight, aren't we? If you ask me, young lady, we'd better remember what will happen if we don't do as we're told!'

Nell's temper flared. 'That will do! You may leave us, Duggan.'

'Leave us, Duggy!' echoed Henrietta.

'Don't be impertinent, Hetty,' said Nell sharply. Then she raised wrathful eyes to the nurse again, who had not moved from where she stood. Ice entered her voice. 'Thank you, Duggan, that will be all.'

The nurse marched to the door, where she turned with a venomous look. 'We'll see what the master has to say, shall we?'

'By all means,' agreed Nell.

Duggan glared, obviously furious that her ploy had not taken. With one last admonition to her charge that she expected to hear that she had drunk all the milk, she took herself off.

Nell heaved a sigh of relief, and turned back to Henrietta. The child was regarding her with awe. Clearly she had never before seen Duggan bested in a battle of wills. The woman would not dare challenge his lordship, and there was none besides Nell to attempt to face her down. She was not at all sure that she had done the right thing, however. It remained to be seen how dangerous the woman was. Meanwhile, she must not waste an opportunity that might never come again.

'Hetty, I want you just to taste the milk, for it seems perfectly normal to me.'

Urged to take the glass, the child reached out, but gingerly, doubt in her face. Nell gently pressed her until she consented to sip the milk. It was immediately evident that the taste was acceptable to her. She sipped again, and handed it back with a decisive nod.

'Mama didn't send it.'

Nell's mind froze. If that meant what she supposed, then the milk was not always as innocent as it appeared tonight. She fastened on the point, trying not to sound too eager.

'How do you know when the milk is sent by your mama, Hetty?'

'Mama say it.' The child pulled a face. 'But she don't got to say it, acos I know. Mama milk is nasty. Don't like it.'

Her chest thrumming unevenly, Nell found her thoughts racing. The milk was the key, just as she had suspected. Only it was evident that its use was intermittent. How foolish of the perpetrators to imagine that Hetty would not taste the difference. And how had she been persuaded that it was her mother who sent the nasty-tasting milk? Her mama said it, Hetty had averred. But her mama had been long dead. To a well-balanced mind this argued yet another piece of unkind trickery.

Under the child's awestruck eye, Nell opened the window and scattered the contents of the glass into the cool night air. Then she set the empty glass down and bade Henrietta settle back under the covers. To her surprise, she was obeyed without question. Nell perched on the edge of the bed and tucked the covers up around the little girl's chin.

'Now, my dear, listen to me. If your mama—or anyone else—should again ask you to drink the milk when it tastes nasty, you must come to me at once. Do you understand?'

Hetty nodded solemnly. Then an unholy gleam entered the black eyes. 'Then will you throw it out the window, Miss Fallyday?'

'I should not be at all surprised,' agreed Nell, although she would be more inclined to take it directly to Lord Jarrow. But she would not trouble Hetty with that threat.

There could be little doubt that someone was tampering with the little girl's milk, with a result that might well be the cause of the child's temper tantrums—and a good deal else besides. She would dearly like to have been able to alert his lordship instantly. But without positive proof, she dared not even whisper it. Already she could not but fear that she had alerted Duggan—if the woman was party to the trick. Nell could not be sure that her dislike was not responsible for her conviction that the nurse was involved. Her fear of it kept her on tenterhooks, however, knowing the ease of access the woman had to her charge. So much so that she determined to remain in the bedchamber—despite setting a foolish precedent—until Henrietta should have fallen asleep.

She awoke to silence and a guttering candle. At first she could not understand why she was lying half across Henrietta's bed. She felt cold and found her limbs were ice. Had she lain here half the night? Memory swept back. The milk! Rising, she leaned over the child in the dim light. Hetty was sleeping peacefully, one plump cheek pillowed on her hand. She looked a very babe, and Nell's heart contracted. At least the child was safe.

Moving with stealth, Nell crept to the door and closed it with care behind her. Then she hurried down the unlit corridor towards her own room. As she reached the corner by the tower, a murmuring of voices ahead made her check. Nell crept forward and dared a peek. From the doorway to the next room—Duggan's bedchamber!—light spilled around two figures, lewdly entwined.

The man's back was to Nell, and she could see that his hair was loose and disarranged. He was in a nightshirt, a dressing robe flung carelessly over one shoulder. Beyond him, Nell recognised the woman Duggan. A thin shift did little to conceal the outline of her figure beneath. Light-coloured hair, hitherto confined under a cap, was tousled about her head and falling around her shoulders. She was looking up at the man with an expression of voluptuous languor, and, as Nell watched, she leaned in to kiss him.

For one hideous moment, Nell thought that the slim figure of the man was that of Lord Jarrow. Her pulse skidded out of kilter and she had all to do to refrain from bursting out of concealment. She pressed back instead, into the shadows, but her eyes remained glued upon the couple. She could hear whispers, but her straining ears could not recognise the man's low tones, nor make out what was said. Then Duggan said something that amused him, and at once Nell knew who he was. There was only one man in Castle Jarrow who had a laugh like that.

Relief and sickening realisation warred in Nell's breast for supremacy. The nurse was the mistress of Toly Beresford. Recalling certain odd looks and instances of cryptic commentary, Nell felt immediately certain that Lord Jarrow was aware of this liaison. But he could have no suspicion that Mr Beresford wanted Nell out of the castle. For herself, everything fell into place. With Nell gone, the man could pursue his game unchecked, whatever it was he wanted with the child. But no trick could be played upon Henrietta without Duggan noticing. Therefore Duggan must be herself involved.

Could she have been the man's spy? Nell's flesh crawled at the thought of those distressingly intimate moments with his lordship being heard and seen by the supercilious nurse. Of one thing there was no doubt. Whatever their purpose, Mr Beresford and Duggan were in it together.

The commotion broke out in the corridor beyond Nell's chamber, catching her in the act of unbuttoning the front fastenings to her gown. She paused as her quick ear detected Henrietta's low grumble as well as the scolding tones of her nurse.

'Come back here, you naughty girl!'

'Won't!'

'Come here! I'll teach you to defy me, I will!'

Swift wrath kindled in Nell's breast, and she stepped at once to the rescue, forgetting in her haste the undone flap at the neck of her calico gown that fell away to expose the swell of her breasts above her white stays. She wrenched open the door.

It was only just turning to dusk, and in the fading light she could clearly see her charge a little way down the corridor. Clad only in her nightgown, Henrietta was struggling in Duggan's grip, trying to pull away. The nurse, with equal determination, was attempting to drag the child in the opposite direction. Hetty was hampered, Nell saw, by her clutch on a half-full glass of milk.

Obedient to her instructions, the child had brought it to her. How long had it been, a matter of days only? Heavens, had they no discretion? She let it pass for the moment, for Hetty was in need.

Assuming an authoritative tone, she intervened. 'What is the meaning of this?'

Henrietta's head turned. 'Miss Fallyday! Miss Fallyday!'

Nell could not be sure, but she thought Duggan cursed under her breath. Aloud, she snapped her fury.

'Nothing to concern you, miss. Miss Hetty, we'll stop this wriggling now, or it'll be the worse for you!'

But the child paid no heed. 'I brung the milk, Miss Fallyday. It nasty.'

The implication shot through Nell's brain as she reached them and took hold of Henrietta's shoulders. The nurse must have seen something in her face, for she suddenly let go of the little girl, instead grabbing at the glass she held.

'Give me that, you little devil, you!'

'Leave her alone!' ordered Nell sharply.

It was evident that Hetty was not going to give up the glass without a fight. The liquid within it sloshed over the rim as she struggled with Duggan for possession. For a second or two, Nell could not think what to do. While she badly wanted to find out why the milk tasted nasty to Hetty, she was loath to demonstrate this to the nurse. Instinct dictated caution.

Her hesitation proved disastrous. Before she could attempt anything at all, the nurse swung her free hand, catching the child a resounding smack across the side of her head. Hetty yelped and the glass went flying, spilling its contents on to the stone floor of the corridor. The importance of the milk went out of Nell's head. She seized the child and clutched her tight against her petticoats, as she loosed the vials of her wrath upon the nurse.

'How could you? What, will you punish the girl for coming to find me? How dare you, Duggan! You are a cruel, spiteful creature, and I cannot think why his lordship has not rid himself of your services long since!'

Henrietta was protesting into Nell's waist, and she was obliged to give her attention where it was most needed. She heard the nurse's shrill retaliation only over the distressing cries and her own attempts to calm the little girl.

'My services, is it, miss? I should think as his lordship will turn you out of doors afore me! He knows as there ain't no one but me as knows how to deal with Miss Hetty. No, and you ain't likely to take my place, I'd say, what with all the screaming and messing I have to put up with. You don't know the half of it, miss, that you don't.'

The insolent tone penetrated Nell's absorption, and she rose up again, spitting fury. 'Be quiet! How dare you speak to me in this fashion? You forget yourself, Duggan!'

Her tone had little effect upon the woman, who drew back her head and thrust her nose in the air. 'I know my place, miss, which is more than I can say for some. Now, are you going to let me take Miss Hetty back to bed, or are you not?'

About to inform the creature in no uncertain terms that she had no intention of handing the child over, Nell found herself forestalled by the irate voice of her employer.

'What the devil is amiss?'

Nell's glance snapped round. She had not heard footsteps, but she found Lord Jarrow standing immediately behind her, the annoyance in his features visible even in the half-light. Hetty's whines dropped to a murmur at the sound of her father's voice. A quick look back showed Nell that the nurse had drawn a step or two away, her mien instantly submissive. Goaded, she turned on him.

'You may well ask, my lord! But let me first assure myself of one thing. Is it by your wish that the nurse you employ to look after your daughter raises a hand to her unchecked?'

Shock leaped in his eyes, and he frowned. 'I don't understand you.'

Nell opened her mouth to inform him exactly what had taken place, but Duggan was before her. The obsequious tone sickened Nell.

'It's true, my lord. I did give her a tap, only—'

'A tap!'

'—she made me that cross I couldn't help myself. I'm sorry for it, as I hope you know, my lord, but it weren't my fault. You know as how she'd try the patience of a saint, often and often.'

To Nell's annoyance, Lord Jarrow merely nodded at this. 'I will speak to you later, Duggan. Take Henrietta back to bed, if you please.'

But Hetty wound her arms about Nell's waist and clung, hiding her face in the fullness of her petticoats. Nell's heart contracted, and she controlled with an effort the hot protests that rose to her tongue, trying for a softer note. But her voice came out more husky than she could have wished.

'Pray allow me to take her myself in a moment or two, my lord. She is still distressed.'

Lord Jarrow was evidently undecided, and Nell shot another look at the nurse. She presented a front that was a model of subservience. Who would believe that but a moment since she had been squawking like a fishwife?

'You may go, Duggan. I will bring Hetty presently.'

Relief riffled through Nell, calming her. She watched Duggan drop a curtsy and then reach down for the abandoned glass. Nell threw out a hand.

'Leave that, if you please!'

The nurse's eyes flew up to meet hers. A dagger look! And she ignored the request. Nell found Lord Jarrow's frowning gaze upon her. Heavens, how to account for her need of the glass without giving herself away to the wretch? She could think of no legitimate excuse, and the woman shifted her attention to his lordship.

'I was meaning to fetch a cloth, my lord, for the milk was spilled. Seems I'd best take the glass downstairs and fetch some more.'

Which brought Henrietta into the fray. 'Don't want no more! Don't like it!'

'Leave it for tonight, Duggan.' And Lord Jarrow signed to the nurse to withdraw.

Nell watched the woman in silence until she had made the turn into the tower. Then she turned to his lordship and found his gaze trained upon her face in mute question. Should she tell him now? Only she no longer had evidence—if evidence there had been in that glass. Nor could she bring the matter up before the child.

Before any word could be spoken, they suffered an interruption. Mr Beresford appeared around the corner, looking a trifle dishevelled with his hair awry and a robe thrown all anyhow over his nightshirt. He was yawning as he came up.

'What's to do?'

Nell felt a shift in the atmosphere. As of instinct, she looked to his lordship and found him stiffening, his jaw line tight. Her heart sank, for she knew that look. The clipped tone bore out his descent into moodiness.

'Scrambled out of your clothes in something of a hurry, did you, Toly?'

The other man's wide gaze opened further. 'Eh? M'dear fellow, can't expect me to look anything but a scarecrow when I'm dragged so rudely from my slumbers. Lord, what a racket! Ah, there's Hetty. Now I understand.'

'You're telling me you've been asleep already? At this hour?'

The dry tone drew Nell's attention, and her mind flew. It could not be much beyond nine, although she had been indulging in reading for some time after dinner. Mr Beresford had been absent, his lordship abstracted. He had excused himself early, she recalled, leaving her to a solitary dessert. Only now did it occur to Nell that Lord Jarrow was dressed for riding. He wore top boots and a frock coat with a spencer atop. And the faint aroma of horses emanated from his person. Where had he been?

'Felt a trifle poorly all day,' Mr Beresford was saying. 'Didn't Keston tell you I'd gone to my bed? Getting too old for the work, poor fellow. I told him to make my excuses.'

'Did you now?'

The disbelief was patent. Nell looked from one to the other, aware of tension in Toly Beresford, despite his air of nonchalance. The man evaded the issue, reaching out to tousle Henrietta's hair.

'And what is it this time, miss? Taking out your temper on poor Duggy again, I'll be bound.'

'Duggy is bad,' stated Henrietta distinctly.

'That will do!' said Nell.

'That's enough!' asserted his lordship at exactly the same moment.

Toly Beresford burst into laughter. 'There's for you then, young Hetty. Best keep your mouth shut, if you want my advice.'

Nell closed her lips upon a sharp retort, and was glad that Lord Jarrow spoke up—for them both, she could have said.

'Hadn't you better take yourself back to bed, Toly, if you are under the weather?'

'I'd not have chosen to come out of it,' protested the other, 'if I'd known it was only Hetty kicking up a dust.'

He yawned again. Ostentatiously, Nell felt. And then he took himself off. Nell's gaze came back to find his lordship once again looking at her. Was there meaning in his glance? She had questions aplenty, if only Henrietta had not been present. She did not know if it showed in her face. Unconsciously she ran her eyes down the clothing that unmistakably showed that he had been out. At this hour? So she might have said, just as he had to his brother-in-law.

His glance caught at hers, and she could not look away. Then—was it deliberate?—his eyes dropped a trifle, and incxplicably held for a moment, before flickering up to her face again. Nell was at a loss to interpret the odd gleam that came into them.

Lord Jarrow said no word, but dropped to his haunches.

'Hetty, come. Time you were in bed.'

To Nell's utter astonishment, the little girl left her instantly, and went straight into her father's waiting arms. Lord Jarrow lifted her up and Henrietta snuggled into his embrace.

'Say goodnight to Miss Faraday.'

Hetty yawned, and flapped one hand. 'G'night, Miss Fallyday.'

Nell managed a smile, and lightly clasped the little fingers. 'Goodnight, Hetty. Sleep well.'

Then she stood aside to let his lordship pass, and watched him depart. Only then was it borne in upon her that her gown was open at the top, and the swell of her breasts had been the focus of Lord Jarrow's steady gaze. Heat rose up, and her fingers fumbled at the flap of her gown, pulling it up. Useless, when he was already gone!

She moved quickly back to her bedchamber, lifting a hand to her burning cheek. An odd odour reached her nostrils. Distracted, Nell sniffed at her fingers, and became aware that they were sticky. From Henrietta? The milk had spilled over the child's hand, had it not? All thought of what had just passed slid out of Nell's mind. She touched her tongue to the stickiness and found a bitter taste.

Her chest hollowed out, and a patter started in her pulses. As if she must be sure, she licked once more. No doubt about it. The flavour was acrid, confirming her suspicions. Duggan was feeding Henrietta with laudanum.

The screams burst loud upon the night and Nell woke with a jerk. She shot bolt upright, listening in a jangle of nerves, her heart beating madly and her thoughts disordered. As the remnants of sleep ebbed away, the disorientation eased and she realised what it was. Henrietta!

Her mind ran on as she slipped from her bed and sought automatically for her dressing-robe on the hook behind the door. Her fingers were all thumbs, for the continuing shrieks shot her through with quivering unrest. It had been so long since the child had given way to one of these hideous tantrums in the night. Yet her apprehension grew as she recalled the episode of Friday evening. Could Duggan have given the little girl laudanum again? It had only been three days. A week since Hetty had first mentioned the milk. Had the nurse dared to lace the drink, when she must know now that Nell was suspicious?

She was dragging on the robe even as her fingers reached for the handle of the door. It turned, but the door would not open.

Nell rattled the handle, a horrid sensation of sick fear wrenching at her stomach. Hetty's shrieks were in her ears, and dread began to mount as she fought with the recalcitrant door. It would not budge. Heavens, was she locked in? Frantic fingers scrabbled for the key, but there was no sign of it. But she kept it always on the inside!

The implication froze her, and she stilled, gripping the handle uselessly, her eyes—which were growing used to the dark—glued to the empty keyhole. Some stealthy hand had removed the key while she slept and turned it from the outside.

Nell leaned her forehead against the door and closed her eyes, anguished by the continuing cries that echoed about the castle. What had they done to the child? What evil act was in progress while she stood here helpless?

She was tempted to cry out. Only that would merely add to the cacophony without accomplishing anything useful. Who would hear her, besides? They must all be about the business of soothing Hetty. This thought calmed her a little. Even were it possible that Lord Jarrow had not heard it—which was highly unlikely now that she thought about it rationally—there was Mrs Whyte on her other side. The housekeeper might leave it to Duggan, but his lordship most certainly would not. If, that was, he was in the house! For all she knew, he could have ridden out again—bent upon heaven knew what hateful mission.

Backing to the bed, Nell sat down upon it, staring at the door, while the harsh cries of the little girl echoed their despair in her heart. Why had she not spoken again to Lord Jarrow? She had left it, thinking—erroneously!—that the nurse must be deterred for a while at least. A foolish assumption. For Duggan did not act on her own determination, of that Nell was certain.

Was that why she had held back from speaking to Lord Jarrow? She must accuse his brother-in-law, if she spoke at all.

A dull ache presented itself in her chest. Self-deceiver that she was! No, Helen Faraday, that was not the reason. Face the truth. She could no longer be certain that it was not her employer who roamed the byways of the forest of a night.

Meanwhile, Henrietta's shrieks began to lessen. Nell was left wondering what could have occurred. She had seen Henrietta earlier and her sleep had appeared calm. Indeed, she had made it her business to check on the child these past two nights, afraid each time of what she might find. The last thing she had expected was a resurgence of these hideous shrieks. She could only sit and listen in growing despair until at last the child quietened.

Nell tried to tell herself that all must now be well, but the unprecedented locking of her door gave her the lie. That this was by Beresford's hand she could not doubt. He might not be Lord Nobody, but he was certainly responsible for what was happening inside the castle. There was no possible reason for Lord Jarrow to be playing tricks upon his own daughter.

It was not to be supposed accidental that the locking of her door should coincide with Hetty's tantrum. It argued instead that the shrieking that had often troubled the child had been somehow induced. Were they even tantrums? Nell could not forget the terror that had underlain the little girl's sobs when she had told her of 'Mama's treasure'. Wrath drove out fear. Whatever was being done, it was intended to frighten the child half to death!

But for what purpose? The seeming insanity of it could by no means be all. Yes, she had doubts of Mr Beresford's mental condition, but Nell was convinced he had both cunning and intelligence. There was motive to these tricks. But *what*? Save only that it had to do with the 'treasure', Nell had no notion what it could be.

The silence was almost as disconcerting as the screams. Rousing herself, Nell got up again and went to the door. It opened at the first try. She stood mute for a moment, incredulous. She had been duped yet again! Now she knew for certain that the culprit was Toly Beresford. Had he not performed the precise same action only a short time since, when she had slipped mistakenly into the wrong tower? That must have been impromptu. This could only have been planned. The thought spurred her into action.

Nell sped down the corridor, moving quietly to avoid being heard. As she went, she wondered just when the door had been unlocked. She had heard nothing, which in all likelihood meant that the key must have been turned while Henrietta was crying out. The thought of Mr Beresford sneaking around outside her bedchamber door made her skin crawl. She determined to be more vigilant in future.

Hetty's door stood partially open, and from within came the sound of a man's voice, low-toned. And apparently cheerful? Nell halted in the entrance, unable to believe that her eyes were not deceiving her.

In a chair by the bed sat Lord Jarrow, clad in a dressing gown and reading aloud by the light of a candle on the bedside table. Henrietta, her eyes fixed upon his face, listened, evidently entranced, to the rise and fall of his voice.

'This speech did not at all abate the Beast's wrath. "Hold your tongue, sir," he commanded, "if you can offer me nothing but flatteries and false titles." The merchant, although in fear of his life, plucked up courage to tell the monster that the rose which he had been bold to pluck was...'

Nell recognised the tale as that of 'Beauty and the Beast' from the book of Perrault's fairy stories from which she was wont to read to the child. But to find her employer doing so astonished her. Yet with a glow at her heart, her suspicions of him lulled, she saw that one of the little girl's hands rested in his as he read, the book balanced upon his knees. So this was how he quietened her fits of screaming. And Beresford had given her to understand that his brother-in-law beat the child into submission. Yet another black mark to be added to his misdeeds, Nell decided grimly.

She stood quietly by the door, unwilling to make her presence felt, until she saw that Henrietta's eyes were sinking. It was apparent that his lordship was aware of it, for although he continued reading, his voice lowered with the child's gradual slide into sleep. He did not cease altogether until it was clear from Hetty's even breathing that she was deep in slumber. He watched her for a moment, and then raised the little hand to his lips and gently placed the errant arm under the covers. Henrietta sighed in her sleep and shifted onto her side.

Jarrow closed the book and set it down. Rising, he tucked the covers more closely around the child, and then moved the chair out of the way and picked up his candle. Giving his daughter one last tender glance, he turned to go and stopped short as he spied Nell standing in the doorway.

Chapter Eight

For a moment Jarrow did not move. Light from the unshuttered window spilled silver over the governess, turning to a ghostly radiance the gleaming tumble of hair upon her shoulders. To see her in *déshabillé* played havoc with his senses, and he was obliged to exercise a rigid control to prevent himself from giving in to base desire. The confinement of her figure within a wrapper caught about her and tied at the waist left little to the imagination. Beneath it he could clearly see the outline curve of her hip and the swell of her breast, and he badly wanted the feel of them under his hand and to taste the wine of her pretty lips with his own. His fingers itched to slide within the silk of her golden hair.

She was regarding him with a lurking smile at the back of her eyes, and the suspicion that she would find it hard to reject his caresses pulled Jarrow up sharply. Let the world believe as it chose, he knew himself for a man of honour. He would not abandon his principles upon a whim. As well sink to the level of she who had played him false.

Motioning Miss Faraday out of the room, he followed her into the corridor and gently closed the door.
She had turned towards him, an eagerness in her face
indicative of a wish to speak to him. Hell and the
devil! He prayed he might cut her short and remove
himself as rapidly as possible from temptation. The
candlelight was more forgiving than moonlight, thank
the Lord! While her face was reflected in the light
from his candle, he could no longer see her figure as
clearly. Only he could feel the warmth from her body
and an elusive female aroma assailed his senses, yet
more arousing. Her words, however, were prosaic.

'My lord, where is Duggan?'

'I sent her away.'

There was a pause. She looked as if she wished to
say something more, but her hesitation gave him the
cue he needed.

'You will take cold, Miss Faraday, if you stand
about in the corridor. All is well now. Go back to bed.'

'Presently. My lord—'

She broke off, and he read concern in her face.
Anxious to be gone, Jarrow spoke more harshly than
he intended.

'What is the matter? If you have something to say,
pray say it and be done!'

Her expression altered and she stiffened. 'I will not
keep you, sir. Tomorrow will do as well.'

'I will not be here tomorrow.'

'You are leaving the castle?'

Jarrow met her incredulous stare and sighed. 'I spoke without thinking. I have business in Collier Row, that is all. I shall not be here before nightfall, and if it is urgent—'

'It is extremely urgent!'

This was so forcefully said that Jarrow became sufficiently intrigued as to overshadow the distracting demands of his body. 'Will it take long?'

Miss Faraday sighed. 'I have no idea. Probably, since I must overcome a good deal of prejudice on your part.'

A low laugh escaped him. 'Am I so prejudiced?'

He received a straight look. 'I do not know, sir. But you are moody and prone to dismiss things that distress you—which gives rise to prejudice, perhaps.'

Jarrow smiled. 'What I dislike so much about you, Nell Faraday, is that you are not afraid to speak your mind! No, belay that. I like it.'

She did not laugh. 'My lord, will you give me a hearing—and with an open mind?'

He hesitated. Did she wish to speak of the tricks Toly had been playing? Lord knew he had enough on his hands with the fellow's more dangerous exploits. Not that he had settled how he was to deal with the man, once he had him cornered.

He eyed the girl's determined features. He had best do what he might to calm her fears at least. Dared he trust her with the truth—as he was coming to believe it—about Toly? Not yet, perhaps. But he could not in all conscience leave her to imagine worse than there was. She had proved not only stalwart in her determination to remain, but obdurate. He made up his mind.

'Why do you not accompany me tomorrow? We could talk on the way.'

There was no mistaking the pleasure that lit in her face. 'Get out of the castle? How delightful that would be!'

Jarrow was taken aback—and inclined to feel a trifle put out. Then he remembered that she had not been outside the walls of Castle Jarrow since her arrival. Lord, how remiss of him to have allowed it.

'That is settled, then. Ten o'clock?'

In a daze, Nell nodded. Away from here—and in his company! The danger to her emotions did not immediately occur to her, though a rise of internal heat threw the reason into her conscious mind. She had never before seen Lord Jarrow in other than black. In his night garments, with his long hair untied, he stirred an inner hunger. Between the open edges of the collar of a white nightshirt, she could glimpse his skin. Her mouth went dry, and her gaze involuntarily rose to his. She found him looking at her in a way that tumbled warmth into her loins. Heavens, but she must not go with him! It was not fitting. He was the father of her charge. Abruptly she remembered her duty.

'Henrietta! I cannot leave her.'

Jarrow was disappointed, and acutely conscious of change. For a moment there, the girl had looked anything but a governess. He found himself seeking a way through.

'She will not be the worse for missing a day of education.'

'It is not that, sir. You do not understand. I cannot possibly leave Hetty here if neither of us is in the castle.'

Arrested, he stared at her. 'Are you mad too, Miss Faraday? What in the world do you suppose happened before you came here?'

Nell clamped down upon a rise of panic—and not entirely due to her fears for the child. She was running all too near to disclosing her suspicions, and that must not be done in the corridor where she might be overheard. Duggan had been sent away, but who knew if she had gone as she was bid. And Mr Beresford had certainly been prowling. She had begun upon this on impulse, her judgement swayed by finding that gentler side in Lord Jarrow. She could not now draw back. A solution presented itself.

'Might Hetty not come with us tomorrow?'

'Why?'

The look in his eyes was compelling and Nell knew not how to prevaricate. She lowered her voice. 'I believe her to be in danger.'

'Is that what you wished to talk to me about? She is a danger to herself, perhaps.'

Nell began to feel desperate. 'Lord Jarrow, I cannot talk of it here!'

'And how will you talk of it if Hetty is with us?'

Nonplussed, she gazed at him. A trifle of amusement showed in his face. 'No matter. We will find a way. I dare say it will do Hetty good to go out. Lord knows how long it has been since she did so.'

This was dismaying news, but understandable in the circumstances. 'Since Lady Jarrow died, perhaps?'

'Longer than that.' Jarrow did a rapid calculation in his head. 'It is nigh on three years since we returned from London. Beyond walking in the forest, I believe Duggan has kept her within doors.'

He then wished he had held his tongue. Wrath exploded from the governess.

'*Three years?* My good sir, is it any wonder that she exhibits signs of instability? It is enough to send any child demented to be incarcerated in such a place!'

Jarrow felt himself pokering up, hot words of resentment hovering on his tongue. Yet he withheld them, torn by an equally hot flush of guilt. He had been unforgivably remiss. Blinded by his own pain, he had ignored the obvious. He should have made it his business to ensure that his daughter spent time away from the castle, at least before he began to suspect her mental condition. After—well, that was another matter. He could scarce be blamed for refusing to show her abroad when her public conduct could not be predicted. But as for this delusion that the child was in danger! The thought checked as he came under further attack from the governess.

'Pray, were you obliged to live here through your childhood, my lord? I shall own myself astonished if that is the case.'

'You are right as usual, Miss Faraday,' he said ruefully. 'I was away at school for the most part, and my holidays were invariably spent with relatives. My father lived here, however, doing all he might to make the estates pay. My mother died, you see, when I was relatively young and my father did not wish me to succumb to such chills or ailments as she had done in Castle Jarrow.'

He came under fire from those unusual eyes. 'It is a pity you could not do as much for your own daughter.'

Triumphant at having reduced him to simmering silence, Nell was just about to walk away when she recalled her mission. Instant remorse attacked her. Why could she not have held her tongue? Now she had alienated him again.

'I dare say you would prefer not to have my company tomorrow, sir,' she said impulsively. 'Never mind. We may speak later, if that is more convenient.'

But Lord Jarrow stopped her as she made to go. 'Let me not be accused of inhumanity a second time! You will accompany me tomorrow—whether or not you wish to!—and you will bring Henrietta. Goodnight!'

Nell watched him stalk off down the corridor, prey to a jumble of mixed emotions. It distressed her to have upset him so—safer though it was to have him back to his usual self. She knew him well enough to believe it would not last. His was a moody nature, brought on no doubt by the vicissitudes of his past life, but she was convinced that Lord Jarrow was at heart a just and a gentle man. A part of her looked forward with a glow of anticipation—and inner unrest!—to the morrow. Yet she also viewed the prospect of unburdening her soul with a degree of apprehension. What if she were wrong? Could she not have waited until she had proof positive? But if she had pricked his conscience over the child, she must be satisfied for Henrietta's sake.

When she arrived back at her chamber, she could only be glad she had forced the issue. The missing key had been replaced on the inside of her door.

Padnall Place was a Jacobean mansion. Purchased, as Lord Jarrow told Nell, in the reign of Queen Anne, and added to in later years, it was a rambling establishment with a great many rooms in several wings. Small wonder his lordship could not afford to live in it.

That he had planned to bring her here was obvious, since he had brought the key, for there was evidently no retainer.

'How do you ensure that it is kept in good order?' she asked, passing into a hall of vast proportions.

'I don't,' he responded briefly.

Henrietta, whose spirits had been exuberant throughout the morning, skipped ahead, bolting up the huge central staircase that swept in two directions from a galleried landing. Nell called after her.

'Take care!' She turned to his lordship, who was in black as ever, but in outdoor garb of frock coat and top boots, a beaver covering his dark hair. 'Are the floorboards sound, or should I recapture her, do you think?'

'She will come to no harm. There is nothing wrong with the fabric of the house. It is the condition of the interior that leaves much to be desired.'

Which, Nell saw, was indeed the case. What furnishings there were had been huddled in the centre of each room and covered in holland covers. Yet there was a film of dust everywhere, the wood floors were stained in patches and much of the wallpaper was peeling. Nell ran her fingers over a doorjamb leading into a large parlour and found the dirt ingrained. Patches of damp gave sign that the roofs were unsound, and there was leakage from some of the closed shutters.

Hetty could be heard clattering about upstairs, and Nell became concerned.

'I had better go after her, sir. She may become lost up there.'

Lord Jarrow headed for the stairs. 'We will follow, and you may call to her from time to time.' He set one foot on the stair and turned. 'Let her roam a little, however. It will give us an opportunity to talk at last.'

Reminded of the purpose of this outing, Nell tried to recapture the feelings that had led her to ask for an interview with him. Irrationally, she began to feel that she had been making a mountain out of a molehill. It must be the influence of the outside world. Away from the castle, she had immediately begun to relax. Lord Jarrow too had fallen into mellow mood, choosing to engage his daughter and her governess in a discussion of the rival merits of Hetty's favoured fairy stories as they drove to Collier Row. He had left them to stroll about the village green while he conducted his business there, and had returned with a toffee apple for the child. Not much to Nell's delight, for she had been obliged to dip her pocket-handkerchief into the pond to rid Hetty's face of the resulting stickiness.

Henrietta had been in high gig from the moment she had heard about the treat. Her surprise had passed swiftly, to be succeeded by a buoyancy that would have been itself a trifle disturbing, were it not clear to Nell that it was induced solely by the release from the tensions obtaining in the castle. If she felt it so strongly, how much more must the little girl feel it? What did surprise her was the ease of the child in her father's presence. But then it had become obvious that she had been deliberately misled—both by Duggan and Beresford. The man who had sat at his daughter's bedside last night, and today laughed to see her plastering her face with toffee, was not one who either beat the child or otherwise treated her with severity. His care of her instead showed him to cherish tender feelings for the little girl.

Yet Hetty's personality underwent no change, for she conducted herself without any idea of polite behaviour—butting in with her non sequiturs upon the discussion of her elders and answering only those questions that she chose. But that, decided Nell indignantly, must be set at the door of her upbringing. If no one thought to teach her how to behave in company, how was the child supposed to learn it?

Following Lord Jarrow up the stairs, Nell found herself reluctant to enter upon the subject that had brought her. Here, despite the dilapidation of Padnall Place, everything was so normal that it felt absurd to talk of vague plots and strange happenings. Prevaricating, she called after Hetty to find out if she was safe. The child's voice echoed back to her, not far away, and Nell was satisfied.

'Now then, Miss Faraday.'

There was command in the tone and Nell suppressed an inward sigh. The moment could not be put off any longer. She paused in the corridor and turned to look at him. The light was dim here, but she thought she detected a return of tautness in his features. Nell drew breath and plunged in.

'My lord, I do not believe that the tricks being played upon me are devoid of purpose.'

Jarrow said nothing. It was precisely opposite to his reasoning, but it would not do to say so at this juncture. Clearly, Nell Faraday had not fathomed Toly's mind as yet. There was uncertainty in her face and he nodded encouragingly.

'Go on.'

'As Hetty's governess, sir, I am thought to be in the way. I do not know precisely why as yet, but I believe the symptoms you see in Henrietta are being deliberately induced.'

A cold feeling crept into Jarrow's bones, but he rejected it. He knew himself to be susceptible to suggestion. How could he not be, surrounded for so long by unpredictable minds?

'How so?'

'With laudanum, my lord.'

Laudanum. The very word was anathema. His tone sharpened involuntarily.

'Nonsense! No one in my household would dare to use it on the child. Julietta was prone to take it—whenever I could not prevent her—and it only added to her difficulties.'

Nell gazed at him, her chest tightening. This was dangerous ground. From Mrs Whyte she knew that his late wife had been affected in similar ways to Henrietta—which might well be attributable to laudanum. Only his lordship was so sensitive on this issue. She wanted to pursue it, force him to recognise the truth. But her heart would not permit it. Hardly realising that she did it to spare him further pain, she softened the tale.

'I may be wrong, but there is the matter of the milk.'

'Milk?'

He sounded blank. He did not recall it. Had she not thought he had been preoccupied when she told him of it before? In an unconscious attempt to keep it light, Nell began to walk again, following automatically in the direction of Hetty's clattering footsteps still to be heard at intervals.

'Hetty dislikes the taste sometimes. And indeed, I think occasionally it has a bitter flavour, for I—'

He interrupted her without ceremony. 'You will have me believe that the child's nightly drink is being laced with that drug?'

Nell halted again. 'Yes, my lord.'

There was a moment of silence. Then Lord Jarrow spoke again, his voice perfectly calm. 'Very well, I will look into the matter.'

With which Nell felt obliged to be content. Not that she was at all satisfied. He would speak to Duggan and the woman would lie. And she had said nothing of her suspicions of Mr Beresford, although she had begun with the tricks.

'Come, we had best catch up with Hetty before she loses herself.'

He had dismissed the subject. Despising herself, Nell refrained from re-opening it. She must keep her own vigil, then. Perhaps the fact that the nurse and Mr Beresford knew it had been reported would be enough to deter them from further assaults upon the little girl. But Nell was not sanguine. The fellow wanted something from the child—but what?

She followed Lord Jarrow through a bewildering collection of corridors, until they came out upon a long gallery, where Henrietta was busily prancing up and down, engaged in the few dance steps she had recently learned from Nell and singing her own accompaniment. She looked anything but demented. Nell wished she had courage to bring the matter up again, but the thought of reviving that haunting bitterness—never far away!—was an effective deterrent. It was all too seductive to be with him in a mood of serenity.

Lord Jarrow opened one of the shutters and light flooded in. They had been lucky with the weather, although the sun was playing peek-a-boo with the clouds. Nell went to join him at the window, looking out upon a vast expanse of trees. His proximity disturbed her, and warmth settled in her bosom.

'There is an orchard somewhere in there, sadly overgrown, I fear.' He pointed. 'And that, if you will believe me, is the start of the lawns.'

Nell saw what appeared more like a jungle. 'Heavens, it will take a mountain of work to set it all to rights!'

'Precisely.'

She eyed his profile as his glance roamed the neglected lands. He was right. He could not afford to live in it, no matter how much he might wish to. Nell had little knowledge of estate management, but even to her untutored eye it was obvious that it would cost a fortune. Not to mention the huge staff that would be needed for its upkeep, once the place was put into order. Nell was struck with a longing to remove at least one of his burdens.

'Why don't you sell it?'

His head whipped round, catching her gaze, a frown between his brows. 'Sell Padnall Place?'

Unnerved by his reaction, Nell hurried on. 'As I understand it, the house forms no part of the Jarrow heritage—unlike Castle Jarrow. If you were to sell it, you could afford to purchase a more modest establishment with the proceeds, and keep it running into the bargain. You might even do so with the servants you now have, and remove from the castle altogether.'

Jarrow was touched at the note of concern. He eyed her expectant countenance under the straw hat she had chosen to sport, together with a modest gown of white muslin under a spencer of the dark green that suited her so well. Inconsequently, he decided that she did not look in the least like a governess. She looked like any pretty young lady he might have squired upon an outing. Suddenly—and desperately!—he wanted to kiss her.

The thought jolted him into reality. He heard again Hetty's clatter on the wooden boards beneath her feet, and took in the repetitive lines of the song, fumbled out in her deep-toned voice. Nell Faraday's hand was resting on the windowsill. Jarrow caught it up and brought it swiftly to his lips.

Nell's pulses leaped. Unaware of the startled look in her face, she allowed her fingers to be kissed. Her hand was released immediately, and she brought it slowly back, covering it with the other hand as if she must hide the imprint of his lips. He spoke, and her quick ear detected unsteadiness in his voice.

'You have made a difference, Nell. Despite your fears, she has changed, hasn't she? Has she changed? Or am I imagining it?'

Disappointment swept over Nell in a wave. Quickly she turned her gaze away, to pass unseeingly over the outer world. He must not see how foolish she had been. What had possessed her to suppose his action to have shown a partiality for her? He was grateful to her for what she had achieved with his daughter—and that was all. She had to force herself to speak, and was astonished at how collected she sounded.

'I don't think she has changed, my lord, so much as become more herself.'

'I wish you will not address me so formally!'

The irritation caught her unawares, and she turned on him. 'How else should I address you, pray? You are my employer.'

'No one would suppose it, from the way you speak to me,' he retorted.

Nell could not deny it. Disconcerted, and still disorientated by having her hand kissed, she became absurdly tongue-tied.

'Well, if you will—I mean, it is not—Heavens, how infuriating you are, my lord!'

He laughed. 'And there it is again! You may as well start calling me Eden and be done with it.'

'Don't be absurd! I could not possibly do so. I wish you will cease this foolish conversation, and return to the point at issue.'

'And allow you to persuade me to sell my house?'

Nell positively glared at him. 'I have no notion of anything of the sort. It was merely a suggestion that happened to occur to me. It is no possible concern of mine what you do!'

One hand waved in agitation and Jarrow recaptured it, holding it fast when she tried to pull it away. 'Be still.'

She abandoned the attempt to recover it, turning her attention instead to controlling her breath, which had taken on a life of its own along with the rapid movement of her heart. With dismay, she saw him frown and knew he had detected her unease.

'You are trembling! Why, Nell? You are surely not afraid of me?'

Of what he could do to her unruly emotions, she was excessively afraid. But she could hardly say so. But her tongue betrayed her.

'You set me in turmoil, Lord Jarrow! Pray let me go!'

The outburst was fatal. Jarrow read the cause of her unrest and his desire for her leaped to meet it. Next instant, she was in his arms and his lips were seeking hers out.

Nell's world exploded into sensation. For several mindless instants, all she was aware of was the intense sweetness in the pressure upon her mouth and the violent beating of her heart against her ribs. Heat coursed through her veins and her legs became jelly. For the first time in her life, she felt her senses slipping away from her. And then it was over.

She stood trembling in every limb, grasping automatically at the windowsill to steady herself. She was aware of a strong hand at her elbow, without which she was sure she would have fallen. Her hazy vision cleared and the features of Eden, Lord Jarrow, swam into focus. She heard hoarseness in her own voice.

'What did you do? Heavens, what did you do to me?' A low laugh spun her mind, and she stared at him stupidly.

'Don't look at me like that,' he begged. 'I assure you I am as much discomposed.'

Another voice piped up. 'What you *do*, Miss Fallyday?'

Nell's eyes shot round to find Henrietta standing to one side, her wide-eyed stare trained upon her governess. Dear heaven! She wrenched herself out of his hold.

'You may well ask, Hetty!' She lowered her voice to a frenzied murmur. 'And before the child, too! How could you, my lord?'

Jarrow was already regretting having allowed himself to be carried away. His senses felt utterly disordered, and he cursed himself for losing control in front of his daughter. He spread his hands. 'What can I say?'

'It is no use asking me, sir,' retorted Nell, endeavouring to straighten the bonnet that had shifted in the late encounter to sit unevenly on the back of her head. 'But you had best think of some explanation that will satisfy her—and fast.'

With which he was in whole-hearted agreement. Only he could think of no explanation that would be likely to pass muster with Hetty. Looking down at his daughter, he discovered that she was holding his hat. He reached to take it, and in a bid to distract the child, dropped down and lifted her into his arms.

'Look, Hetty! See the big gardens? Would you like to see outside the house?'

The wide stare—so much associated with the Beresford taint!—passed over the view and returned to his face. She was Julietta to the life, even to the heavy brows that frowned upon him now. Was that why he could not believe otherwise than that she resembled her mother in the disorder of her mind?

'Miss Fallyday come too?' Was it suspicion in the deep voice, or accusation?

'We will all go.'

To his relief, she nodded her satisfaction and he set her down. Replacing the hat upon his head, he took the girl's hand, and signed to Nell to follow. Then he led the way to the main staircase and out again through the front door, which he took care to lock behind him. The respite afforded him all the time he needed to formulate his explanation and apology. That both were due was undeniable, in despite of the unnerving reaction he had surprised in Nell Faraday. Had he not guessed it? She had tried to conceal it, but at a level where he need not inspect it, he had been aware for some time that she was attracted to him, which in itself behoved him to keep his distance. The more fool he for inviting her to come with him today!

He waited until they were arrived at a spot close to the overgrown lawns, into which Henrietta immediately leaped with a shout of joy, swishing her way through the high growth of weeds and laughing immoderately at the trail she left behind her of half-crushed grasses.

When Nell would have followed her, Jarrow reached out to detain her, grasping her by the arm. 'Wait.'

He pulled her round to face him. There was reproach in her eyes, and he let her go, rushing headlong into speech.

'Look at me like that if you will, for I have deserved it. I apologise unreservedly, Nell, for my conduct was disgraceful. What else can I say but that you are a pretty girl, and I have been for too long alone.' He detected a change in her expression, and held up a hand. 'No, I don't mean since my widowhood, but for so much longer. I don't know what you may have heard, but I am sure it must be enough for you to appreciate that much at least.'

Nell could not deny it. Despite every effort to subdue the feeling, her heart went out to him. She spoke her thoughts unchecked.

'More than anything else, I could not wish to add to your burdens, my lord. Let us forget it, if you please.'

Not that she would! She had recovered her composure, but she was sure it would be long before she was able to recall the incident without a resurgence of the sensations it had invoked. She was gratified to see a lessening of the trouble in his face, and could not resist smiling at him. To her unacknowledged chagrin, he did not return the smile, but turned quickly away, training his gaze upon his daughter. There was reserve in his tone.

'The worst aspect of the matter is my having forgot Hetty's presence. Do you suppose she will forget what she saw?'

Nell thought it highly improbable, but she felt obliged to reassure him. 'If she does not, at least she is not likely to speak of it. She does not confide in Duggan, and there is no one else.'

He was sure she had not meant to reproach him, but Jarrow felt it as if she had. 'I am aware. If I could be assured that she would behave properly, I would do what I might to bring her into company with other children.'

Since Nell knew that under present circumstances there could be no such guarantee, she refrained from answering. Overset by recent events, she sought this way and that for a diversion, and found one.

'You had nothing to say to my suggestion of selling this place, sir. Are you attached to it?'

Jarrow glanced about the grounds. It was a moot point. 'Since I have never lived here, I cannot claim an attachment. Yet—' He broke off, abruptly recognising that there was no real reason why he should not sell. He turned to look at her. 'I never thought of it until you put it into my head.'

'Putting the place up for sale?'

He nodded. 'Before I succeeded to the title, I made a vow that when I did I would build up the estates and restore Padnall Place.' The familiar bitterness crept into his chest. 'That was before I met Julietta, of course. After...' After, he might whistle for it! Though he had not known it when he married her.

'I could not wish anyone to break a vow, I suppose.'

He turned to find Nell examining her surroundings with a critical eye. Jarrow could not blame her. 'Vows are made to be broken.'

Nell looked at him. That bitter note again? He must have had enough of shattered vows. 'If they are not solemn, perhaps.'

He threw off his sombre mood. 'I should employ you for my manager, Miss Faraday, rather than a governess. Have you any more advice for me?'

She laughed. 'Besides selling the house?'

'If I could find someone to buy it!'

'There can be no difficulty about that. It is a pleasant place, if a trifle unwieldy. Although it is obviously too big and expensive for your present circumstances, it is just the place for some jumped-up tradesman wishing to lionize.'

'Now why didn't I think of that?'

'You had not thought of selling at all,' Nell reminded him. With a gleam of fun, she added, 'And once you have disposed of it, I know exactly what you should do.'

There was distrust in his face. 'Indeed?'

'The castle, my lord. On no account think of being rid of it. Instead you must fill it with ancient armour and weapons—in fact, all the historical memorabilia you can find—and turn it into a museum. Which, when all is said and done, is all it is fit for!'

Nell warmed to his laughter, and the lifting of the shadows in his face. His tone was dry. 'I thank you, Nell Faraday. Should the time ever come, I shall not hesitate to seek your no doubt expert assistance.'

It was but a short respite. Before long, Lord Jarrow pointed out that they must leave now if they were not to be late for dinner. He turned to call out to Henrietta, and Nell could only be glad he was not looking at her. If her features reflected the dulling in her breast, he would see how little she wanted the interlude to end. She would not have suspected that the thought of returning to the castle, with all its mysteries and pain, had the power to depress her. Or was it that outside it she had been, for just an instant, something more to Lord Jarrow than the governess?

Nell would not have believed, a couple of days earlier, that she could feel this restless. Had she not made up her mind that her presence was necessary to protect

Henrietta, she believed she must have given in to despair and left Castle Jarrow. She tossed again in her bed, shifting her limbs in a bid to drive out the devils in her womb. Oh, that fatal kiss!

Again and again she had pounded the Duck's warnings into her unwilling brain. Nell had never a suspicion that the lady's vast store of wisdom could become useless in the face of the unrelenting longings that physically wracked her in these nightly raids. Yet the warnings had been truer than she knew. She had given in to temptation, and the consequences were shattering. He had begun it, but Nell knew she had been remiss in not pushing him away at once. As if she could have done so! She had never been less in control in her life. And all at the hands of a man who might well have disposed of his own wife.

At that moment, Nell had forgotten all of it. His moods, the tortures of his past, and the wholly unsettled question of Lord Nobody—even now, these matters failed to change the way she felt. Indeed, she acknowledged guiltily, instead of being glad that his lordship showed no sign of repeating the offence, she was both chagrined and disappointed at his obvious withdrawal.

They had met only at dinner, and his manner had been reserved to the point of rudeness. His taciturnity had drawn comment even from Mr Beresford, but Nell had caught the latter sneaking surreptitious looks in her direction that made her wary that he might have guessed something of what lay between the governess and Lord Jarrow.

While she did what she might to discourage such suspicions by adopting an attitude as close to normal as possible, in the privacy of her bedchamber Nell could no longer contain her deep involvement with her employer. How it had happened she was no longer able to fathom, but she was hopelessly lost. Useless to deny that her heart was touched—she had known it these many days!—but she had not bargained for the intense physical yearning that inflamed her with the unquenchable memory of the sensations induced by the touch of his lips upon her own. Nothing in Mrs Duxford's teachings had prepared her for the bodily ache that tugged in the confines of her secret well, presenting her with disturbing images that came from she knew not where, and forced her to recognise the dreadful truth. Despite all the doubts she had of him, she was passionately in love with Eden Jarrow.

No sooner had she reached this hideous conclusion than Nell was roused by a soft footfall outside her door. She had taken to sleeping with the curtains partially open on that side, so that she could not be taken by surprise. By the time the handle was turning, she was already out of bed. A small figure slipped quietly into the room.

About to call out the child's name, Nell hesitated. Henrietta had not seen her, for she walked past her and made directly for the bedside, standing there in the same manner that she had done upon the first occasion. She was sleepwalking again.

Could it be laudanum-induced? Had his lordship not spoken then to the nurse? Nell cursed herself briefly for her preoccupation. She should have made some effort to find out. Her thoughts veered as she leaned down to take the child's hand.

If there had been laudanum in the milk, why had Hetty drunk it? Or had the commotion over her attempt to refuse it a few nights back destroyed her confidence? Perhaps she thought Nell could not prevent the nurse from giving it to her. There was no knowing what the wretched creature might have said to scare Henrietta into obedience.

She led her out of the room, and stopped short, suppressing a sharp gasp.

A little way along the corridor stood a wraithlike figure in diaphanous grey garments, with a mane of long, flowing dark hair. A face shone marble white, with features that were mere openings of mouth and eyes. It was—or was meant to resemble?—a ghost.

Nell's heart began to thump uncomfortably, but she stoutly refused to accept it. The thing raised one white hand and beckoned, and a whisper snaked towards her, an eerie hiss in the quiet of the night.

'*Come, my love. Come, my dearest.*'

Instinct caused Nell to catch at Henrietta's shoulder. 'No,' she told her firmly.

'*Come, dearest. Mama wants you. Come, my love.*'

The little girl struggled against Nell's hold, and she had perforce to let her go. But she kept close behind Hetty as the 'ghost' turned away and floated on down the corridor. It waited at the turn, and Nell's breath shortened in spite of her disbelief. As they neared, it took off again and, on making the turn, Nell saw that it was disappearing through the door into the tower. Nell was disorientated, but a sixth sense warned her. As Hetty made for the door and would have followed, she seized the child and pulled her back, just before the door slammed shut. In her inner eye, Nell could see the broken interior and knew it for the same tower that she had fallen into by accident.

Who or what had tried to lure Hetty in there was a question that did not long exercise her mind. For the child had woken as she grabbed her, and was whimpering with fright. Nell soothed her as she picked her up bodily.

'It's all right now, little one. Nell is here. Don't cry, Hetty.'

Without pause for thought, Nell took off with the child in the direction of Lord Jarrow's chamber. She hoped she had judged it aright, for the incident had jarred her sense of direction. She crooned to the distressed Hetty as she went, but her mind was wholly concentrated upon reaching her employer.

Halting by the door she thought to be his, she opened it and called out.

'Lord Jarrow! My lord? Are you there?'

No reply came. Nor could Nell, listening intently, hear any sound within. Was he asleep, or had she the wrong room? The darkness in there was impossible to penetrate.

Choosing the lesser of two evils, she proceeded along the stone corridor, bearing her burden whose tears continued to soak into Nell's shoulder. Her eyes had become accustomed to the minimal light seeping in at the windows that let on to the courtyard. Nell negotiated the turn and found herself near the staircase. Then she had correctly identified Lord Jarrow's room.

She shifted the child's weight in her arms and made to move on, but a sound from without the castle halted her. Hoofs upon the cobbles! Nell crept to the window to one side of the stairs and looked out in time to see a horseman riding in. The figure was little more than a silhouette, but it had the same look she had seen weeks ago when one of the gentlemen had ridden out.

A figure detached itself from the shadows at the side of the house and went to the horse's head. Detling again? The rider dismounted. Nell heard a murmur of voices and then whoever it was entered by a side door, leaving the groom to take care of his mount.

Nell became aware of increased weight and discovered that Henrietta had fallen asleep. Through the turmoil in her mind, she found the way to the child's bedchamber, hastening her pace. Better if she was not found loitering here. If she had intended to accost Lord Jarrow, she could not do it now. He had been out in the night, and she could no longer doubt it was he. For Mr Beresford, without any doubt at all, had been busy playing at ghosts only a few moments since.

She soon had the little girl safely back between sheets. But there was no question of leaving her, for Hetty awoke again and it was evident that the child was terrified.

'Mama comed back. Don't go, Miss Fallyday, or Mama come back again.'

Inwardly cursing the miscreants who had inculcated this belief, Nell reassured her charge, and quickly slipped into the bed beside her. She fell asleep with the plump little body pressed closely into her own.

It had taken a deal of courage for Nell to request the interview. But her employer's tactic to create distance, though hurtful, proved efficacious. He had bade her take a seat at the table near the window, and placed himself several paces from her at the end of the parlour, resting a hand on the mantelshelf above the fireplace. The black garb emphasised the pallor of his countenance, causing Nell to feel chilled, though the day was warm.

She banished the little pain engendered by Lord Jarrow's tight-lipped refusal to give any sign of remembering the intimacy they had shared. Nell did not believe it to be forgotten, but she was forced to recognise that he wished it so. Since she had herself suggested they forget it, she could not blame him for that. Nevertheless, the icy front was distressing. It was a far cry from that fatal outing, and her resumption of plainer garb—the brown calico had never before felt drab!—increased the gap that yawned between them.

He was apparently unmoved by her recital of the night's events. 'You would have me believe that someone is pretending to be my late wife's ghost?'

'I certainly don't expect you to believe that your wife's ghost is walking the castle!'

Lord Jarrow stiffened, and his glance flicked away, and then returned. 'You saw this apparition up close?'

'It was not an apparition, sir. Give me a nightgown, a mask and the correct type of wig, and I will engage to present a like appearance.' Nell thought a faint amusement gleamed in his eye, and was a little cheered. 'My lord Jarrow, I am not here concerned with the effect upon me, but upon Henrietta. She was sleepwalking at the time, but it is evident that she saw it, for she believes that it was her mother, and is severely frightened.' Almost as an afterthought she added, 'I had no idea they would go to such lengths.'

He took her up at once. 'Who is they? Who is it you suspect?'

Nell hesitated. If she told him, she must disclose everything she knew. 'The same person—or perhaps I should say persons—who have done all the rest. I don't pretend to understand their purpose.'

He hit the mantelpiece with the flat of his hand. 'Hell and the devil, Nell! Are you going to make an accusation, or are you not?'

She was betrayed into retort. 'I would, if only I could be sure of you, Eden!'

Nell regretted it at once, for he went white. 'That again? Why don't you come right out with it and call me a murderer? That is what you meant, isn't it?'

She got up swiftly. 'What am I to think? You were out last night, for I saw you! I came to your room with Hetty and you weren't there. Then I saw a man ride in, and I knew it must have been you.'

'You think I killed her.' Suppressed violence under the half-whispered words.

Nell could not endure it. 'I don't! I think nothing of the kind.'

'But you are not certain.'

She was silent.

He turned away, fixing his gaze upon the portrait. A dcfcatcd note entered his voice. 'After all, why should you trust me? You know nothing of my life, and I don't doubt you have heard enough to horrify you. From my own lips, too,' he added, turning to look at her.

The protest was dragged from Nell. 'Eden, I want to believe in you! Only you are so extremely sensitive that I can't open my mouth without you taking it amiss. And you had doubted me, with less reason.' He said nothing, and Nell continued more moderately, 'Perhaps you think I imagined the ghost as well.'

He was no longer looking at her. 'No, I don't think that.'

She regarded his profile with dawning suspicion. 'I believe you know more than you allow me to believe,' she said slowly. 'You cannot have been ignorant of such things if, as I suppose, they had been going on before I came.'

Jarrow knew not how to reply to this. She was all too shrewd. He did not himself know why he was reluctant to open up to her. Why the secrecy? If Toly was playing at ghosts now, then he must have doubled back last night. Had his brother-in-law seen him following and fooled him on purpose? Or had it been a ruse to draw him out of the house?

Which presupposed that there was something in Nell's suspicions. Yet the seriousness of his dilemma made him reluctant to say anything. Better, perhaps, that she suspected him. She must not become involved.

Lurking at the back of his mind was the thought that such an involvement must inevitably lead to a commitment he was not equipped to make. It had been difficult enough to hold off from her. That one taste of her lips had roused such a demon of want in him that he knew not how to subdue it, save by keeping her at a distance. Hell and the devil, but he could not drag her into this! The more he allowed Nell Faraday into his inner life, the less he would be capable of allowing her out of it. And that was unfair.

He turned to find her with an arrested expression on her face, looking over his shoulder. He flicked a glance back and realised that she had been caught by

Julietta's portrait. Glad of the excuse of a change of subject, he shifted to one side.

'Hetty is very like her, don't you think?'

Nell started. She had been unaware of him for several moments, struck by the realisation that had come to her. Absently she agreed, coming forward to stand before the portrait. But it was not at Julietta Jarrow she was staring. Her eyes were instead fixed upon the painted necklace about her throat. It was gold and studded with emeralds. Here, without a doubt, was Hetty's treasure! And Lord Jarrow had known the moment she told him.

'Had she seen this necklace? Henrietta, I mean. She must have done. Perhaps her mama showed it to her. It could not be that she imagined what she told me from this portrait.'

His lip curled into his most bitter look, and Nell's heart sank. His eyes had shifted to the portrait and he reached out, one finger tracing the green drops that hung from the heavily encrusted gold band.

'She may have seen a necklace, but it was not the one in this portrait. That was stolen from me. The theft is thought to be the cause of my wife's death.'

'Thought to be?'

His voice hardened, and his brow grew black. 'Lord Nobody seized the jewels from her throat, after he shot her.'

Chapter Nine

For a moment Nell could not speak. The immediate remembrance of Papa's death must weaken her. But the words seared her heart. Could he speak so of the highwayman if he had himself pulled the trigger? Then why did he ride out at night, and yet not tell her the reason? It made no sense. Why should he pretend that a theft had taken place and speak of it in a manner that showed it still had power to hurt? He could not be guilty! It was only her desperate need to know him for innocent that made her doubt.

Lord Jarrow shifted away from the portrait to pace the parlour floor.

'I had it in mind to sell the emeralds myself. They are ancient, an heirloom. Or were, should I say. I hesitated too long. I thought to use the proceeds to restore Padnall Place, but I had difficulty reconciling it with my conscience to do what no other Jarrow had done before me, despite any temptation they might have had through one misfortune after another.'

He halted, turning to look at Nell, grimness in his face. 'It was sacrilege and I had my deserts.'

He might have been trying to prove his own guilt!
What, was she to think he had killed his wife for the
emeralds? Absurd. And she could not bear his pain.

'Merely for thinking of it? A harsh judgement, sir,
if that is so.'

'Life is harsh. You are young, and have not yet had
time to find it so.'

Nell suffered a reversal of feeling, eyeing him now
with some resentment. 'If you have suffered, sir, you
need not make the arrogant assumption that others
have not!'

Arrested, Jarrow stared at her. Belatedly, he remembered her calling and the place from whence she had
come to him. The Paddington Seminary was peopled
by orphaned young ladies. Seized with remorse, he
crossed quickly to her, catching at her hands and holding them fast.

'Forgive me, Nell! You carry your own misfortunes
so lightly, one is apt to forget they exist.'

Her smile seemed to him unbearably poignant. So
much courage as she possessed! Had she not borne
with fortitude all the fearful inadequacies and horrors
that had been poured upon her hapless head in this
dread place he was forced to call home? She had almost told him that she did not trust him, yet she did
not recoil. He was moved to hope a little. There was
a hint of the wry humour that characterised her as she
replied.

'Well, I can scarce claim to rival your problems,
but I have had my share.'

'And more—if only in taking up this post.'

She laughed out at that. 'We have yet to discover how much of a misfortune that will prove, my lord.' Her hands tugged a little and he released her. 'As for my youth, I take leave to doubt that you have yet attained thirty yourself.'

Jarrow was obliged to smile. 'Very nearly.'

'Then you have the advantage of me by only seven years.'

'Seven years of hell!'

The beat of Nell's heart, already in disarray from the circumstance of his holding her hands, became positively flurried at the resurgence of bitterness in both face and voice. A feeling of desolation crept over her, at the damping of an unacknowledged hope. Had she secretly thought to redeem him from his parlous state? A man whose past actions she must continue to view with reservation. She was dismayed to find herself no less foolish in ambition than her friend Kitty. She sought for a change of subject, and could think only of probing the hidden meaning of his words.

'You have hinted as much before.'

The familiar kick of guilt made Jarrow shift quickly away from her. His instinct was to keep it all buried. Why should he burden this girl with the sordid tale of his unlucky marriage? Yet had he not already done so with his moods and ill temper? If there was an added reason that spurred him, he did not give it room in his mind. He found himself standing by the table, and threw himself into a chair to one side.

'It is not a pretty story.'

In the periphery of his vision, he saw her approach and take a seat across the table. Jarrow turned to look at her. The sun fell upon the halo of honey-gold hair, but he was the more taken at this moment with the intelligence that shone in her eyes. A rare quality in a woman. It was madness not to trust her, despite her doubts of him.

He shifted his chair so that he faced her, and leaned one elbow on the table. His eye went over her shoulder to Julietta's portrait. A stronger contrast would be difficult to find.

'She was in every way your opposite,' he said impulsively. 'Dark and sultry in looks, with curves so voluptuous that I lost my head. My father was against the marriage, as well he might be. He knew more of the Beresfords than I.'

'The taint of madness?'

It was spoken in a murmur, but Jarrow caught it. He nodded. 'He tried to warn me, but I was obdurate. I married her in the teeth of his prohibition.'

Nell nodded sagely. 'Parents invariably go the wrong way to work in such matters, so I have been told.'

He gave a shrug. 'I doubt anything would have stopped me. Have you ever been infatuated? No, of course you have not. It is akin to madness, but it does not last. My eyes were opened soon enough, but by then it was too late. The deed was done.'

Nell found the unemotional flatness of his tone more revealing than if he had railed. It was plain that he had lived in torment from the moment of realising his mistake, and then having condemned himself, to discover little by little that his wife was suffering from a malady that could only deepen his torture. Almost she could forgive him if he had taken her life!

'What happened, Eden?'

She was unaware that she had used his name again. As if it was the most natural thing in the world, she reached her open palm across the table. He looked at it, and then lightly brushed his hand across it, catching at the tips of her fingers. He held them so, his thumb lightly caressing them. There was affection in the gesture, and a riffle of warmth slid through Nell.

'Julietta treated me with much evidence of devotion, but it was a childish thing, insincere. She was like a child, wayward and exacting. Then came the flirtations. At first she behaved as if she enjoyed my jealousies; I felt that she taunted me with her laughter. Later I realised that it genuinely amused her to see me raging, and that she felt no vestige of remorse. I, on the other hand—'

He broke off, and it came to Nell that his regret encompassed not only his error of choice, but also his failure to change the creature he had married. A normal woman would have responded to his jealousy and abandoned her faithlessness. He had no need to tell her that Julietta's conduct had gone beyond flirtation, for his evident agony bore out what Mrs Whyte had told her.

'With my father's death, I had to return here,' Jarrow went on. 'Julietta hated it. There was not yet enough in her behaviour to alert me to her mental state. Or the disease had not yet advanced so far as to be noticeable—except in the occasional tantrum. Besides, she was with child, and women are prone to megrims in pregnancy. When Henrietta was a few months old, I yielded to Julietta's pleas to return to town.' He released the fingers he was holding as the memories crowded in. 'We spent two or three seasons there—I forget now, for the time rolled into one long era in my mind, with Julietta's vagaries and Toly's constant presence.'

'You lived in his father's house?' Nell was recalling what Mrs Whyte had said about Mr Beresford's influence on his sister.

'For my sins. But my in-laws were rarely there, though Toly was. He was close to Julietta, and I imagined he might serve to steady her.' His lips tightened. 'I was mistaken, but let that pass. At length the situation became untenable. I could no longer ignore the signs that told me Julietta was unbalanced. Her conduct made us both a laughing-stock, or an object of pity. Neither case was to be tolerated. I brought her home, and forced her to remain in this Godforsaken place.'

Nell had no words, either of comfort or compassion. She was the more moved by what he left unsaid than by the little he had told her. It was clear that he had expected to be forever locked in the castle, tied to a woman he could no longer love and who put him through every kind of hell from which her death had conveniently released him. The thought threw hollows into her chest.

'It did not answer.' Again, the flat note that gave all too much away. 'Deprived of those outlets for her restlessness that London provided—albeit such actions as caused us both the gravest harm—Julietta became more and more unbalanced. We were treated day and night to the same shrieking tantrums in which Hetty indulges. She too began to walk the corridors in her sleep. I would find her stretched at her length somewhere, sleeping like the dead, with just that labouring breath of which you have spoken in the child.'

He passed a hand tiredly across his face. 'If fate had not intervened in the person of Lord Nobody, I dare say she might have ended her days in some other fashion. By falling from the battlements, perhaps, where she was wont to walk. Or down that broken stairwell you mistakenly stepped into the other night. At all events, so I tell myself when the demon of memory proves too gruesome to be endured.'

Nell found her tongue, spurred by her own dread remembrance of the past. 'You are talking of the accident?'

His eyes caught at hers, and held them. 'Was it an accident?'

She clasped her hands tightly together to still their sudden trembling. The moment she had dreaded had arrived. She had wanted this moment. Only now did she recognise that she had been avoiding it. To hear it would be to relive the worst moments of her life. Yet she must know!

'What did happen that night, Eden? You were there, were you not?'

Jarrow nodded, the memory sharp and clear, etched into his mind from that moment, as if it had been caught by an artist's brush and left standing on the wall of his memory.

'I was riding behind the coach. Julietta had given me the slip, and cajoled Grig into taking her to a ball at Chadwell Heath. Detling would never have done so, but he was off that night. By the time I had discovered her absence, it was too late to stop her. I guessed at once where she had gone, for I had refused the invitation from Lady Guineaford only a few days earlier.'

'You rode after her?'

'To fetch her back, yes.'

He recalled the wild ride through the night, his heart in his mouth as his imagination tumbled over the havoc Julietta might have wrought among a public consisting of his immediate neighbours.

'I did not show my face, but sent a servant for the hostess. She was a friend of my father's and knew a little of our story. She persuaded Julietta to come into the vestibule and I took her away.'

'She came without protest?'

Jarrow gave a grim laugh. 'On the contrary. She threatened to undo us both with a screaming fit. I was obliged to put my hand across her mouth and carry her out to the coach. I took to horse, for I had no mind to be treated to a barrage of abuse—and Julietta would not have hesitated to use her nails.'

'And that was when you were held up by Lord Nobody?'

Nell saw his lip curl. 'Or, as some hold—perhaps as you believe, Nell!—that was when I took on the persona of Lord Nobody and shot my wife in the head.'

The taunt washed over Nell, for the image of her father was stirring. She thrust it down. 'Tell me, pray.'

'There is little to tell. Grig saw the fellow and must have pulled on the reins, for the horses plunged badly. To his credit, he managed to control them. I could not see the man myself, but even as I rode around to find out what was amiss, he had come in to the other side of the coach. I heard Julietta cry out, and rode around from the front. He had pulled open the door and had the pistol trained upon the inside.' He ran his fingers over his dark hair in a gesture of frustration. 'I hardly remember what happened next. I know I tried to ride him down. He must have hit out at me with the pistol for I felt a blow and came off my horse. The pistol exploded. By the time I had got to my feet—my head was none too steady at the time—Lord Nobody was riding away. I found Julietta lying dead, and the jewels she had been wearing had been torn from her neck.'

Nell was trembling violently, but she managed the one word. 'Torn?'

'There was blood where the necklace had ripped her flesh, besides that which was running from the wound in her head.'

Nell could no longer control the sensations that were churning in her bosom. The horror of her childhood was there in full, but overlaid with the release of an even greater pressure. He had not done it! Eden had not killed Julietta.

She slumped in her chair, throwing her hands to her temples. Distantly, she heard Lord Jarrow's sharp intake of breath.

'Hell and the devil, I should not have told you! Nell? Nell!'

She tried to reassure him with a faint wafture of one hand, but her teeth were chattering too much for speech. In a moment, she could feel him above her, and his hands caught at her shoulders. Then he was down beside her, trying to see her face.

'Nell, look at me! Nell, for God's sake!'

She made a supreme effort, dragging herself upright. One wavering hand caught his arm, and she pushed the words through a sandpaper throat.

'I am...all right. It—it is not...'

He left her abruptly, and she heard his hasty footsteps crossing to the door. Another door slammed, and there was quiet for a space. Nell rested her arms on the table and laid her head upon them, willing herself to recover. Then Lord Jarrow was back again, urgency in his tone.

'Drink this! Come, lift up your head.'

She had perforce to do as he wished, for his hand was forcing her head up. She felt the cool of glass at her lips.

'It's brandy. Take a little.'

The tone was peremptory, and obediently Nell sipped at the liquid. The taste was strong but pleasant. But as she swallowed, she felt as if her throat was on fire. She was urged to take another sip, and did so only because she had no will to resist. Presently the faintness left her, and the tremors died down. She was able to sit up at length, and gave the concerned features of her employer a reassuring smile.

'I beg your pardon.'

'Don't! I should beg yours for burdening you with my harrowing tale.'

Nell shook her head. 'It is not that.' She drew a breath. There was no further need for that long-held secrecy. Not with the man she loved—and trusted. 'You see, my father was killed in just such a fashion.'

Shock leaped in his eyes. 'And I was patronising about your sufferings! Nell, can you forgive me?'

'Readily. But there is no need. My experience was nothing to yours.'

'Who is to say so? How old were you?'

'Not much older than Hetty is now.' A little sigh slipped out. 'My mother had died from an illness, and

Papa took care of me so well. It was unfortunate that we were held up that day.'

'Unfortunate! You have a gift for understatement, my girl.'

Nell became aware that one of her hands was held in his strong grip and that he was on one knee beside her chair. Confusion swamped her, and she shook herself free.

'Pray get up, sir! There is no need to—to—'

He rose swiftly, and his tone hardened. 'You appear to be recovered.' He pushed the glass towards her. 'Another sip?'

Nell shook her head. 'I am perfectly well now, thank you.'

Jarrow lifted the glass and tossed off the brandy himself. Setting it down with something of a snap, he shifted away from her, feeling distinctly rebuffed. Did she disbelieve him? Or had the history with which he had regaled her given her a distaste for him? He could scarcely blame her if it had. The whole business was sordid in the extreme. But he must not dwell on his own troubles. It was that which had caused him to distress her in the first place. He turned to look at her, and caught a faint flush upon her cheek. She looked away from him, and he felt certain he had guessed aright. Perhaps he should not have been so frank. He thrust down the thought, concentrating instead upon her story.

'What happened to you afterwards?'

She did not look at him, and her voice was low. 'My aunt took care of me for a while. But she was herself widowed and with little means of support, once Papa died. He was her brother and had taken it upon himself to assist her, for her portion was meagre.'

'But did not your father's heirs assist you?'

A tiny grimace crossed her face. 'He had none, sir. He was not landed, and all his family had been soldiers. Mama and I followed the drum.'

'Ah, so that is where you learned your self-sufficiency.'

She laughed, glancing up at him briefly, and he felt a degree lighter. 'By no means. It was instilled into me at the Seminary, where my aunt at length sent me so that I might have a means to earn my own living. I could not blame her. She was barely able to keep herself, poor dear, let alone a niece. I have come to be glad of her common sense.'

Jarrow watched the play of expression in her face and found in himself a strong desire to pull her back from the future that she faced so cheerfully. She was both resilient and resourceful, and he could not imagine that she had need of a knight errant. It was rather he who had need of her! She was speaking again, and in an odd tone that gave no clue to her thoughts.

'I have never told anyone of this before—not even my closest friends know the secret of Papa's death.' She looked up and met his eyes, a light in her own that spoke to something so deep inside him that Jarrow could not give it a name. 'I was haunted for years by my helplessness—I could do nothing to save him. Indeed, I sat mumchance and terrified, thereby probably saving my own life, as my aunt once said. I resolved never to speak of it, you see, so that the memory might be blotted out.'

Every good intention flew out of his head. The familiar distress closed in upon him, throwing him out of temper. 'Impossible! There is no blotting it out. There are griefs involved, and griefs should not be suppressed. Better to let it roam the mind so many times that at last it ceases to have the power to hurt.'

Nell eyed the changed countenance with deadness in her chest. She had lost him again—Julietta would ever win. Nevertheless, she could not withhold it.

'Has it ceased to hurt, Eden?'

He turned away from her, crossing to the portrait. Harshness was rife in his voice. 'It is no longer that sort of hurt that I feel.'

'I do not believe you. Your whole life is an agony!'

He swung round. 'Because I have not resolved it! Because the truth is so unpalatable that I have refused to confront it. Suspicion is one thing. Confirmation means that I must do something about it, and I don't know what to do!'

Impelled, Nell rose from her chair and went to him. 'What do you know? Does it explain what I have experienced in this place? You know something is awry, yet you will not give credence to the one thing I know to be true.'

Jarrow frowned. Was she at that again? 'You mean Hetty? That I have resolved. Duggan says she had put the veriest sip of laudanum in the child's milk, only in hope that she might sleep soundly. I have forbidden her to repeat it.'

'Then why was she sleepwalking last night?'

'For the same reason Julietta did,' he uttered, exasperated. 'Leave it, Nell!'

She wrenched back, away from him. 'I cannot. You think it is all innocent trickery, Eden, but I do not. Yet you have all but accused Mr Beresford of—'

'Don't speak of it.'

The harsh tone arrested Nell, and she stared at him, dimly conscious of a depth of hidden distress. Then he did think his brother-in-law had killed Julietta, his own sister. Her breath felt constricted. If he could believe that of him, how could he not see that the man was a danger to his daughter? Clearly she had no choice but to pursue it herself.

A burgeoning thought surfaced. A question only Eden could answer. She forgot all the rest, and threw it at him.

'Tell me this, if you please, my lord. If the emeralds were stolen when Julietta was killed, has no attempt been made to recover them? So important a piece ought to compel the authorities to make a thorough investigation.'

Jarrow stared at her, confused by the sudden change of subject. 'So they would have done—had I allowed it.'

'Why didn't you?'

He was goaded into response, unable to prevent the bitterness that rose up into his gorge to choke him. He almost spat the words. 'Because I would not have them waste their time and energy. The emeralds were worthless!'

Confusion set into Nell's mind. 'But you said—'

'That I had not sold them, yes. I did not say that they were not sold.'

'I don't understand. If Lord Nobody stole them—'

'What he stole were not the Jarrow Emeralds. The necklace was a carefully constructed fake, and the emerald drops were nothing but paste.'

Nell's brain was reeling. 'Paste!'

There was impatience in his tone. 'You still don't understand, but why should you?' The dark eyes flicked back to the portrait of Lady Jarrow. 'How could you guess that all hope of repairing my fortunes had been gone forever, well before the tragic end of my lovely wife? The irony will not escape you. Julietta was murdered for the sake of the emeralds. Only she had long since secretly disposed of them— selling them jewel by jewel.'

Henrietta was in one of her black moods. Nell found her wearing, for she could neither say nor do anything to the child's satisfaction. She had not realised how exhausting had been her interview with Lord Jarrow until she was obliged to endure in addition the ill temper of a six-year-old child. Attempting to pacify her with the wooden doll failed. Hetty threw it across the room. Nell knew she must be patient, for it was undoubtedly due to last night's unhappy adventure. The difficulty was that Hetty remembered nothing about it.

There was proof in the little girl's state that laudanum had been administered last night. If she could glean confirmation from the child's own mouth, would Eden believe her at last? That was, if his obsession elsewhere could allow him to grant a little thought to this far more pressing matter. Heavens, she was becoming as sardonic as his lordship!

Her careful questions met with no satisfactory answers.

'Did you drink your milk last night?'

'Don't 'member.'

'Perhaps it tasted nasty again, is that it?'

'I told you, I don't 'member!'

Unwilling to recall to Henrietta's mind a happening that she would prefer to forget, Nell had found herself at a loss. But the urgency of the child's safety was paramount. She had to try.

'Did you have bad dreams, perhaps?'

Hetty knuckled her eyes, growling in her throat. Nell sharpened her tone.

'I cannot understand you when you insist upon talking like an animal! Speak up, if you please.'

The hands dropped and a pair of black eyes regarded her with a smouldering fury that reminded Nell irresistibly of her father. 'I did dream, I telled you!'

'Thank you. Would you like to tell me about the dream?'

'No!' said Hetty baldly.

Nell gave it up. 'Very well. Then I shall read you a story.'

'Don't want a story!'

'Then we shall sit in silence.'

Folding her arms, she sat back in her chair and trained her gaze upon Henrietta's own. For several moments, the little girl stared back in defiance, her plump cheeks crushed in a scowl, pretty lips mulish and pouting. Then her gaze dropped, and she sank her temples onto tight clenched fists, resting her elbows on the desk. Nell heard the stirrings of tears, and could not help relenting. Her voice softened.

'Hetty, won't you tell me what is wrong?'

A muffled sob, and a frantic kicking at the footrest below. But no response.

'Hetty?'

The fists came down with a crash, beating on the lid of the desk, and rage issued forth. 'My head ache! *My head ache!*'

'Then you did drink the milk last night!' uttered Nell involuntarily.

'I don't know, I don't know. I don't *'member!*'

The protest ended on a burst of sobs, and Nell hastily left her seat and went to catch the child up. She said nothing, but only held Henrietta in a gentle embrace, not wishing to add to her frustrations—which were undoubtedly increasing the pain. The very thing that could possibly soothe her must be denied. At the Seminary, laudanum was infrequently but judiciously used to alleviate severe pain.

'Come, my dear, try to stop crying,' Nell urged. 'You will only make the pain worse.'

'It hurt, Miss Fallyday!' sobbed Hetty. 'It *hurt*.'

'Yes, I know, little one. I understand, truly I do.' She glanced out of one of the windows and saw that the sun had gone in. 'Let us go out onto the roof. The fresh air may clear your head a little.'

Still whimpering, the little girl allowed herself to be persuaded to remove from the schoolroom and walk up and down the battlements for a short time. It was warm, but the light was dim with the sun behind cloud, so that she need not fear it might worsen the child's pain.

While Nell soothed aloud in response to the grumbles of her charge, inwardly she was seething. Why could Eden not look at what was under his nose? Had he examined Hetty's conduct with an open mind—impossible in the circumstances!—he must have seen that those precise symptoms he took as showing Hetty's tendency to dementia were in fact caused by laudanum. The Duck had deprecated excessive use of it, citing just those instances of conduct that had alerted Nell to the possibility. Sleep that resembled a stupor was an initial result, often accompanied by nightmares. But it was then as the effects wore off that the moodiness set in, which in turn led to tantrums and rages. What Hetty was experiencing was the type of headache that came after a heavy bout of liquor consumption, for excessive laudanum had the same effect.

Of those who used it on the little girl for their own nefarious ends—would she might discover what they were!—she blamed Duggan the more. Beresford had the callousness of the insane. But what was the nurse's excuse for indulging in so wicked a proceeding? What had she to gain? Which brought Nell full circle.

The object could not be merely to make Henrietta believe that her mama had returned to the castle. There must be some purpose behind that—and this morning Nell had suddenly thought that she had it. Only Lord Jarrow had blown that theory out of the water. If the emeralds were paste, there could be no future in setting Hetty to search for them. Yet some sort of 'treasure' undoubtedly existed.

She looked down at Hetty's bent head, as the little girl trotted along where she led her, quieter now. The child could not remember where it was. Did Beresford hope that the drug and a dreamlike state would jog her memory? But in any event, there was no point in going down that road now. Unless Mr Beresford did not know that the emeralds were paste?

She found herself once again going over Eden's uncompromising reaction. He had known what she was about to say—and stopped her dead. Faced with the necessity to believe in his lordship's innocence, Nell had only one other option for the identity of Lord Nobody. There could be no doubt that Mr Beresford had pulled the trigger. But had he done it deliberately? Was this what tortured Lord Jarrow? Had he been certain, Nell could not believe he would tolerate the presence in his house of his wife's murderer.

It was a terrible dilemma, and Nell felt for him with her whole heart. She recalled that night—far off now, it felt—when she had first mentioned Hetty's treasure. Eden had identified it, only he had first sat staring through her. It must have been this question revolving in his mind. Nell had no question. She did not know whether Toly Beresford had intended to kill his sister, but she could not acquit him of complicity in the matter of Henrietta. Alone, Duggan could have no motive. As Toly Beresford's paramour, the motive became immediately visible.

Hetty was dragging at her hand. Nell halted. 'Are you tired?'

The child nodded, moving to place herself in one of the gaps in the battlements. Nell went with her, afraid of her falling in her present state. Loath to mention the headache, Nell skirted it with a general question.

'How are you feeling now?'

Henrietta sighed. 'Hurting not so much.'

'That is excellent. And have you remembered anything about last night?'

The black eyes looked up at her. 'Didn't sleep good. Dreamed and dreamed.'

'Yes, you told me. Only you did not say what the dreams were about.'

'Don't 'member.'

That road was effectively closed.

Nell judged it time to drop the subject. She wished she could think how to prevent the child from taking the drug again. Heaven knew what threats had been made to stop her from attempting to sue to her governess for help! But Hetty would be unlikely to remember them. In the grip of fear, would she recall anything other than the so-called demands of her dead mother?

A curious thought struck Nell. Sleeping—or sleep-walking—Hetty was malleable. Awake, she fought back. How had they overcome her resistance? If she was encouraged to follow the 'ghost' in her sleep, and now could remember nothing about it, how was it that she had become convinced that her mama was in the castle?

Nell glanced down at the little girl where she sat quietly in the battlement ledge. Henrietta was yawning, her dark head resting against the stonework. She looked like any ordinary weary child, and not in the least like a deranged one. That she believed in the presence of her deceased mother had no bearing on the case. Any child might be persuaded to believe such a thing. Only how?

Hearsay was not evidence. No amount of telling would serve with children, as Nell well knew. They must be shown before they would accept. Could it be that the 'apparition' that had called to Hetty in the corridor last night had come to her while she was awake? Nell could easily picture just such a possibility. If the child woke up to find that ghostly *thing* apparently floating by her bed, would it not be enough to throw her into shrieking hysterics? And having set the household by the ears, why should the thing not vanish into some hidden recess and await its moment to escape unseen? Just as someone had done that day when Nell had herself been lured into Lady Jarrow's room by the playing of the clavichord.

'Are we wishful to fall off the roof, Miss Hetty?'

Duggan's shrill tone startled Nell quite as much as it did the child. Without thought, she caught at the little girl and pulled her up from where she sat, holding her against her petticoats as the nurse came up. She attacked Nell forthwith.

'No concern of yours if we come to grief, is it, miss?'

Nell snapped. 'Don't be stupid! Hetty was perfectly safe.'

'Oh, was she now? And who's to say we wouldn't up and jump before you could stop us? You know well we ain't right in our mind and can't be trusted to do as others might.'

'Be quiet!' ordered Nell, low-voiced. 'If that is how you speak in front of—'

'Come, Miss Hetty,' interrupted the woman, ignoring her and seizing the child by the arm, 'it's time and past we was having our nap. We'll get a bite to eat and then it's off to our bed without no more argybargy.'

'Didn't argy-bargy!' protested the child, unwillingly allowing herself to be pulled away from Nell. 'Want to go to bed. Got a headache.'

'And why wouldn't we have an aching head when we do nothing but grump and growl and throw tantrums, eh? Now come along.'

Even had Nell tried, there was little hope of blocking the woman's flow of complaint. As it was, she was stricken to silence by a realisation. The first time Hetty had broken out screaming in the night—on Nell's very first evening—Mr Beresford had been in the dining-parlour throughout. When Lord Jarrow had returned, he had stated that Duggan was with the child. Was it then Duggan masquerading as Lady Jarrow's ghost?

Nell had all along supposed Mr Beresford had been responsible for the tricks played upon her, and upon Hetty. Although it must be Duggan who administered the drug in the milk—if indeed it was drugged. Only if Duggan had dressed up as the ghost, how had she freed herself from the garments and—

Of course! As if she saw it played out in her mind's eye, Nell knew how it must have been done. Duggan need not dress up in the clothes. She had only to hang them upon some object—a broomstick, perhaps?— waft it before her, and then wake Hetty. The child would be half asleep, the room dim with the light of a single candle. How would she realise that what she saw was merely an empty gown topped with a mask and wig? And having terrified the little girl into screaming, what need was there for more? Duggan had only to dispose of the thing in some convenient place—under the bed?—and resume her proper role so that Lord Jarrow would discover her there when he came into the room. How simple it was.

Yet the ghost she had seen last night had been solid enough. Inhabited, Nell was convinced, by Bartholomew Beresford. She could not believe that Duggan had the necessary skill to carry off the fraud. Mr Beresford, on the other hand, had proved himself a most accomplished actor.

Recalling the last occasion upon which Hetty had woken in a fit of screaming, Nell remembered that her own door had been locked. How easy for him! He had only to dress up, lock her door, and take himself off to Henrietta's room. Once the child had been terrified, he might make good his escape before Lord Jarrow could arrive. His own room was next door to Hetty's. He had no need to hide himself from Duggan. He had only to unlock Nell's door at his leisure, hoping to bewilder her.

So that she did not unravel his scheme? Or to frighten her into quitting the castle? Like last night's ghost. A little reflection had told Nell it had been meant for her, rather than Hetty. The child had been in no real danger from the broken stairwell in the tower, for Beresford must have known Nell would prevent her entry there. Had Duggan led the sleep-walker to Nell's chamber, leaving Toly Beresford lying in wait?

The sheer cleverness of these proceedings left her breathless. But the wickedness made her ache with distress for the defenceless little victim. Whatever his motive—what *could* he want if it was not the Jarrow Emeralds?—there could be no forgiveness. And no more time! Nell determined to thwart him. And without delay.

The housekeeper was aghast. She sat staring at Nell with horrified eyes, her teacup held between her motionless hands.

'I have no proof,' Nell said wryly. 'It is all supposition.'

Mrs Whyte found her tongue, setting down her cup with a snap that clashed in the saucer. 'Proof! No, and nor you won't get it, as clever as they both are! Capering about in the night dressed up like the mistress? He must be all about in his head!'

Of which Nell needed no convincing. Yet it was not insanity that drove Toly Beresford to pose as the ghost of his dead sister. He had a tangible purpose, if only she could put her finger upon it.

'But you've no need of proof with me, ma'am,' went on the elder woman, 'for I've long suspected him as taking more interest in the little 'un than was warranted. I'd a notion he wanted the child to seem like to her mama, though I couldn't reason out why—except as it had to be for his own gain—nor how he did it.'

'Yes, but he didn't do it, Mrs Whyte,' argued Nell. 'He made Duggan do it for him.'

'Well, as to her, ma'am, she's no better than she should be, and I've known that for a fact any time these two years and more.'

Nell became impatient. 'I am not concerned with her morals!'

The housekeeper clicked her tongue. 'Yes, but you can't deny—though it's what a body can't forgive— that it's why she did it for him.'

'Is it?'

Mrs Whyte stared. 'Why else?'

'I only wish I knew.'

Nell fidgeted absently with the spoon in the sugar bowl, sifting the grains in an aimless fashion. The housekeeper reached out and stayed her hand.

'You've an idea though, haven't you, my dear?'

'I thought I had.' Releasing the spoon, Nell picked up her cup and swallowed another mouthful of the soothing beverage. 'I was convinced it had to do with the Jarrow Emeralds.'

Mrs Whyte stared. 'But they were stolen by Lord Nobody.'

'Yes, so I understand. Besides, Lord Jarrow tells me they were nothing but paste.'

It was evident that this was not news to the house-keeper. 'I suspicioned as much. Didn't seem to me as the master would let her flaunt them all round the castle the way she did if they'd been real. Used to wear them all day and half the night, and his lordship said never a word against it.'

A faint tattoo built up in Nell's veins, and she caught at a random thought at the back of her mind that refused to settle. Was there a clue to be found here?

'Then that is how Hetty came to see them,' she said slowly. 'She told me that her mama showed them to her, and I took it that it had been only the once.' Like a lurking cobweb, the thought flittered into sight. 'Or did she mean that Lady Jarrow showed her where they were hidden?'

The housekeeper's eyes popped. 'Lordy, Miss Faraday! Are they wishful for young Hetty to find them?'

Nell frowned, for the thought had fluttered out of reach again. 'It's what I had thought. Only it does not make sense. Only consider, Mrs Whyte. Mr Beresford is perfectly aware that the jewels were stolen by Lord Nobody, in which case he either knows they are gone for ever or—'

'Or he's already got ahold of them!' said the housekeeper grimly.

'Pray hush, Mrs Whyte!'

'One of us had to say it,' pursued the other stubbornly.

'Yes, but—'

'But nothing! We both know as he's the one as done it.'

'But we don't know if it was deliberate. It might have been an accident.'

The housekeeper looked sceptical, but Nell was thankful that she chose to drop the subject. 'Well, and you were saying?'

Nell let out a laugh. 'I have forgotten my train of thought.' Then it came back again. 'Yes, I have it. I was going to say that the second possibility is that Mr Beresford, like his lordship, must know the necklace is worthless. In which case, I cannot account for his using Hetty to find it. Unless it is some other jewel altogether. Or perhaps he does not know that the emeralds were copies.'

Mrs Whyte nodded vigorously. 'He knows all right. If the mistress sold 'em, as I suppose, who do you think did it for her? She can't have arranged it herself. Setting aside she wouldn't have the nohow, she'd not the wit to do it with discretion.'

'There you are, then,' declared Nell tiredly. 'We are left with an insoluble enigma.'

The housekeeper lifted the pot and poured more tea into Nell's cup. Picking it up, she put it into Nell's hands. There was silence for a space, and Nell sipped at the tea. It was lukewarm, but it had the desired effect. Her pulse began to settle. Yet the niggling idea that would not form still troubled her.

'Will you tell his lordship?'

She met Mrs Whyte's penetrating gaze, and sighed deeply. 'I did. He will not take it seriously. He has his mind on—other matters.'

Nell felt unequal to explaining the ramifications of her relationship with Eden Jarrow, although she could not but suppose that the housekeeper had an inkling that there was something between them. She had hinted as much before this.

'Well, he's a deal to think of.' Mrs Whyte sipped at her tea. 'Still, there's one thing I can do.'

'And what is that, pray?'

'Why, stop sending milk up for the mite. And if Joyce comes in my kitchen demanding it, I'll tell her to her face that it's the master's orders.'

Nell had to smile. 'She would not believe you. I am afraid I have given myself away, and she will guess at once that it is my work.'

'Let her. Nothing she can do, even if she does think it.'

But Mrs Whyte was mistaken, as Nell discovered early upon the following morning. She was in the schoolroom preparing when the outer door crashed open and Lord Jarrow strode in, white-lipped with fury.

Chapter Ten

Through his black rage, Jarrow saw her only as a symbol of base betrayal. Baffled hurt consumed him. All their dealings would not have made him suppose her capable of an act so detrimental to the mental health of his only child. He could barely get the words out.

'How could you? How *could* you do this?'

How dared she stare at him with those innocent green eyes? As if she was not well aware of her guilt! Would she now lie, to add fuel to the flames that already wreathed his brain?

'Of what do you accuse me, sir?'

Jarrow was obliged to muster all his self-control. He could hear the harshness of his breath, the rough tone of his own voice as he tried to speak without blasting her where she stood.

'After all that has been said between us, to tell Henrietta the truth!'

'What truth? I don't understand you.'

Almost he was persuaded by the innocence of her tone. But it would not do. 'Pray don't be guileless,

Miss Faraday, it does not suit you!' He flung away, wrenching himself from the sight of her.

Nell stared at his back. What new turn was this? What was she supposed to have done to enrage him so disastrously? Alarm bells began to ring in her head. If Mrs Whyte had carried out her determination about the milk—

Eden had turned again, a look in his eyes of brooding contempt. Nell's heart plummeted and her mind froze with distress.

'Well?'

The harsh monosyllable jerked her into retaliation. 'Well what, sir?'

'Are you going to explain yourself?'

Nell stiffened involuntarily, hurt pride coming to her rescue. 'Not until you explain my crime, my lord Jarrow.'

The word struck him to silence. Yet it was a crime. Perhaps she did not see it as such. His anger dulled, leaving him prey to the old cynicism.

'I suppose you will tell me that you meant it for the best. No doubt you had your reasons. You always do! Will you try to make me believe that you thought it could resolve this ghost business?'

Not much to his surprise, Nell lifted her chin. Defiant to the last! He might have expected it.

'In this mood, sir, I will not attempt to make you believe anything!'

'As well! I would not have thought it of you, Nell. No, nor believed it, had I not heard it from Hetty's own lips.'

Bewilderment slew Nell's defiance. 'Hetty spoke to you?'

'Naturally I went to her the moment Duggan said it. I had little expectation of finding it to be the truth, the more fool I.'

Nell heard it with scant thought of her own alleged involvement. What had they done to Hetty? It must be in retaliation. Heavens, she might have guessed it! Why had she allowed Mrs Whyte to act? But it was too late now for regret. Wholly forgetting Lord Jarrow's dangerous mood, she approached him with urgency.

'What was it? What did Duggan tell you?'

Jarrow's temper flared. 'As if you didn't know!' He seized her shoulders as she reached him, shaking her hard. 'You fool, Nell! Didn't I tell you myself that I had kept it from her? She is distraught! I knew how it would be the moment she learned the truth about Julietta's death. And all she could say was, "Miss Fallyday said it! Miss Fallyday said it!" over and over. And I thought I could trust you!'

He released her, almost flinging her from him. She staggered back, and he half put out a hand. She slapped it away.

'Don't touch me!'

There was no room in Nell's head now for Henrietta's pain. All that occupied her was the hideous reality that Eden Jarrow accepted this fabrication without question. It did not occur to him that the same creature that gave him the news could have poisoned the child's mind. Oh, no. With all the evidence against Joyce Duggan and his own heartless brother-in-law, he chose to take his stand against the one person who had his daughter's interests at heart. Hurt fury washed over her. Her hands were clenched upon the petticoats of her brown calico gown, and her voice shook with effort as she strove for calm.

'It is obvious, my lord, that we have nothing more to say to each other.'

Jarrow regarded her, prey to a sense of hungry frustration. In the midst of his anger, he discovered in himself a shocking desire to kiss her with all the violence at his command. He shifted back, but he could not walk away.

'You have nothing more to say? Have you no explanation, no excuses? Defend yourself, woman, for the Lord's sake!'

Her voice was ice. 'Why should I? You are judge and jury, sir, and have condemned me. I repeat, I have nothing to say.'

Jarrow wanted to seize her, and shake her until the teeth rattled in her head. Surely there must be some mitigating circumstance? She could not have meant to hurt Henrietta. A sense of desperation crept into his breast.

'You must have had a reason! Nell, *tell me*. I can forgive anything, only to know why you would do such a thing.'

He could forgive? Well, she could not. She had done everything in her power to protect his child, and this was his return. And she had been fool enough to believe he was beginning to care for her. Her heart had betrayed her, and she was desolate. She said the only thing appropriate in the circumstances.

'I believe the time is right for us to part, Lord Jarrow. I will ensure Henrietta is soothed before I go, but—'

It was the ultimate betrayal. Heat flared in Jarrow's breast and he was no longer master of his tongue. 'You will go nowhere near the child! Go directly to your chamber and pack your things, if you please. I will arrange for Detling to take you to the coach office.'

Nell heard him almost with indifference. She did not intend to obey him. She could not possibly leave the castle without ensuring that her charge was safely disabused of whatever dread tale had been told to her. She was certainly leaving—but in her own good time. He need not know it, however. She dropped a stiff curtsy.

'As your lordship pleases.'

It was the final straw. Jarrow strode furiously to the door and turned there. 'I will, of course, pay you until the quarter. Keston will give you the money. We will not meet again.'

He was gone. Nell was glad of it, for she knew she could not have contained her spleen had he remained. How dared he reduce her in that dismissive fashion? What, had he kissed a mere governess, and confided his soul to her? And she, fool that she was, had dared to dream of a bridal! She was well served for her foolishness, for Eden assuredly had no use for a female who had neither understanding nor compassion.

Compassion? Nell sat down abruptly, her anger rapidly dissipating. What had she done? That fatal Faraday pride! How the Duck would scold her—and deservedly. She would not have believed she could be so stupidly arrogant, so self-obsessed.

The reversal of feeling left her weak. Had she given her heart only to snatch it away at the first hurdle? And what of Henrietta? The poor child was suffering in shock and despair, while she—whose first concern it should have been!—indulged herself in misplaced self-righteousness.

The thought threw her into realisation. Beresford had acted swiftly! She had been neatly outgeneralled. The man must be desperate to have gone to such lengths to be rid of her. With her sanction, Mrs Whyte had clamped down on the milk, cutting off his route to give Hetty laudanum. He must know it was owing to Nell's interference. What was she to do now?

She must see Hetty, but that had become secondary. It was of the first importance now to find out what drove him. But how? From the nagging question that had persisted at the edges of her mind, the answer

came. And only one person could help her with it—
Henrietta herself.

She found the child sobbing on her bed, deaf to the
pleas of the housekeeper, who bustled up the moment
she spied Nell entering the room.

'Thank the Lord, ma'am, for I can't get a word out
of her but that Miss ''Fallyday'' said it!' Turning back
to the bed, she called over Henrietta's crying, 'Give
over, Miss Hetty, do! Here's your Miss Fallyday, she's
here. Only look, child!'

By this time, Nell had reached the other side of the
bed. Without further ado, she tugged at Hetty's shoulders, pulling her face out of the pillows. The sobs were
augmented by a protesting shriek.

'Hetty, you goose, it's me! Hush, my dear, Nell is
here. Do you hear me? It's Nell.'

She was obliged to repeat herself several times before her words penetrated the frenzied weeping. But
at length they did, for Henrietta ceased her lamenta-
tions abruptly, jerking her tear-stained face about to
look. Nell smiled encouragingly at her.

'Come, my love, tell Nell all about it.'

Upon which, Hetty uttered a squeak of joy, scrambled up and flung herself into Nell's arms, bursting
out into sobs all over again.

'Duggy told me you said it! Duggy said you
goned away!'

Over her head Nell exchanged a glance with the
startled Mrs Whyte. Question was in the house-

keeper's face. Nell gave her a rueful look, expressive of the current state of affairs. Mrs Whyte set her arms akimbo, looking extremely pugnacious. Nell thanked heaven she had at least one champion.

She was relieved to find that Hetty had no blame for her. Indeed, it was clear from the first outpourings that the child was more distressed by the intelligence that her governess was going away than by anything other.

Guilt swamped Nell all over again. She had been preparing to desert the child, all on account of her own pride! With a secret riffle of dismay, she heard herself promising that she would not leave Hetty. A mountain loomed before her, if she was to make good the vow. But for the present, there was a more urgent matter demanding her attention.

'Hetty, what is it that Duggy told you about me? What was it that I said?'

'Did you said it, Miss Fallyday?' The child's black eyes were bleak all at once.

'I am sure I did not, but I don't know until you tell me what it is,' Nell pointed out.

She glanced at the puzzled features of the house-keeper and put a finger lightly to her own lips to engage her silence. Mrs Whyte nodded and turned her attention to the little girl. Henrietta's pretty features were crumpling.

'Duggy told me you said Mama killeded with a gun. That's why she comed back. Mama cross 'acos Papa killeded her.'

A sharp gasp from the housekeeper brought the child's head round. She pointed a chubby finger. 'Whytey knowed it! See, Miss Fallyday.'

'I did not, indeed!' protested Mrs Whyte strongly. 'The idea!'

'Pray hush!' begged Nell. She took the child's hand and held it tight. It would not serve to lie now. The child was far too intelligent. If it had been needed, here was proof that she was wholly in her wits.

'My love, it is true that your mama was killed with a gun, but it was an accident. Your papa did not do it. On the contrary, he tried to save her. And I am afraid Duggy lied to you. I did not say it.'

The child frowned. 'Then why Mama cross? Why she comed back?'

Nell slipped one arm about the child's shoulders and hugged her. 'My darling, your mama did not come back. She is peaceful in heaven now. I'm afraid someone has been tricking you.'

In a small voice, Hetty responded. 'Duggy?'

Nell nodded. 'And one other. I promise I will tell you all about it later. But you see, my love, I need your help. We must find a way to show your papa that Duggy is bad. Do you agree?'

Hetty needed no urging. 'Duggy *is* bad. She said you done bad things and Papa don't like you no more. She said he throwed you out.'

'I'll give her bad things!' threatened the housekeeper *sotto voce*.

Nell frowned her down. 'Your papa was very cross, because he thought I told you about your mama. But when he sees that he has it wrong, he will change his mind.'

Hetty eyed her doubtfully. 'Will he like you again?'

'He does not dislike me now, child. You have been cross with me too, remember. But I believe you have not stopped liking me, all the same.'

It was plain that this view of the matter had weight, for the child began to look more cheerful. 'Yes, and you cross with me, Miss Fallyday. But you like me?'

'I like you very much indeed,' averred Nell, hugging the little girl tightly.

'I like you, 'acos you like a princess.'

Spying a telltale gleam in the housekeeper's eye, Nell was obliged to smile. 'That is praise of no common order I will have you know, Mrs Whyte. Princesses are the be-all and end-all with Hetty.'

She received a grim look in response. 'Aye, and has this one reckoned on her next move? For I don't doubt as there are those as think they've bested her.'

Recalling the urgency of her need, Nell detached herself from Henrietta and rose from the bed. She spoke with determination. 'They will find they are mistaken.'

'What do you mean to do?'

'That must depend upon whether Hetty can help us.'

The little girl immediately jumped up from the bed and came to her side, slipping one hand into Nell's. 'I help you. What you do, Miss Fallyday?'

Nell hesitated. Whatever she did, it must be done quickly. She heard footsteps coming down the hall. Duggan? It was evident that both Mrs Whyte and Hetty had heard them too. It was the housekeeper who acted. She hustled them towards the head of the bed.

'Quick, get behind the curtains there. I'll get rid of the wench.'

Without thought, Nell slipped to the back of the four-poster and slid behind it with Henrietta, giving the child's clutching hand a reassuring squeeze. They were just in time, for someone entered seconds later.

'Mrs Whyte! What are you doing here?'

'Checking on your work, my girl,' came from the housekeeper in an authoritative tone. 'When was the last time you swept under the bed?'

The nurse broke into instant protest, asserting that Mrs Whyte had no right to interfere in her domain, to which a heated reply gave the woman to understand that the housekeeper considered no area of the house to be outside her jurisdiction when it came to cleanliness. The argument raged for several moments, but Nell gave it scant attention. It had occurred to her that there was adequate room behind this bed for a man to conceal himself.

How often had Mr Beresford stood here of a night, having terrified the bed's occupant into hysterics? Perhaps even while Eden Jarrow sat reading her a story, unknowing that his brother-in-law, masked and bewigged in a nightgown belonging no doubt to his late wife, stood listening in the shadows. The thought brought her out in goose bumps.

Or had he waited here, after the little girl had swallowed the evil potion he had ordered, and called to her in a semblance of her mother's voice? Called to her to come. *Come, my love. Come and find Mama's treasure.*

Nell's blood froze. It was true. Hetty had not dreamed it. Only she was either sleepwalking or half asleep, drugged with laudanum. She would be in no case either to recognise the fraud or to fight it. Up she would get, wandering in the night, following the voice and the beckoning finger, searching, searching—in the hopes that she would finally remember. And to crown it all, today he had burdened her with a horrible lie about her father, alongside a truth.

She became aware of violent movement behind the curtain, and the shrieking protest of Duggan.

'What are you doing?'

'I'm taking these disgusting sheets off the bed!' responded the housekeeper in a suitably irate voice. 'You'll take them right this minute, and get yourself down to the laundry, do you hear me?'

'I won't do any such! Put them sheets back again, I say!'

'You'll do as I tell you, or Miss Faraday won't be the only one to be walking out the door of this castle today!'

There was a silence. Nell held her breath, looking swiftly down to the child. Henrietta's black eyes were trained up at her governess, ablaze with unholy glee. Nell could not in all conscience blame her. She put a finger to her mouth and received a conspiratorial grin from her charge. It was plain that there was little amiss with Henrietta's mind!

Hasty footsteps were followed immediately by the slamming of a door. Seconds later, Mrs Whyte's face peered round the edge of the bed curtains.

'She's gone.'

Nell gave way to weak laughter as she pushed Hetty out of their hiding place and followed her back into the room. 'What a tartar you are, Mrs Whyte!'

The housekeeper looked gratified. 'If I've put her off the scent, that'll do us for the moment. But you'd best remove from here before she ups and smells a rat.'

'I see she didn't take the sheets,' Nell said drily, finding the bedclothes awry and the sheets thrown all anyhow into the middle of the floor. Hetty was gazing at them in bewilderment.

But Mrs Whyte was already at the door. Cautiously she opened it, peering up and down the corridor. She beckoned. 'All clear. What do you mean to do?'

'I will take Hetty to the parlour. No one will think to look for us there, and there is something I want to show her.'

'I'd best get back. We don't want Keston wondering where I've got to. You'll find me in the kitchens if you need me.'

Holding Henrietta firmly by the hand, Nell followed the housekeeper to the main staircase, where they parted company. She slipped into the parlour, and looked worriedly down at her charge. But it was plain that Hetty had done a volte-face. From black despair, she had shot into alt, riding high on all the excitement. Her plump cheeks were flushed and her black eyes fairly sparkling.

Thanking heaven for her established influence that had made Hetty take her at her word, Nell ushered her to the portrait above the mantel. She pointed to the necklace, abandoning all attempt to tread warily. Only bluntness would serve her now.

'Is this the treasure, Hetty?'

Henrietta stared up at the picture, a deep frown forming between her brows. 'Not the treasure. Is a picture.'

'Yes, but is it a picture of the treasure? Does it look like your mama's treasure?'

The child nodded solemnly. Nell's pulses leaped into life. She had been right! The necklace was indeed their goal. Excitement rose in her to match the child's. It had to be the original! Why else would they have put Hetty through all that determined searching? It made no sense at all otherwise.

Beresford must know that they were the true emeralds, for Mrs Whyte had assured her that he would

have been the one to sell the jewels. Had he and
Julietta set out to deceive Eden into believing the real
emeralds were lost in order to put him off the scent?
Or was it Julietta who had, in the madness that possessed her, attempted to conceal them?

A horrid thought sent a shiver down Nell's spine.
What a motive for murder! If Julietta had hidden the
jewels, not from her husband, but from her brother—
then everything fell into place. It not only solved this
mystery, but also the dilemma that was torturing Eden.
Her breath caught. It had become imperative to find
the necklace.

Could she push Hetty through the next stage? In her
drugged mind, she had sought for the thing without
result. And suffered agonies of frustration. Could she
remember it now, without the spectre of her dead
mother pursuing her?

Nell sought in her mind for some method that might
help the girl to break through the waywardness of her
memory. Make a game of it? But how?

She glanced down and found Henrietta watching
her gravely. Was there a hint of apprehension in the
dark eyes? She *could* not put her through any more
hell! Besides, she decided ruefully, if she tried to push
her, there was no doubt Hetty would create a song and
dance. A song and dance?

Inspiration hit and she seized the child's hands.
'Let's sing a song, Hetty.'

The child frowned. 'Don't know any song.'

'It does not matter. We are going to make one up. We'll sing a song about the treasure. Listen!' She caught at the first rhythmic tune she could find, and swiftly put simple words to it.

'The treasure is in the parlour, the treasure is in the parlour.
Hey-ho, fiddle-de-dee, the treasure's in the parlour.'

'See, Hetty? We can put the treasure anywhere we like. Come on, sing with me.' She repeated the song, beginning to move in a circular motion, stepping in time with the song. It took several attempts, and Nell had to caper with energy and sing as brightly as she dared without becoming loud enough to be heard all over the castle. But at last Hetty became caught up in the song.

Once she had the child participating, Nell put the treasure somewhere else. *'The treasure is in the schoolroom.'* Then it went to the kitchen. It travelled through a series of rooms, and then Nell put it in the window, the desk and the candlestick. Henrietta began to introduce her own inventions, which was exactly what Nell wanted.

Almost Nell lost sight of the object, for the game became so much fun to Hetty that it warmed her to see the child lost in enjoyment at last. The dancing slowed, and the song became a competition, each throwing out a single place for the treasure in turn, using just the one line. They finished up sitting on the carpeted floor, the treasure veering wildly to the most unlikely places.

'Treasure's in the water jug,' challenged Henrietta.

'The treasure's in the chamber pot,' countered Nell, making Hetty roll about with mirth. When she had recovered, she thought for some time before her eyes lit with triumph.

'Treasure's in the pudding!'

'Yum, yum,' said Nell. 'The treasure's in the cake.'

'In the pudding!'

'No, you can't have pudding again. Think of something else.'

'Treasure's in the…in the beef!'

'Oh, very good. Hmm, now let's see. The treasure is in the bone.'

Hetty brightened at the new trend. 'Treasure's in the leg.'

'Oh, dear, what else? I know, the treasure is in the foot.'

'In the toe.'

'In the arm, then.'

'In the hand.'

'How about in the finger?'

Henrietta gave a sudden gasp, and her black eyes widened. Nell's heart skipped a beat. She dared not speak. The child's gaze left hers and settled upon her own hands. She cupped her fingers as if in prayer. And then her deep voice came, shocked almost into a whisper.

'In the hands. I 'member! Treasure's *in the hands*.'

'Oh, well done, Hetty!'

The child beamed, the dark eyes shining. 'In the hands. I 'member. Mama showed me. Treasure's in the hands.'

Nell's heartbeat quickened, but she held her excitement back. She must not frighten the child, nor force the memory. But, *what hands*? She schooled her countenance to normality, catching at the little girl's own hands.

'That's wonderful, Hetty! You do remember. Now, let's see if we can find out where the hands are.'

The child's brow suddenly lowered. 'I know where.'

'How stupid of me,' said Nell quickly. 'Will you tell me then?'

'On the lady,' said Hetty scornfully.

'Oh, I *see*,' said Nell, just as if she did. She adopted a musing tone. 'Now I wonder which lady she is.'

The frown intensified. 'Don't 'member.'

Nell curbed a natural impatience. She tried another tack. 'Does the lady have a name?'

'Course she does. Like yours.'

'You mean she is called Nell?'

'N-ooo.'

'Helen?'

The child shifted her shoulders. It was plain that this point eluded her. But they had made progress. She gathered the little girl into a close embrace.

'Aren't you the clever one?'

The child returned her hug with enthusiasm, and Nell's heart warmed. Even as she crooned, however, her mind was racing. Where did they go from here? Should she approach Lord Jarrow with this? A stab at her heart reminded her of his last words. No, she could not go to him. Not yet. He was likely seething in his turret study. Unless he had truly arranged for her departure? If so, someone must have been searching for her. Well, she was not yet ready to be found.

And Duggan, no doubt, would be looking for Hetty. Then let her look! Nell would take the child with her, and seek refuge with the housekeeper until his lordship's temper should have had time to cool.

Mrs Whyte was found to be fidgeting in the kitchens, unable to settle to her work. It was evident that she had begun upon her preparations for dinner, for a collection of vegetables had been randomly thrown on the large table, ready for chopping, and to one side was a basin of flour and a hunk of butter on a platter. The housekeeper waved a vague hand.

'I thought to make a pastry for a pie, but I can't think what I need. My brain seems to have frozen.'

Nell had no time to waste on frivolities. 'Never mind that. Hetty has recalled where the treasure is hidden.'

The housekeeper stared at the child. 'Treasure? Mercy me, I didn't know there was any such!'

'Is Mama's treasure,' piped up Henrietta.

A wildly enquiring eye found Nell's, and she nodded. 'Yes, it is the one Hetty's mama wears in the portrait.'

Mrs Whyte sat down plump upon a kitchen chair, closing her lips with obvious difficulty upon exclamations that she could not make before the child. Nell bent a meaningful eye upon her, with the object of making her understand more than the words that came out of her mouth.

'I think this may be *real* treasure, Mrs Whyte, and so it is most important that we help Hetty to find it.'

The housekeeper gasped outright, clasping a hand to her plump bosom. 'Lordy! Do you say so, indeed?'

'Mama showed me,' announced Hetty proudly.

'She did?' asked Mrs Whyte. 'When?'

'When she not dead. She comed in the night and she show me. Down the stairs.'

Alert, Nell seized on this new information. 'Which stairs, my love?'

'Round ones.'

'She means one of the towers, I expect.' The housekeeper had gone a trifle pale. 'Do you say she's been trying to go down those horrid winding stairs in the middle of the night?'

Nell quickly brushed past this, not wishing the child to recall the circumstances of her fruitless drugged searches. 'It does not matter now, Mrs Whyte. Only think, if you please. Hetty says the treasure is in the hands and on the lady.'

'In the hands and on the lady?' echoed the house-keeper blankly.

'Just so,' agreed Nell with a swift little smile. 'But Hetty cannot quite recall the lady's name. She thinks it is like mine—on the order of Nell or Helen.'

For a moment Mrs Whyte sat in puzzled silence. And then her eyes popped. 'Eleanor!'

Henrietta jumped excitedly. 'Nellenor! Nellenor hands.'

'Is there an Eleanor?'

Mrs Whyte rose from her chair. 'Was, my dear. One of the Jarrow ancestors. I know there's supposed to be a statue of her lying on one of the tombs in the crypt.'

'Crip!' cried Hetty. 'Nellenor got the treasure. She's in the crip!'

Nell's heart skipped a beat. The mystery was un-ravelling. If what she suspected proved true, Mr Beresford had a good deal of explaining to do. She dared not begin to contemplate how Lord Jarrow would take it. Soft, she counselled herself. It might still be that Henrietta was mistaken. She did what she might to control the rise of mingled apprehension and excitement in the flurry in her veins.

'Where is this crypt?'

'Why, below stairs, ma'am,' said Mrs Whyte, and shivered. 'Horrid place it is! Damp and gloomy—full as it can hold of rats, I should think. It's under the stables and the laundry on the far side.'

'How does one reach it?'

'Usual way is to go through the courtyard to the laundry—'

Nell cut her short. 'That's no use. We must not be seen.'

Mrs Whyte grabbed her arm. 'You ain't thinking of going down there?'

'I don't see that I have a choice.'

'I come, Miss Fallyday?'

Nell took the child's hand. 'Of course, Hetty. I need you to show me where to find Eleanor's hands.'

But the housekeeper set her arms akimbo. 'I won't let you go, either of you! It's a nasty, smelly hole and no light to speak of.'

'Then we shall take a candle.' Nell laid a hand on the older woman's shoulder. 'Mrs Whyte, you must recognize that I have gone too far to back out now. Come, tell me how to get there without being seen.'

Mrs Whyte shook her head. 'I'd best come with you. It ain't safe down there.'

Nell rejected this with firmness. 'It will be thought odd if we are all found to be absent. You must stay here and pretend ignorance if anyone asks after Hetty or myself.'

The housekeeper grumbled her dissatisfaction as she hunted for candles in one of the capacious kitchen cupboards. She stuck one into a pewter stick and took a taper from the range to light it.

'And what, pray, am I to tell the master if he comes looking for you here?'

A twinge caught at Nell's breast. Almost she was tempted to go in search of Lord Jarrow and tell him what had been discovered. Yet if she were to meet either Duggan or Toly Beresford, she would be undone. And if she were truthful, a trifle of resentment yet lingered. No, she had best be sure of her ground before she tackled his lordship! She took up the candlestick and a firm grip of Henrietta's hand, and confronted the housekeeper.

'You have not seen me, Mrs Whyte. That is all you need say, no matter who asks. And to say truth, I have scant expectation that Lord Jarrow will trouble his head about me today.'

The confined space of the study was too small to contain him, prey as he was to conflicting emotions. Instead Jarrow paced the roof walkway, haunted by intrusive images of Nell Faraday.

His imagination placed her everywhere. Standing at the battlements with the light making a halo of her golden head about the strong features. Dangerously leaning into the broken tower in a way that had sent his heart into his mouth—he had suffered visions of her falling helpless, to be lost in the blackness at the bottom of the central well. And walking, walking, head bent, as she paced the roof just as he was doing now, when he had watched her unseen, wondering over and over with apprehension in his breast if she would decide to go.

Now he knew that the thought of her leaving had dictated much of his conduct towards her. All the while fearful of her departure, he had done his best to hasten it! Because, deep down, he had known he was becoming involved—and he had felt it with loathing. Had he not sworn that he would never again succumb to the wiles of a woman? Fate had cast him for a hapless fool, blinded by desire to the detriment of his interests and the ruin of his life. And had he learned of this? The devil he had! Within a few short months of an unlooked-for release, he was once more entwining himself in feminine coils with the first pretty female to come within striking distance—and his daughter's governess to boot!

Well, it was over. He had let his guard down, and received his deserts. He would ensure that the next creature would be impossibly outside the realms of his romantic fancy. Forty-five at least, and of as unattractive an appearance as he could contrive. There would be no more Nell Faradays!

Something stabbed in his chest and he caught at the battlemented wall, staring out across the green forest below. He must be rid of her! Was she yet gone? If his orders had been attended to, Detling would have the cob harnessed to the gig, and she must by now have packed up, ready for departure. His breath caught in his throat, and he was obliged to grip the grey stonework until his knuckles whitened.

Hell and the devil, but he had to let her go! He could not again endure that agonising betrayal of trust.

If she could do a thing so thoughtless towards his child, she could as readily injure him in other ways. He wanted to believe that. Why should he not? Despite that all her attention had been on discovering dangers that she supposed were threatening Henrietta, she had herself done more to destroy the child's mental state than anyone. However innocently done, it was the height of stupidity. And Nell was not stupid!

The thought, blinding in its simplicity, hit him squarely in the solar plexus, stopping his breath. For several instants, he could not even formulate the conclusion. But he knew it as surely as if he had. Nell was neither stupid, nor guilty.

The reversal of feeling swept him with remorse as all consuming as had been his anger. He had done her the grossest injustice. Whoever had told Hetty the truth, it could never have been Nell. In an excess of emotion, Jarrow immediately decided that he had known it all along. He had known it, used it, because he wanted to get Miss Helen Faraday out of his life. *He did not want to love her.*

From the instant of realisation, Jarrow acted purely on impulse. He sped across the roof walkway, shot through the schoolroom and threw himself down the winding stairs two steps at a time. He was outside Nell's door and hammering before thought even began to enter his mind.

No answer. His control in tatters, Jarrow turned the handle and thrust the door open. He stood in the empty room, staring about him, unable to take in the implication of what his eyes were telling him. There was a curious silence in the chamber that echoed in his head as thunder. Nothing had changed. The bed was neatly made, a candle set ready upon the bedside cabinet along with a leather-bound book. Jarrow snatched it up.

It fell open upon a page covered in writing. A feminine hand without doubt, its curlicues and flourishes indicative of an artistic or passionate nature. Was it Nell's hand? He read a line or two, and found it to be notes of instruction upon her role.

Jarrow stared at it stupidly, aware of a thumping in his chest. Dispassionately, had he been asked, he would have expected to see neatness and control in Nell's handwriting. But what he was looking at became immediately right in the woman he had come to know. This was Nell indeed—boldly individual, with a strength that must fell all vestige of opposition, and a depth of heart that he had only begun to probe. And she had not left him!

He cast a swift glance round, finding her dressing robe on a hook at the back of the door, and upon the dressing table, a wood-handled set of brush, comb and mirror. Crossing to the press, he opened the doors and tugged out drawers one by one, reassured by the piles of clothing within that Nell had done no packing. She was still here.

Relief swept through him, to be immediately succeeded by alarm. If she was here in the castle, then where was she?

For the first time it occurred to him to think rationally about what had happened. Duggan had accused Nell, saying that the child was in tears. Miss Faraday had claimed the nurse had revealed the truth about her mother's death. Shock had sent him flying to Hetty's chamber, although even then his mind had refused it. But when, at sight of him, his daughter had thrown herself anew into her pillows, screaming her own accusation, he had not stopped to consider possibilities.

What a blind fool he was! Had not Nell herself given him ample reason to distrust the nurse? She had tried to warn him, and he had paid no heed. There was the matter of laudanum for one thing. Had the woman been deliberately drugging the child?

His gorge rose. Whatever Duggan was doing, he knew well whom he had to thank. Whatever the nurse did must be at the instigation of his brother-in-law, whose bed she had been warming since nobody knew when.

Concentrated as he had been on his conviction that Toly had been responsible for Julietta's death, he had ignored the nearer danger. Why he should target Hetty was a matter passing Jarrow's comprehension, which must be why he had paid no heed to the warning signals. Did Toly wish him to think his daughter had inherited her mother's insanity? If so, it must be some product of his warped mind. The same that had driven him to destroy his own sister! A matter that Jarrow had tried in vain to set aside, knowing that the truth could only land him in a resounding scandal and bring Toly to the hangman's noose.

Had he shrunk from that only to leave his daughter prey to the tortures that could be inflicted by a mind devoid of true humanity? For Toly was undoubtedly subject to snatches of insanity including such vagaries as capering about in ghostly garments, or fooling Nell with his playing of the clavichord. Only Jarrow had refused to recognise that the man could be truly dangerous, only because he must then accept the truth he had not wanted to believe.

And with that realisation, he had left Nell, too, endangered. It was plain enough now that Toly wanted her gone. The implication of this morning's fracas became sinister. His heart lurched. Nell was not gone, after all. Toly had failed. It became a matter of supreme importance to discover the present whereabouts of his brother-in-law.

Yet, as he left the bedchamber, instinct sent him searching after Nell. He tore down the corridor towards the back of the castle, meaning to try the parlour and then the kitchens, for it was common knowledge that his housekeeper had befriended the governess. Making the turn, he failed to see his butler approaching the head of the stairs, and almost cannoned into the man as he made for the parlour door.

'Hell and the devil, Keston, what are you doing?'

The fellow was breathing hard, evidently unable for the moment to answer, and Jarrow looked at him with astonishment.

'What the devil is the matter, man?'

Keston was holding to the knob at the edge of the balustrade. He struggled to express himself over the heaving at his chest. 'I was—coming—to find you, m'lord.'

Dread caught at Jarrow's heart, sending his pulse into high gear. He seized the butler's arm. 'Tell me!'

'Mrs Whyte, m'lord,' gasped Keston. 'Found her—on the floor in the kitchen.'

'What, has she fainted?'

'Knocked on the head seemingly.'

Jarrow released him, his brain afire. 'Is she still unconscious?'

The butler shook his head, speaking more easily now. 'Gave her some brandy, m'lord, and left Grig to mind her. She sent me to fetch you straight, m'lord. Said I were to tell you it concerns Miss Faraday.'

The way had been distinctly unpleasant, taking them down through dank cellars below the kitchens and into a dark and freezing corridor that followed the castle interior. Nell suspected the hem of her gown was gathering both wetness and dirt, but she cared nothing for that. She had kept tight hold of Henrietta's hand as she crept around the base of a tower and along a dreadful collection of broken-down cells that could only have been dungeons in former times. Skirting the second tower, she had frightened them both with the opening of a heavy wooden door that creaked ominously.

As she moved through, the air struck damp and chill, and a heavy aroma of must and decay enveloped them. Henrietta, who had been dumbly obedient until this moment, was moved to a squeal of protest.

'Hush!'

'Is the crip,' replied Hetty in a whisper. 'It stink. I 'member.'

'You remember this smell? Then we are in the right place.'

Nell held the candle aloft, spreading light across a series of boxlike tombs of heavy stone. To her dismay, nearly all had a long statue lying across the top. Despair gripped her.

'Where in the world are we to find Eleanor?'

She glanced down at the child by her side, and found Henrietta's eyes gazing apprehensively up at her. Evidently she had no memory of the location of the particular tomb they sought. Nell released her hand and gave her shoulders a quick hug.

'Never fear, my love. We will find her.'

Moving forward, Nell was startled by a sudden slithering in the darkness at her feet. She could not withstand a gasp of fright, and pulled back sharply.

'Is a rat, I 'spec,' opined Hetty in a matter-of-fact tone.

'I dare say, but I had rather not know.'

'I 'spec there's spiders too, and cockaroshes. We prob'ly tread on them.'

'Thank you for that nice thought,' said Nell drily. 'However, whether there are cockroaches, spiders or rats—or even all three—we will not regard them, for we must look for Eleanor. Do you agree?'

Hetty nodded. 'I'se not afraid.'

Nell refrained from telling the child that she was! 'Excellent. Then let us go forward.'

Squaring her shoulders, Nell took hold of Hetty's hand again and moved to the first tomb to one side. She held the candle to its edge and read the inscription. She had done this two or three times before the little girl reminded her that they were looking for the hands.

'How silly, of course we are.'

Thereafter, she held the candle high to check at each tomb whether its stone hands were positioned in such a way that they might conceivably form a secret compartment. Several sets of fingers were discovered folded in prayer, but no pair Nell examined gave sign of any hiding place. She began to wonder if she had allowed her imagination to be carried away. Only Hetty had been so positive.

Mrs Whyte had intimated that the crypt ran the full length of one side of the castle, and it began to seem endless as she and the child shifted from one tomb to another, Nell desperately trying to ignore the giveaway patters and slithers that indicated the presence of crawling things she would prefer not to identify. The atmosphere was oppressive, and the darkness closed in all around them as the spill from the single candle travelled slowly along the tombs of mouldering stone, cracked with age.

All at once Henrietta uttered a cry. Nell turned quickly to her, half expecting to find that some creature had run across her foot or made its presence felt in some other horrible way. But she found the little girl already moving, into the far spill of the candlelight.

'Take care!'

She followed quickly, and came up behind the child to find that she had halted before a tomb carrying the long figure of a woman in medieval garb, her head covered in the traditional wimple held on by a coronet. Cupped hands rested at her breast.

Nell searched along the tomb's edge for the inscription, and her heart leaped when she found it. '*Eleanor Jarrow*. This is it, Hetty!'

Henrietta ran to the head of the tomb and tried to jump up. 'The hands! Nellenor hands! Look this side, Nell.'

In the midst of her own excitement, Nell took in that the child had used her given name and her heart warmed. She saw that Hetty had managed to pull herself up and was climbing on to Eleanor's head. She moved forward.

'Wait, Hetty! Show me first.'

She looked where the little girl pointed, and sure enough, just above the two thumbs in an arc made by the fingers was a small opening. Nell caught her breath. The thought flittered through her mind that Kitty ought to be here for this. She would have been in her element.

When Henrietta would have poked a finger in the hole, she seized it to stop her. 'There may be some insect nesting in there.' Holding the candle close, Nell tried to peer into the interior of the hands. She thought something winked in the light, and the blood abruptly drummed in her head. But her common sense did not desert her.

'I must find something to poke into the hole,' she muttered, and lifting the candle thrust it this way and that.

A shadow crossed her vision, and she paused, looking intently into the darkness. Henrietta exhorted her to hurry, and she dismissed it. She had probably caused the shadow herself with the movement. Bending a little, she searched the floor and located a sliver of stone that might be of use.

Her caution proved justified, for the instant she poked the end of her implement into the hole, some sort of beetle ran out. Both she and Hetty started back as the thing paused in the glare of her candle. Then it turned about and sped off down a stone fold of Eleanor's age-old gown, disappearing out of the light at the end of the tomb.

Nell let her breath go, and again applied her implement to the hole. No further emanations occurred, but there was undoubtedly some obstruction within that shifted with a soft clink as she poked.

'There is something there, Hetty,' she uttered, unable to keep the excitement from her voice.

'Get it! Get it quick,' squeaked Hetty, her voice loud in the cloistering silence that surrounded them.

A riffle of alarm swept through Nell, but she shook it off. The prize was too close! She inserted her finger into the hole and felt about. There was indeed something inside, cold to the touch, and moveable. Try as she would, Nell could not hook anything with her finger to fish it out. She gave it up in despair.

'You try, Hetty. Your fingers are smaller than mine.'

Henrietta was sitting on Eleanor's face, and she had only to lean forward to the opening. Nell blenched as her entire hand slid inside. The child gasped, and with a little difficulty tugged her hand out. Clutching in her fingers, a mess of green and gold came sliding from the hole, rippling in the light of Nell's candle.

Nell caught at it, and Hetty let it go. 'Is the treasure, Nell! Mama's treasure!'

From behind them, a voice spoke, shattering the moment.

'I will take that, if you please.'

Shock rode a river of ice down Nell's back, and she whipped round. Standing just within the perimeter of the candlelight stood Toly Beresford, eyes wide and triumphant, with a pistol in his hand.

Chapter Eleven

For what felt an age, Nell could neither speak nor move. She was aware of Hetty behind her, still sitting astride the stone head of Eleanor Jarrow's statue. She cursed herself for a fool. He must have been following them. Then she had seen something shift in the shadows!

'Come on, Miss Faraday, hand it over!'

His voice was pleasant, but there was an edge to it that Nell at least recognized. He meant business, and it was plain that he was not afraid to use his pistol. Nevertheless, she could not give in so tamely. She found her voice, and was dismayed to hear in it the rasp of the fear that gripped her.

'I believe this belongs to Lord Jarrow.'

His smile was a snarl. 'Eden doesn't even know it exists. It's mine, and I mean to have it. I've not waited this long to lose it all over again.'

Nell's thirsting curiosity got the better of her. Lifting the candle higher, she caught his glance and held it. 'Again?'

He threw back his head and laughed. 'Think you're clever, don't you? Keep me talking and make good your escape with the booty, eh? I think not, Miss Faraday.'

To Nell's horror, the child here intervened. She had risen to stand upon the statue, and her voice came over Nell's shoulder, close to her ear.

'Is Mama's treasure, Uncle Toly! Mama showed me.'

'Quiet, brat! I know she showed you. The witch told me so, or I wouldn't have known. She had the cunning of the insane did your mama, my girl, and she paid for it.'

Nell's mind leapt, flying past the meaning hidden in his words. She had guessed right. The words were out of her mouth before she could stop them. 'Then she did employ you to copy it! Only she did not sell the real emeralds.'

Beresford's features became suffused with colour, and his eyes sparked. 'Of course she didn't. She was supposed to hand the thing over to me to take abroad. I knew I couldn't sell it here. But she double-crossed me, daughter of Satan that she was, and hid it.' His mouth curved cruelly and there was a blaze at his eyes. 'Anyone else would have left it lying here safe, but not my sister Julietta. Oh, no. She took to wearing it to taunt me. I told her I would have it, aye, and keep all the proceeds.' His teeth ground together. 'But she wasn't wearing it that night, blast her eyes!'

'She foiled you,' Nell found herself saying, 'and you used Hetty to try to find the necklace.'

His tone became fretful. 'Stupid girl couldn't remember, what else could I do? And you,' he added, turning on Nell, 'interfering busybody that you are. Knew I'd got to either get rid of you, or push you into investigating for yourself.'

Then he had been one step ahead of her all the morning—creeping after her, and listening at doors! Nell's flesh crawled. She glanced at the child and found her both round-eyed and perplexed. No more talk. She must act!

'I think we have heard enough,' she said flatly. Moving back, she caught Hetty up, lifting her to the ground. Toly Beresford cursed and again ordered her to give him the necklace.

'I'm not afraid to use this,' he warned her, waving the pistol in a way that alarmed Nell more than when he had merely pointed it at her. 'Wouldn't be the first time I've blown out a parcel of feminine brains.'

Nell heard it only in the periphery of her mind, for she knew she had only one card to play. She had the necklace in her right hand, the candle in her left. Lifting the jewels, she made as if to hand them over. A terrible gleam danced devils in his eyes, and he uttered a guttural noise as he reached out to take them.

In that instant, Nell dashed the candle to the ground and ducked, crying out to the child as the place was plunged in darkness.

'Run, Hetty! Hide yourself!'

The pistol exploded above Nell's head, and a grunt of rage emanated from the madman. She heard the ricocheting whine of the bullet and a scrabble as the little girl dropped out of sight. A hand caught at the back of her gown, and Nell hit out at it with her free hand, dislodging it from the material. She began to crawl away, as swiftly as she dared, and as silently as she could, clutching the necklace.

She could hear Toly Beresford blundering and cursing in the dark as she sought for the sides of the tombs and marked them to their edges, turning corners she cared not where, as long as they took her further away from the hunter. Nell knew that her hands were scraped, that her gown was ripping, for she could feel the tug as the fabric caught and hear the tears as she frantically freed herself. She had Beresford himself to thank! Instead of remaining quiet and listening for some sound of her whereabouts, the man was raging like a beast in torment, crying out his frustration.

'Witch! Wait 'til I get you! I'll blow that pretty little head off your shoulders!'

Nell stilled, crouched between the sides of two great blocks of stone. She was trembling and sore, but she had the emeralds. She knew not how she was to come out of this, and she could not but fear for the child. Common sense came to her rescue, riding in over the thumping in her chest.

Hetty had sense enough to conceal herself, and she was smaller than Nell. Beresford had no light, and he had discharged his pistol. For all she knew, he had

another, but he could not aim safely in the darkness
of the crypt, which did not prevent him stumbling
from place to place, swearing revenge.

Her fingers were quivering, but Nell managed to
unfasten the flap at the neck of her gown. Then she
stuffed the emeralds deep in the cleft between her
breasts, pushing them down into her stays. She could
feel the cold of the stones against her chemise beneath,
and they dug into her skin. But they would be safer
there than in her hand. But how to escape?

A muffled sound of shouts and footsteps came to
her ears. Outside the crypt! Someone was coming.
Had Mrs Whyte alerted the household? But how did
she know?

Silence had fallen on the place, and it was clear that
Beresford had also heard the noise. Listening intently,
Nell was sure she could make out the turning of a key.
A door scraped against stone, and a sudden access of
light was followed immediately by an oath from Toly
Beresford.

'Nell! Nell, are you in there?'

Lord Jarrow! Without thought, Nell leaped to her
feet, shouting a warning in response. 'Take care,
Eden! He has discharged one pistol, but he may have
another.'

There was the sound of speedy footsteps, and she
looked quickly across to the edge of the much larger
pool of light than had been thrown by her single candle. She could see Toly Beresford plunging in the direction of the tower door at the other end of the crypt.

'There! He is escaping!'

But Lord Jarrow was already thundering down, his footsteps loud on the old stone floor. Nell saw that it was Keston who was holding a massive candelabrum.

Her glance flew back in time to see Beresford disappear through the door, with Eden after him. There came a cacophony of oaths, thuds and grunts, and Nell ran as best she could through the tombs towards a faint light within, calling for Henrietta.

'Hetty! Hetty, where are you?'

The child materialized close by, and Nell halted. 'Oh, thank God! Are you all right, Hetty?'

'Uncle Toly fighting with Papa,' announced Hetty, ignoring the question.

This intelligence sent Nell moving to the tower door, calling out to Keston to bring the bigger light. She reached the doorway in time to see Lord Jarrow fell his brother-in-law with the butt end of the man's own pistol. Beresford slumped to the floor and lay still.

Panting, Jarrow stood looking down at the inert figure, the murderous thoughts in his head dying down with his triumph. He felt a touch upon his arm and turned to find Nell at his side. His heart jerked, and he caught her by the shoulders.

'Nell, are you hurt?'

Vaguely he took in that Keston had come up, for light flooded the chamber, showing him the wavering smile on her face as she shook her head.

'I should rather ask if you are.'

Jarrow released her and rubbed his jaw with one hand. 'He caught me a glancing blow, but that is all.'

'It sounded as if all the devils of hell were fighting in here!'

He grinned. 'I had a little help.'

Nell looked where he gestured, and discovered the beaming Grig standing in the shadows, his fists still clenched in the pose of a prizefighter. From the corridor beyond came another voice, a trifle cracked. Detling appeared, carrying a shaded lantern.

'Shall we tie 'un, master?'

'Have you brought rope? Then do so, Detling, and keep him in the stables. And take this pistol.'

It appeared that the whole household had become involved. Nell turned back to Jarrow. 'I suppose Mrs Whyte told you we had come down here, but how did you know to expect Mr Beresford?'

'My poor housekeeper had been attacked in her kitchens when she tried to prevent his following you. A foolish thing for him to do, for he should have known I must discover it. But then, my brother-in-law is not noted for his wisdom.'

An interruption came from Hetty. 'We got Mama's treasure.'

Lord Jarrow's eyes went straight to Nell, a burning question in them. 'It is true, then! The emeralds were hidden here.'

Nell nodded, but she was forestalled by Hetty, who had come up to catch at her father's hand. 'I 'memberded. Mama showed me.' She began to pull him back into the crypt. 'Treasure in Nellenor's hands.'

A tattoo had begun in Jarrow's chest. He suffered himself to be led down the crypt by his daughter, unable to take in the possibility that was burgeoning in his head. But a footfall sounded at his side and Nell was there.

'I have them, Eden. We extracted the necklace, and Mr Beresford tried to take it from me.'

He halted. 'You have it safe?'

Her nod sent the blood fleeing down his veins, but bewilderment wreathed his brain. Had Julietta not then sold the emeralds? Hetty broke into his thoughts.

'Come see, Papa!'

Jarrow stared at the hiding place, a tumult of emotion in his breast. How had Julietta found it? What compulsion drove her warped mind to steal the thing from him, only to conceal it here? Yet he was not convinced that the emeralds were real, despite the intense efforts of his brother-in-law to recover them. After all, his sanity was as much in question as Julietta's. Who knew if either would not do all they had done even though the jewels were long gone?

Impatience gnawed at him. And the necklace was the least of it.

'Come, let us leave this place.'

Mrs Whyte was found seated on the side of the round stone vat in the laundry. The heat of the room struck Nell the moment she entered, in stark contrast to the chill of the crypt they had just left. It was light in the laundry and, with the addition of the huge candelabrum borne by Keston, Nell fairly blinked at the glare. An array of white linen hung from ropes suspended between the roof beams, and several tubs gave evidence of the industry involved in keeping the clothing of the castle inmates in good order.

The housekeeper rose eagerly. 'You are safe! Thank the Lord! And what's happened to that devil, if I might make so bold?'

'He will not trouble you again, Mrs Whyte,' said Jarrow. 'Grig and Detling have him in charge. What of Duggan?'

Nell started. 'Heavens, I had forgot her!'

'Don't you fret, ma'am,' came grimly from the housekeeper. 'I went up to her room as you bade me, my lord, and found her stuffing her belongings into a portmanteau as fast as she could.'

'I trust you ensured that she could not leave?'

'Locked her in, sir.' A note of satisfaction entered her voice as she turned to Henrietta. 'She'll not get the chance to harm the mite no more. Poor little thing! I'm that glad to see you safe, Miss Hetty.'

'Uncle Toly is bad,' announced the little girl importantly. 'He brung a gun. Papa bash him with the gun, didn't you, Papa?'

Jarrow swung her up into his arms and held her close. 'I did, and I would do it again.'

Nell's eyes pricked as she watched him plant a kiss upon the child's chubby cheek. His tone gentled.

'My sweet, you are very right. Uncle Toly is bad and so is Duggy. It is Miss Faraday who is good and I want you to listen carefully to what she tells you.' He glanced at Nell as he spoke, a message in his eyes. 'Tell her the truth, Nell.'

But before Nell could say a word, Hetty spoke up. 'Nell told me already, Papa. She said Mama did be killeded with a gun, but you never done it. She said Duggy telled a lie.'

'And so she did.'

Nell caught his rueful glance and looked quickly down, unwilling to venture upon delicate ground in public.

'Duggy said you cross with Nell and she goned away. Only Nell comed and she didn't goned away. You cross with Nell, Papa?'

Jarrow kissed her again and set her down. 'No, sweetheart, I am not cross with her. I am very grateful to her.'

'So I should think!' muttered the housekeeper under her breath. 'But wait a bit, Miss Hetty. Did you find the treasure?'

'The treasure!' exclaimed the child, running to Nell. 'You got it, Nell! Where you got it?'

Nell found Eden's gaze upon her and all at once recalled how she had been obliged to open the flap at her gown. Looking down, she was relieved to find that she was not entirely exposed, and was annoyed to feel herself blushing nevertheless. With a muttered excuse, she turned her back. Then she dug her fingers deep

into her bosom, reaching into the curve between the
swell of her breasts to where she had stuffed the necklace. Aware of silence from the onlookers, she became
even more heated, for it took some effort to extract
the piece from the tightly fitting stays.

Only Hetty shifted to find out what she was doing,
and Nell prayed she would say nothing. In vain.

'Is the treasure down there?'

A stifled exclamation from the housekeeper behind
her made Nell protest aloud. 'I do wish you will be
quiet, Hetty!'

'But treasure is down there,' objected the child.

'Yes, but there is no need to tell the whole world.'

To her relief, the necklace came tumbling forth, accompanied by a shout of triumph from the little girl.
Nell turned with the jewels between her fingers.

'See, Papa. I telled you we found the treasure.'

Jarrow's fingers quivered as he reached out to take
the emeralds. He was conscious only of numbness, but
his heart jerked oddly as the jewels fell into his hand.
He spoke his thought aloud. 'They are unexpectedly
warm.'

Nell flushed, and he realised what he had said. Heat
rushed into his veins and he could no more keep his
gaze from straying to her bosom than fly to the moon.
He saw her quickly reach to pull the flap across, con-
cealing that tempting sight. Urgency engulfed him. He
dropped to his haunches and put an arm about his
daughter.

'My sweet, go with Mrs Whyte for a while. I am sure she will like to hear all about your adventure in the crypt.' He glanced significantly up at his housekeeper. 'It is quite like one of Hetty's fairy tales.'

'Is like Aladdin! I tell Whytey about the crip.'

Briskly nodding, the housekeeper stepped forward to take Henrietta's hand. 'That's right. I'm agog, child. We'll go to my kitchen and have a nice drink of—'

Nell could not help smiling as Mrs Whyte broke off, her mob cap wobbling comically. She intervened. 'Not milk, for Hetty dislikes it.'

'Don't want milk! Hate milk!'

'Then you shan't have it, my love. I am sure Mrs Whyte has some lemonade, or—'

'I know what you'd like,' interrupted the housekeeper. 'Hot chocolate.'

Hetty's eyes lit at the notion of such a treat, and she fervently approved the offer, adding a rider. 'And cake?'

'All you can eat,' said Jarrow, a hint of impatience in his tone. 'Off you go now.'

'Nell come?'

'Not yet.' With firmness. 'Nell and I have a great deal to discuss. Have we not, Miss Faraday?'

A rosy glow settled in Nell's bosom at the gleam she spied in his eye. Her heartbeat out of rhythm, she scarce knew how she responded. 'I believe there are one or two matters outstanding, my lord.'

She received a straight look that she was at a loss
to interpret. 'Then let us repair to the parlour. Keston,
I don't wish to be disturbed.'

Eden was in the parlour before her and had laid the
emeralds on the table. Insistent upon first changing her
soiled and torn gown, Nell had hurried into her bronze
calico and quickly done up her hair again before join-
ing him there. Now she stood looking down at the
jewels as he tidied the gold casing, his finger caressing
the green stones. The suspense caught in her chest.

'Is it the real one?'

'I can't tell. They are intact, which the false ones
were not. But I can't be sure.' His head turned. 'I shall
have to take it to a jeweller.'

Their eyes met, and the emeralds went out of
Jarrow's head. He caught her hand.

'Nell, can you forgive me?'

A smile wavered on her lips. 'I was as much to
blame. There is nothing to forgive.'

'Oh, but there is!'

He released her and shifted out into the room. How
to tell her? Could she possibly fathom the double-
edged sword that had driven him? His gaze returned
to her face. There was a troubled frown there and he
longed to kiss it away. But that was impossible—until
he had won the right.

'You thought me obtuse, unfeeling, when I accused
you. Indeed, I am sure you must have thought me a

fool to believe for one moment that you had thus betrayed me.'

Her voice, tentative, reached across the space between them. 'Not a fool, sir. Only obsessed.'

Jarrow looked away, shamed by her truth. 'You are right, as always. I could not think beyond the events of that night. For months they have tortured me—the truth staring me in the face. Only I did not want to face it. The consequences...'

He left it hanging in the air, and crossed restlessly to the mantel, staring at the portrait. 'She did not deserve that of him.' Jarrow did not know he had spoken aloud. Nell's clear tones startled him.

'You make no allowance for his own state of mind, my lord.'

'What mind?' he demanded savagely, turning. 'That of a fiend!'

Nell saw the bitterness re-enter his features and her heart sank. But she did not shrink. 'The mind of one who has no grasp upon reality. Don't you see it? Julietta may have been demented, but her brother is truly insane. He killed her without compunction, and only because he said she had cheated him. He did it to get the emeralds, for he told me so. But she had thwarted him.'

She saw horror in his face. Had he truly not believed it until this moment? She took an involuntary step towards him, and halted.

'Eden, no one but a madman would have taken the path he chose. Using a child! You must see that.'

'I should have seen it long since.' Low-voiced, and filled with self-blame.

Nell longed to go to him. But she was uncertain yet. Abruptly, she felt the onset of exhaustion. It had been a difficult day. She dropped into a chair by the table, rubbing absently at a graze on her hand as her eyes shifted to the necklace.

'He is an accomplished actor. And he has cunning. You were too close to him to see through him, perhaps. It was easier for me. Coming here a stranger—and untouched by these events—I could look with an open mind.'

But not for long, she might have added. The pain still visible in his drawn features tore at her heartstrings.

Jarrow looked across at her. The halo of honey-gold hair shone in the light from the window. The tug of his conscience faded. Her voice came at him like a ripple of music.

'What are you going to do with him?'

He moved without realising it, his eyes on the strong-featured face. He spoke automatically. 'I have no idea, Nell.'

The fate of his brother-in-law had somehow ceased to be important, a vague shadow in the dimness of his mind. But he entered into it none the less, feeling an odd sense of unreality, of distance.

'If we remain here, I must get rid of him—somehow. If it turns out instead that I now have the wherewithal to remove from the castle, then I don't know.'

Nell reached out absently to finger the jewels. 'I wish you would remove, for Hetty's sake.'

'Only for Hetty's sake?'

It was softly said, and Nell turned quickly to look up at him. A faint pulse beat at her, but she spoke in as normal a tone as she could. 'For your own also. To remain where your memories must torture you seems foolish to me. Especially now that you know the truth.'

'The truth, yes.' An echo of that familiar distress gnawed at him. 'I had long suspected it. For months I have known that Toly was playing at highwayman. What I did not know was whether he had begun before or after Lord Nobody fired that fatal shot. Nor could I be certain that he had indeed that identity—which is what sent me riding out after him. I hoped to catch him in the act. But the moment I began to believe it, I had to struggle with the possibility that he had shot Julietta deliberately.'

She did not speak, and he crossed to the table with sudden impatience, seizing up the necklace. 'Had I the faintest inkling that this was what he wanted—!'

'Why did you think your wife had sold the jewels?'

Jarrow felt only a trace of the bitterness that had been a part of him for so long. Strange. Where had it gone? He answered almost absently.

'Julietta told me so. When I brought her home, and she was angry enough to wish to hurt me.'

'And you believed her?'

He shifted his shoulders, a trifle discomfited. 'I had no reason not to believe it. And every reason to do so, for she showed me the paste copy and smashed one of the stones before my eyes, so that I could see it was but glass.'

'But how vindictive!' Nell caught herself up, giving him a contrite look. 'I should not have said that.' To her relief, Eden looked rather bemused than angry.

'She could not have been wearing the paste ones in the castle. It must have been these, or I should have noticed the missing jewel.'

Nell caught his meaning and her eyes met his. Her tone was hushed. 'Eden, they must indeed be the real emeralds you hold in your hand.'

She saw his fingers tighten on the gaud and they trembled a little. His voice became tight. 'I will not believe it until they are seen by an expert.'

How much it meant to him! Nell rushed headlong into speech. 'I am sure, if you are not, Eden, else why should Mr Beresford covet them and do so much evil only to recover them. He must have known the true worth of the necklace she hid from him. Only what I cannot fathom is what Julietta thought she would do with the emeralds if she did not allow her brother to sell them.'

Jarrow dropped the necklace to the table again and sat down opposite. 'You are trying to fathom the workings of a diseased mind, Nell. It likely amused her to think that the jewels were intact when I supposed them to have been lost to me.'

There was a silence. Nell found his gaze upon her and could not return it. She saw him reach out, and next moment her fingers were imprisoned within his own.

'Nell, I owe you a debt of gratitude which I can never repay.'

Heavens, let him not take that road! 'You owe me nothing, sir.'

'On the contrary, there is no way I can express—'

Goaded, she tugged her hand away. 'The last thing I wish for is your gratitude, Eden! I had rather you turned moody and snarled at me!'

She was on her feet, and he rose to match her. 'Why, Nell? You must know how much it means to me to know that Hetty's mind is untainted. Or at least as far as I can be sure at this present.'

'I believe you will find her ever to be so. She is free of that curse, I am certain.'

'Then I am more than ever in your debt. For your future care also. I know you will not desert her.'

Nell felt torn. He had tried to apologise for his mistake and she would have none of it. But now she was conscious that she still cherished a grievance. He had evidently realised his mistake, but it had made no difference in the way he regarded her. She was Henrietta's governess still, and she wanted to leave this place forever! The words felt forced from her.

'You will have to find a new nurse.'

'A new nurse, and a new governess.'

Nell stopped dead, staring at him in shock, her heart thumping in her chest. Her voice was a thread. 'You want me to go?'

He was before her, reaching towards her. Nell evaded him, but he caught her easily. 'Be still, my dear one!'

The endearment caught at her and she let out a sound somewhere between a sob and a laugh. 'Eden, don't tease me, pray!'

'I was never more in earnest,' he assured her, and captured her into his embrace. 'I don't want you for a governess, Nell. Can't you guess why?'

The next instant, Nell was deprived of all power of thought, for his mouth descended upon hers and his fierce kiss quite melted her bones.

She emerged in a state of desperate confusion, her heart fluttering like an imprisoned bird. Since she felt as if she were about to fall, she had no recourse but to cling to the arms that cradled her, but the chaos of her mind sought instant expression.

'You must not, Eden! It is not right, you know it is not.'

The brown eyes were close to hers, alight with a passion Nell felt as keenly as her own. His voice had a quality of hoarseness.

'Then we must make it right, for I can no longer tolerate your presence in my house without abandoning every precept by which I call myself a gentleman.'

Nell did not pretend to misunderstand him, but it was not the declaration for which she had secretly yearned. She tried to pull away. 'Then I have no choice but to leave.'

Jarrow abruptly released her, prey to an unreasoning hurt. 'Do you take it for an insult, Nell? I am asking you to marry me, not to become my mistress!'

'I know.' She backed away. 'I should say that I am honoured, should I not? Only I cannot, Eden, for you don't mean to honour me, do you?'

'No, I mean to make you mine because I must, because I cannot bear to be without you. Does that count for nothing?'

Nell shifted away, trying in vain to control her churning emotions. 'You are lonely, that I understand. And Henrietta needs a mother, that too I appreciate.' She turned, gazing back at him with longing in her heart. 'You tempt me very much, but I dare not yield. I could not endure to be so close—and yet not close enough.'

For several moments he said nothing, but the dark eyes showed his hurt, and Nell was hard put to it not to retract her words and give in. He turned away at last, and moved slowly to the window. He spoke without turning round.

'I see what it is. You have seen my wounds, and you are afraid of the risks.'

Nell could not deny it, but she did not speak. She could not bear to hurt him further.

'I cannot blame you,' he went on, low-voiced. 'Nor can I promise that they will not ride me from time to time.' He looked at her over his shoulder, and the bitter look was pronounced. 'The scars run deep, Nell. I don't even know if I am capable of mending.' Then he turned to face her again, and the hunger at his eyes was unmistakable. 'What I do know is that I need you. I tried to be rid of you today because I have fought against what you do to me. I swore that no woman would beguile me again.' A faint smile crossed his lips. 'I had not bargained for the wiles of Miss Helen Faraday—a governess and as irresistible as water to a man dying of thirst!'

A laugh escaped Nell despite the tug and thrust of feeling in her bosom. Everything in her yearned to give in to him. But that hard core of common sense held her back. The barrier was insuperable. She came to him, holding out her hands. He took them in his and lifted them one by one to his lips. Nell watched this proceeding with tenderness, but her determination was not shaken.

'Eden, I am not afraid of your past.' Despite herself, a tremor entered her voice and her eyes filled. 'But you see, I love you. There is nothing you can say that will make me put myself in a situation which can only give me pain.'

Jarrow was staring at her blankly. 'I don't understand. How should it give you pain? Except by my exposing you to my black moods and bad temper?'

'How can you ask me? A love unrequited can only—'

'Unrequited! What the devil are you talking about, you idiotic female? Haven't I been telling you for the last half hour at least that I love you to distraction?'

It was Nell's turn to stare. 'Are you mad, Eden? You have not said so once!'

'Not in so many words, perhaps, but virtually everything I've said—' He broke off and swore roundly. 'Hell and the devil, Nell, come here!'

And then she was in his arms again, with a pressure that threatened to break her ribs.

'Eden, I can't breathe!'

'Then you are well served for being so foolish!'

But his grip loosened a trifle, and he gathered her close as his mouth found hers again. This time, Nell withheld nothing of herself, allowing him to probe the velvet sweetness within so that a flame seared through her veins and she groaned aloud. Jarrow paid no heed, but only intensified the fire of his kiss until Nell lost all capacity for thinking, and had neither the will nor desire for speech.

When she did speak again, she found herself squashed into one great chair by the wall, half seated upon his lordship's lap, and firmly entrenched within his grasp. Somehow her hair had become loosened from its moorings, for Eden was playing within its heavy golden folds, winding them about his fingers. He reached into her hair and gently pulled her head back, his lips tracing a path along the column of her throat.

Nell squirmed, grasping at his free hand, which instantly twined with hers.

'Did I mention that I love you?' he enquired, breathing fire into the hollow below her ear.

Nell wriggled uncontrollably and, unable to bear the intensity of desire, pushed him away. 'Oh, stop! We should not be doing this—not yet.'

Jarrow kissed her. 'My darling, you had best accustom yourself, for we are going to be doing it—a great deal, and frequently.'

She caught at his wandering hands. 'For shame, sir, will you cheat the marriage bed?'

'Yes,' he averred baldly, and his glance caught at hers. 'The question is, will you?'

Nell hesitated, eyeing him doubtfully. Was he in earnest?

'Don't you trust me? Do you think I will take you and then refuse the consequences? Have no fear, Nell. We will be married with all due ceremony, as soon as I can contrive.'

She pulled herself out of his arms and sat up. 'But we have not settled anything, Eden. And only look at how carelessly you have left the necklace lying there!'

'To the devil with the necklace!' Receiving a reproachful look, he sighed, allowing her to remove the comfort of her warmth, and rise. 'I warn you, I shall not be so accommodating when we are married.'

'When we are married, my dearest, I shall do just as you bid me.'

He laughed, getting to his feet and slipping an arm about her. 'I sincerely doubt that. But I am glad that you are moved at last to call me your dearest.'

'Well, you are my dearest,' said Nell, escaping from him to the table. 'But we have still too many matters awaiting settlement before I can allow you to cajole me into further dalliance.'

Jarrow groaned. 'I see I shall be living under the cat's foot. What a managing female you are, Nell! Very well, let us attend to these matters, if we must.'

Nell took a seat at the table and picked up the emeralds, holding them to the light. 'If only we knew for certain whether these are real.'

'Even if they are,' said Jarrow, coming up behind her, 'I believe I must keep them in the family.' He reached either side of her, and took the necklace, bringing it to rest against Nell's throat.

She quickly reached up a hand and pulled it away. 'No!'

Eden let go, and Nell thrust the jewels from her, dropping them upon the smooth walnut surface. She watched him as he came around to the other side of the table, puzzlement in his features as he slowly sat, the brown eyes never leaving hers.

'Why, Nell?'

She could not repress a shiver. 'I cannot wear them. There are too many shadows, Eden. Too much pain.'

Jarrow was frowning, his gaze shifting to the necklace. 'Then I had best be rid of the thing.'

'No, that you must not! It is an heirloom.'

The sensations that had driven Nell were easing. She could not have named them, she only knew they would not let her wear the emeralds. She reached out, and Jarrow took her hand.

'What would you have me do, Nell?'

The answer came readily. 'Keep the jewels for Hetty. Perhaps it is what Julietta intended, for it was to Hetty that she entrusted her secret.' She smiled at him. 'And Hetty will be over the moon, for she will be just like a princess!'

Jarrow's breath caught and he kissed her fingers. 'How is it that you have always just the right solution?' Releasing Nell, he picked up the necklace. 'Poor Hetty suffered enough on account of it, I dare say she deserves it.' The emeralds slipped out of sight and into his pocket. 'Besides, you need no adornment, Nell. You are extraordinarily beautiful, did you know that?'

She shook her head, unable to speak for the lump that rose in her throat. 'I believe you are prejudiced, my lord.' She did not add that he had said much the same of Julietta.

He evidently felt her discomfort, for he caught at her hand again. 'I know what you are thinking. But it was different, Nell. It is different! Your beauty shines from within. Yes, your hair is magical and your eyes are glorious—but it is not that. It is your truth, Nell. And that is past price.'

Her eyes pricked and she shook her head. 'Pray don't make of me a paragon, Eden. You can only be disappointed.'

Jarrow grinned at her. 'You will regret having thus accused me! Paragon? A pestilential female who routs me at every turn? I think not, my dear one.' He became serious again. 'But a woman of honour, that you are, Nell. And I believe that is half the reason I fell in love with you.'

'Thank you.'

Aware of a husky note in her voice, she thrust her attention hastily elsewhere. And recalled the use he had meant to make of the emeralds. 'Heavens, Eden, you can't give Hetty the emeralds! Have you forgot your wish to restore Padnall Place?'

Jarrow shook his head. 'It would be a waste, and you know it. Your plan is the better one. Besides, we can adopt that without sacrificing the emeralds, and my conscience will be the easier.'

Nell warmed to that word 'we', but her mind was already working at the scheme. Jarrow found himself deep in discussion of several proposals towards the sale of Padnall Place and the purchase of a comfortable but modest establishment. But it was not long before Nell brought up the vexed question of Toly Beresford.

'What will you do with him? You cannot leave him to languish in the stables indefinitely. And yet I believe you will not wish to give him up to the constables.'

'And face a resounding scandal? By no means.' Jarrow's frown deepened. 'I am sorely tempted to let him roam the highways and byways until he is taken for a footpad and hanged.'

'But you won't,' Nell said with certainty.

'No.' He smiled lovingly at her. 'What shall I do, dear counsellor? You tell me. I feel sure you have some scheme which you are dying to present to me.'

Nell was obliged to laugh. 'Well, I have, as it chances. At least, it is only possible if you indeed mean to sell Padnall Place and remove elsewhere.'

'That is already settled, dear one, so cut line!'

'If his own family will not offer him shelter, then I think you might let him remain in the castle.'

'What, alone? As good as a prison! Nell, I could not.'

Nell frowned. 'When he has injured you in so many ways? Eden, if he came by his deserts he would either go to the gallows or end his days in Bedlam. But he knows this place, and it is a fitting retribution. You may pay a servant to support him. Or let Duggan keep house for him. She deserves to share his fate.'

'And if he continues to maraud the countryside?'

'You will tell him that you are going to inform the magistrates that Lord Nobody has retired. Once Mr Beresford knows that you will not support him should he be taken, I am persuaded that he will give it up. He may be insane, but he is not without cunning and intelligence.' Jarrow was silent, and Nell wondered a little uneasily if he was dismayed by what she had said. 'You must do what you think best, my dearest.'

The old haunted look came into his features, and harshness to his voice. 'The best? There is no other best than his death! While he lives, there is no justice and my daughter will never be safe.'

Nell's heart contracted. 'Hetty will be safe, dearest, for we shall keep her so. Remember, he has no reason now to harm her.'

Jarrow looked at her. 'But will he leave us alone? If he is in the castle, what is to stop him from pestering us?'

'Then perhaps you must instead pass the problem to his family. He said there are Beresfords enough. Are there?'

He shook his head. 'No, I could not inflict him upon them for they have enough to bear. Julietta was not the only sufferer. And how could I burden his parents with the knowledge that their son had murdered their daughter? No, the more I think of your castle scheme, the better I like it. And it is fitting.'

'Then I am glad I thought of it.'

Jarrow was filled with a burst of impatience. He got up, and came around to pull Nell to her feet. 'Have we now settled everything to your satisfaction, Miss Faraday?'

Nell smiled at him. 'I believe so, Lord Jarrow.'

'You have not forgotten anything?'

'If I have, I care not.'

Jarrow gathered her into his arms. 'Then at last we are of one mind.'

Upon which, he demonstrated the precise manner in which their minds were attuned. And Nell, abandoning all present attempts to bring him to a sense of his duties, gave herself up to the sensations of extreme pleasure aroused by his passion. After some little time, she bethought herself of Kitty Merrick, and resolved to write that the Gothic castle had yielded up a baron for a princess.

* * * * *

HISTORICAL ROMANCE™

LARGE PRINT

THE EARL'S PRIZE
Nicola Cornick

Miss Amy Bainbridge is a lady of honour, but when she finds herself the recipient of a surprise windfall her whole life changes! Now Amy can not only re-enter society, she's also secured the attention of London's most notorious gambler and rake!

Joss, Earl of Tallant, is everything Amy despises in a man, but she's utterly intrigued by him. She's certain Joss isn't attracted by her fortune, so why is this renowned rake pursuing her with such intent? Amy's finding his amorous attentions all but impossible to resist…!

NELL
Elizabeth Bailey

Practical Nell would never be so fanciful as to believe a mysterious Gothic castle and a darkly enigmatic baron would bring her a fairytale romance…

The star pupil from the Paddington Charitable Seminary, governess Miss Helen Faraday, prides herself on her common-sense approach to work. But Lord Eden Jarrow's imposing abode is enough to test the steadiest of nerves—and the brooding man enough to test the steadiest of hearts! Can one with such a shadowed past be capable of love, and loving a governess at that?

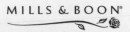
MILLS & BOON®

HIST0303 LP

HISTORICAL ROMANCE™

LARGE PRINT

SAFE HAVEN FOR CHRISTMAS
Three seasonal short stories

A Christmas Rose by Paula Marshall
Fleeing to Yorkshire, her reputation in tatters, Rose
was tempted to play the reckless courtesan with
Sir Miles Heyward…

The Unexpected Guest by Deborah Simmons
When a mysterious, seductive young widow sought shelter
at Campion Castle, the head of the mighty de Burgh
family found his yuletide peace shattered…

Christmas at Bitter Creek by Ruth Langan
The man was trouble, but Laura Conners could no longer
cope alone on the ranch. Would Matthew Braden stay and
make this a Christmas to remember?

GIFFORD'S LADY
Claire Thornton

Miss Abigail Summers watched in shocked fascination from
her window as a man leapt stark naked from his bed in the
house across the way. He looked to be fighting the worst of
nightmares. Embarrassment rapidly overcame female
curiosity when they were introduced the following day.

Sir Gifford Raven was a man of action, not at all
comfortable in Bath's polite society, which was why
the penniless Miss Summers intrigued him. Her dress
was dowdy, but beneath her shyness he detected an
impulsive young woman, a kindred spirit who could
help drive his devils away…

MILLS & BOON®

HIST0403 L